"That was crazy as hell," Jason said. "That guy could have killed us."

Oddly enough, now that they were safely inside, Lucy felt calmer. "I know. Thank you for not letting that happen."

Her comment made him laugh. "Yeah. I guess I'll be making another report to Sheriff Jeffords." He dumped the contents of his bag onto the kitchen table and shook his head. "There sure is a lot of stuff here. Mostly junk mail."

"I see that," she replied, unable to take her gaze from the manila envelope. "Aren't you curious to find out why you were served?"

He met her gaze. "I am. But I'm also dreading opening it. I mean, how much weirdness can happen in one day? I can't help but wonder what the hell I did to piss someone off. First the break-in, and now someone tries to kill us. None of it makes sense. This is as crazy as when I'm working the war zone over in Kabul."

Again, she had the unshakable suspicion that all of this was because of her.

* * *

If you're on Twitter, tell us what you think of Harlequin Romantic Suspense! #harlequinromsuspense

Dear Reader,

Snowbound Targets was a fun book to write. I haven't written anyone with amnesia in a long, long time and learning the reason for Lucy's memory loss fascinated me. And Jason Sheffield is my favorite kind of hero, a man's man with a world-weary air. He's seen too much darkness and is ready for some light.

Add in Colorado (one of my favorites of all the places I've lived) and snow (yes, I love winter) and, of course, the ever-present element of danger, and you've got a story. Oh, what a story! Because to me, there is nothing like love and light triumphing over darkness.

I hope you love Lucy and Jason and the fictional town of Cedar, Colorado, as much as I did.

Happy reading!

Karen Whiddon

SNOWBOUND TARGETS

Karen Whiddon

HARLEQUIN

ROMANTIC
SUSPENSE

HARLEQUIN®
ROMANTIC SUSPENSE™

Recycling programs
for this product may
not exist in your area.

ISBN-13: 978-1-335-62650-9

Snowbound Targets

Copyright © 2020 by Karen Whiddon

This edition published by arrangement with Harlequin Books S.A.

For questions and comments about the quality of this book, please contact us at CustomerService@Harlequin.com.

Harlequin Enterprises ULC
22 Adelaide St. West, 40th Floor
Toronto, Ontario M5H 4E3, Canada
www.Harlequin.com

Printed in U.S.A.

Karen Whiddon started weaving fanciful tales for her younger brothers at the age of eleven. Amid the gorgeous Catskill Mountains, then the majestic Rocky Mountains, she fueled her imagination with the natural beauty surrounding her. Karen now lives in north Texas, writes full-time and volunteers for a boxer dog rescue. She shares her life with her hero of a husband and four to five dogs, depending on if she is fostering. You can email Karen at kwhiddon1@aol.com. Fans can also check out her website, karenwhiddon.com.

Books by Karen Whiddon

Harlequin Romantic Suspense

The CEO's Secret Baby
The Cop's Missing Child
The Millionaire Cowboy's Secret
Texas Secrets, Lovers' Lies
The Rancher's Return
The Texan's Return
Wyoming Undercover
The Texas Soldier's Son
Texas Ranch Justice
Snowbound Targets

The Coltons of Roaring Springs

Colton's Rescue Mission

The Coltons of Red Ridge

Colton's Christmas Cop

The Coltons of Texas

Runaway Colton

The Coltons of Oklahoma

The Temptation of Dr. Colton

The Coltons: Return to Wyoming

A Secret Colton Baby

Visit the Author Profile page at
Harlequin.com for more titles.

To my family, many of whom are not related by blood. You know who you are and I love and appreciate you.

Chapter 1

Any other time, the sight of the snow-capped craggy Colorado mountain peaks would have filled Jason Sheffield with joy. Tonight, with the stains of war coloring the edges of his vision with blood, he gave a grim nod toward their majesty and continued on up the twisting road. A few miles ahead, he'd reach his sanctuary. Only then would he allow himself to let down his guard, an instinctive, protective reaction the result of spending far too long in the volatile war zones of Afghanistan and Syria.

Home now, he reminded himself, turning off the two-lane blacktop onto the narrow gravel tract that climbed through evergreens and aspens. Finally, he caught a glimpse of the red metal roof of his cabin, perched on the side of the hill looking out over the valley below and the mountain range stretching into the distance.

This was where he came when he wasn't working, traveling around the hot spots of the globe and reporting right in the middle of the action. When he'd been younger, the danger had filled him with adrenaline. These days, he just felt weary.

After parking his four-wheel drive Jeep, he grabbed his heavy duffel bag, hefted it over his shoulder and started up the path toward his front door. His refuge. Since he hadn't been back here in six months, one week and three days, he anticipated there'd be quite a bit of dust to deal with. At least he'd stopped in Walsenburg and picked up food along with a bag of ice and a large ice chest in which to stash the perishables. Since he didn't plan to go anywhere for at least a week, he'd brought plenty. And with the ever-present possibility of snow, he'd made sure to grab enough to last two weeks minimum.

About to insert his key in the front door, he frowned. The door was already unlocked. Odd. He checked the fake rock on the side of the path where he always kept a spare. The key was missing.

Damn. He froze. He felt as if he'd somehow stepped back into a house in a back alley in Kabul. Dropping his duffel bag on the front porch bench, he drew his pistol. Heart pounding in his ears, he shoved open the front door and sidestepped inside, gun raised. At first, as his eyes adjusted to the interior lighting, he saw nothing that appeared amiss. Except a lamp was on. He swiveled left and right, his weapon following his movement.

There. A lump of various-colored ragged blankets on his couch. They weren't his. And judging from the shape, someone or something hid underneath.

"Show yourself," he barked. "Hands up. Now."

The lump didn't move. At all.

Mouth dry, he gave the order again. This time, the pile of blankets stirred. A sleepy pair of long-lashed, ice blue eyes peered out at him. He noted the silky shoulder-length dark hair, the heart-shaped face and swallowed. His intruder was female. A stunningly beautiful female. With a huge purple bruise on the left side of her face.

That didn't make her any less dangerous. He'd learned that early on in the Middle East. Of course, this woman wasn't wearing a burka. And they were in Cedar, Colorado, not war-torn Afghanistan. Still, he kept his gun trained on her as a precaution. Years of living on the edge of danger had taught him that.

"Who are you and what are you doing in my cabin?" he demanded.

Instead of answering, she simply stared at him, unblinking and solemn. Again, he noted her beauty, but discarded the thought instantly.

"Do you speak English?"

Sitting up and stretching, a graceful movement that drew his unwilling attention to the swell of her breasts under her baggy gray sweatshirt, she slowly nodded. "I think… Yes. I do.

"Why are you pointing a gun at me?" A slight frown creased her forehead as she eyed him. "And who are you?"

"I might ask you the same question," he drawled, lowering his pistol to his side, but keeping it out just in case.

But she looked beyond him, her gaze taking in the polished oak paneling, the rustic furniture, even the high ceiling with the deer antler chandelier that hung over the dining table. "Where am I?"

Had he imagined the faint touch of horror in her silky voice?

"In my cabin," he told her. "Which leads to another question I have for you. How'd you get in here? I assume you found the hidden key, but how'd you get up here? I didn't see a vehicle, and I find it hard to believe you were out hiking and stumbled across my place."

If anything, her frown deepened. "I...don't know." Confusion turned to fear as she pushed to her feet, shoving her hair away from her face. She turned in a circle, swallowing hard, taking in her surroundings with barely concealed panic before facing him. "I'm sorry. I have absolutely no idea who I am."

Stunned, Jason stared at her. Whether he was being played or not, she clearly believed every word she said. He sighed and holstered his gun. "Did you hit your head?"

Her hand went up, an almost involuntary motion, sweeping under her hair. "I don't think so. At least, it doesn't hurt." Again, she swallowed, drawing his gaze to the graceful lines of her throat. "I don't understand. How is this even possible? How can I be in a place I don't recognize, with a man I don't know and have no idea of my own name?" Her voice rose slightly with each word and he saw how her hand shook.

"I have no idea," he answered, fighting back his own exhaustion, which was winner over his skepticism. "But I've been traveling for a long time and I need to get some rest."

"Friend or foe?" she asked, her expression serious as she caught and held his gaze.

Caught off guard, he wasn't sure how to respond. "That depends," he finally answered. "On which you turn out to be." Then he pointed toward his bedroom. "I'm going to get some sleep. I will be locking my door. If you're still here when I wake up, we'll talk some more and try to figure this out."

When she finally nodded, he managed a tired smile. On his way past her, he went to squeeze her shoulder, intending to offer her some sort of reassurance that everything was going to be okay.

Before he could, she yelped, as if his touch had hurt her. And then, as he gaped at her through a haze of exhaustion, she yanked him, put her shoulder under his armpit, and somehow flipped him past the couch, past her and onto the floor. Hard onto his back.

"Don't. Touch. Me."

Stunned, he managed to scramble back to his feet, first checking to make sure she hadn't managed to grab his pistol. Nope, still in the holster.

Silent, they faced off. This time, he knew to be on guard.

"What do you want?" he asked.

"Want?" Eyes huge, she stared back at him. Her mouth trembled. "I don't know what just happened."

"You attacked me," he pointed out.

"No." Slowly, she shook her head. "I defended my-self. You touched me." Her voice shook.

Fear. More than that, absolute terror. Like some of the rape victims he'd met in Kabul.

"I wasn't trying to hurt you," he said, speaking

slowly, his voice calm. "That was meant to be reassuring."

"OK." Her too-vigorous nod attested to her continuing agitation. "Just don't touch me again, all right?"

"All right," he agreed. "I'm going to walk past you and go to bed."

With all of his movements deliberate, he sidled around her, taking care to keep his holster side away. She stood frozen watching him, her haunted expression achingly familiar. What the hell had happened to her that she'd ended up here alone and shaken, with absolutely no memory?

And mad self-defense skills.

He kept his gaze on her while walking backward all the way to his room. While there was nothing he enjoyed more than solving a good mystery, right now his entire body screamed for sleep. He felt hollowed out, almost as if he were sleepwalking. He needed rest. Then he'd be much better equipped to face his mystery guest.

As soon as the door closed, she heard the quiet click of the lock. Letting out a breath she hadn't even been aware of holding, she allowed herself to sink back down into the soft warmth of the blankets on the comfortable couch.

Inhale. Exhale. Attempt to calm her racing heart. Try to contain her panic, to center herself. Even so, it took a moment or two for her entire body to stop shaking. Another for her to clear her mind enough to even attempt rational thought.

What had she gotten herself into? How had she ended up here? The big man who claimed to own this cabin, whoever he was, had seemed serious. And he'd had a gun. Did that mean her life might be in danger? Had he been hinting as to what he might do to her when he'd said if she was still here when he got up? Her face throbbed. She reached a hand up to touch it, wincing at the pain. She had no idea how she'd injured herself, but judging from how tender her cheek was, it had been recent.

If she'd been afraid before, the idea of leaving brought on a different sort of terror. Still, she forced herself to pad over to the door and open it, taking a look outside.

A blast of chilly air made her shiver. Despite her lack of a jacket, she stood in the doorway and took in the surroundings. Craggy mountains with snow-capped peaks. Lots of trees, mostly aspen, though some pine and spruce, interspersed with the occasional Poplar. How could she know this, what the trees were called, and not know her own name?

Briefly, she considered. If she left this place, this small cabin that appeared to be pretty isolated, where would she go? And how would she get there? Did she have any money, or any personal items? Would she even recognize them if she saw them? If she truly was in some sort of danger, would she even recognize her enemies if she saw them?

The answer unfortunately came back a resounding no.

Closing the door and locking it, she knew she had no choice but to stay put. The big man might be a bit intimidating, but she'd pick the devil she knew over the unknown. At least right now. For all she knew, he could be her enemy or her captor. She might not know her name, but she knew enough to watch her back. She'd be careful and keep her guard up. Hopefully soon, some of her memory would return.

Still, she looked around, hoping to see maybe a purse or something personal of hers. Wouldn't that be wonderful, especially if she found a wallet with identifying information?

But there wasn't anything. Apparently, she had nothing but the clothes on her back. Super soft black leggings and an oversize sweatshirt. And while she wore a pair of socks, she didn't see any shoes. Her head ached. How was that even possible? Then again, she supposed anything might be possible since she had no idea of her own identity or how she'd gotten to this remote rustic cabin.

Memory loss. How? Why? What could have caused that? Again, she felt her skull, using her fingers to probe for any bumps or lumps. She found a few, none of them too big. A little tenderness rather than pain. Not enough to explain this.

Had she been ill? Like with a brain tumor or something? The thought didn't ring a bell, but then what did?

Instead of taking stock of what she didn't know, she decided to list what she did. Precious little, actually. She'd been awakened by a man she didn't know, apparently for trespassing in his cabin in the mountains. As for what state, she knew there were several that had mountains like those. She found it odd that she could list all the mountainous states but not her own name or where she'd come from. Or what had happened to get her here.

Once more she fought a rising tide of panic. A blank slate could mean anything. She didn't even know what kind of person she might be—good or bad. She had no idea if she was married or single or divorced. If she had any children or siblings or parents who might be worried at not hearing from her in too long.

This was not helping. Then what would? She needed to think. As tempting as crawling back under the blankets and hiding from the world might be, doing so wouldn't solve anything.

Instead, she paced, hoping the simple act of moving would bring a glimmer of…something. After a few minutes of stalking the interior perimeter of the cabin, she realized this wasn't helping either. Apparently, one couldn't simply will their memory to return. Not even in bits and pieces.

Trying not to feel utterly defeated, she sat back down on the couch. She glanced at the smoldering woodstove, wondering if she should add a few logs. As dusk settled in over the mountains, she knew the temperatures would continue to drop. How she knew this, she couldn't say.

In the end, she settled for burrowing back under the blankets.

She must have dozed off, because the next thing she knew warm sunlight streamed in, warming her face. Stretching, she yawned and tentatively searched the void of her memory to see if anything had returned. No such luck.

Her long-sleeved sweatshirt fit loosely. She pushed up the sleeves, startled to see her arms were covered in bruises of various shapes and sizes. The colors ranged from plum to a deep purple, almost black. Gingerly, she touched her arm, which made her wince. She had no idea what had happened to cause these.

Glancing around her at the now brightly lit room, she noticed the bedroom door remained closed. The big man must still be asleep. Which suited her fine, since she didn't trust him.

She padded down the hall, looking for a bathroom. Once there, she eyed the shower longingly before deciding she might as well. But first, she locked the door. Only then did she strip off her clothes and glance in the mirror.

As she'd feared, in addition to the massive one on her face, more bruises decorated her legs and hips. She even had a huge one covering part of her stomach and back. Though she hadn't been aware of them before, now that she was, they hurt. Especially if she pressed her fingers into them. Which she immediately stopped doing.

Instead, she grabbed a couple of towels, located a new bar of soap under the sink, and stepped into the shower.

The small room had filled with steam by the time she'd finished. Clearly, she liked her showers hot. As she toweled herself dry, she realized she felt better already. Clean, at least. If only she had a change of clothes. Maybe the man would know where she might obtain these.

Thinking of the man must have made him manifest. Because when she walked back to the kitchen combing her fingers through her still-damp hair, she nearly ran into him. Only a quick jump back kept them from colliding.

As she gazed up at him, her heart rate once again going double time, she realized he appeared larger than he had last night. And more muscular. In fact, judging by the hard stare, he seemed much more intimidating.

She refused to let him see her quaking. Instead, she dipped her chin in a cool nod. "Good morning."

"Mornin'." He narrowed his eyes. "Do you drink coffee?"

Did she? Considering the question for a moment, she settled on a shrug. "I don't know. I guess I'll find out."

He turned and led the way to the kitchen. She followed, feeling slightly calmer. She needed to remind herself that, as of yet, he'd given her no reason to be afraid of him. No sense looking for trouble before it started, as her grandmother always said.

My grandmother. Eager to capture a memory, she froze, waiting for her mind to supply images of a face and a name. But nothing else came and she finally sighed in defeat.

The man waited at the counter. He'd gotten down two large mugs. "Would you like to try it black or with cream and sugar?"

How she wished she could answer him.

"Just pick one," he said, noting her hesitation. "Let's go with cream and sugar."

"Okay," she allowed, watching as he put some kind of pod into the machine, placed a mug under it and pressed a button.

She realized she didn't even know his name. Which should be okay, since she didn't know hers, but she was getting tired of thinking of him as *the man*.

"I'm Jason Sheffield," he told her, startling her. "And since we don't know who you are, I'm thinking we'll call you Lucy. Would that be okay?"

Lucy. Considering, she tried out the name inside her head. "I guess that'll be as good as any," she replied. "At least until my memory comes back."

"Great." He flashed a smile and handed over the mug. "Here you go, Lucy. Careful, it's hot."

Grateful, she accepted it and carried it over to the kitchen table, where she took a seat. Taking a tentative sip, she smiled as the rich flavors filled her mouth. "This is good. I think this is how I like it."

"Good." Carrying his own mug, he pulled out the chair across from her and sat. "How are you feeling?"

Again, she had to stop and reflect on a seemingly simple question. Finally, she settled for honesty. "I'm not sure. I have a few lumps and bumps, plus bruises all over my body. I have no idea how I got them."

"Let me see," he ordered. Then, softening his tone, he amended his request. "Please."

Slowly, she pushed up her sleeve. First one, then the other, exposing the pattern of purple, black and blue. "My legs look the same. And my stomach and back."

His harsh intake of breath made her tense. He swore, low enough that the curse word was almost imperceptible. "It looks like someone hit you, numerous times. By all rights, you should have a broken bone or two to go with those."

She shivered. "Nothing is broken that I can tell. I'm a bit stiff and sore, but the hot shower helped with that." Taking another sip of coffee, she managed a small smile. 'And this is helping me feel better too."

"You don't remember what happened either?" His watchful gaze held enough compassion to make the back of her throat ache.

"No. I wish I did."

"Any dreams that you can recall? Maybe your subconscious might try to communicate that way."

She thought for a moment. While she sensed she'd dreamed, to her best recollection those dreams were a swirl of chaotic colors and seemingly unrelated movements. "Nothing," she finally admitted.

At her response, he dragged his large hand through his unruly hair. Somehow, this only made him look more dangerous. Was he?

"It was worth a shot," he said.

She took a deep breath. To trust him or not, that was the million-dollar question. However, in the end, what choice did she really have?

"I need your help," she admitted. "I'm beginning to see that you didn't ask for any of this, but then neither did I. I feel like I might be in some sort of danger."

He stiffened, his gaze instantly alert. "From whom?"

"That I don't know. Like everything else. Maybe I shouldn't have said that, but I just have a gut feeling. A sense of lurking danger, if you will. There's no logic or reasoning behind it. I could be wrong." She sighed. "Honestly, there's no way to tell without my memory."

She watched him while he considered her words. His sheer size could have made him seem intimidating, though for her she found it made her feel safe. He'd been nothing but kind to her, even though he would have been within his rights to toss her out the door.

"I think I'll go into town and do some investigating," he finally said. "Will you be okay here alone?"

Would she? "I suppose so. But are you sure you trust me enough to leave me alone in your home?"

He laughed at that, a warm masculine sound that managed to coax a smile from her. "You were alone here before I got home. I don't see the difference."

As Jason drove slowly down his steep drive, he couldn't help but glance back at the cabin. This place had long been his refuge, a place known to only a few select friends. How, then, had the mysterious woman he'd try to call Lucy gotten there?

Of course, everyone in the small mountain community of Cedar knew about his place. His family had been coming here for decades before he'd purchased it from his parents. Maybe the mystery would turn out to be as simple as that. It was entirely possible Lucy might turn out to be a local who'd known the cabin sat empty most of the year and decided to use it as her refuge.

Though Jason hadn't planned on being around people for at least a week or two, he needed to check with the sheriff and see if any missing-person reports had been filed. That would be a good place to start in his quest to determine her identity.

Main Street in Cedar, Colorado, could have been a Christmas-card photo. The storefronts were meticulously maintained, even though they experienced far less tourism than other parts of the state due to their distance from any ski resort. With buildings constructed of red brick and wood, the aspen-lined street gave off a homey, welcoming feel.

He parked in front of Joe's Hardware, grinning at the thought of saying hello to Joe after his many months' long absence. *Too long,* he thought.

A bell over the door jingled as he went inside.

"Be right with you," Joe called out without looking up from a box full of tools he had on the counter. Due to the time of the year, snow shovels and a snowmobile were on display, along with Christmas lights.

Jason prowled the aisles, enjoying the sense that he'd returned home. Unlike many of the locals, he hadn't grown up in Cedar, though his family had owned the cabin high on the mountainside for decades. They'd routinely made the trip from Colorado Springs, spending a few weeks in the cabin every summer.

After his father died, his mother had decided to sell the place. Jason had promptly bought it. He'd done some extensive renovations, updating the roof and plumbing and heating system. Though he spent much of his life traveling due to his career, he enjoyed having a place to return to where he could find a modicum of peace.

Joe finally looked up. When he caught sight of Jason, he let out a loud whoop. "Well, look at you," he exclaimed. "About time you decided to pay us a visit."

After some back clapping and a one-armed guy hug, Joe asked Jason what he could help him find. "They're predicting a snowstorm," Joe supplied. "You got enough firewood up there?"

"Nope. How soon can I get a cord delivered?"

"For you, I'll try to get it done this afternoon."

Since Jason already had all the other winter essentials, he paid for the wood. "Anything new in town?" he asked casually. While he knew hoping Joe would tell him about a missing woman was a long shot, he figured it didn't hurt to try.

"Not really." Joe shrugged. "We've had a few more tourists this summer than usual, but after August, things settled back down to the same old, same old. But it's good to see you again, Jason. How long are you here for this time?"

"I'm not sure. I'm thinking at least a month." Truthfully, he'd been toying with the idea of longer, maybe even giving up war reporting for good. His soul ached with weariness from all the bloodshed and savagery.

"Through Christmas then." Joe grinned. "You know me and the missus do our annual misfits' dinner for Christmas. Everyone and anyone is invited to come eat with us. The only thing you have to do is bring something. Food, wine, beer, whatever."

Jason nodded. "Thanks. I'll let you know." He barely remembered the last time he'd celebrated Christmas. Most times he'd either been traveling or stuck in some foreign hotel. The best holiday he'd had in recent memory had been when he'd found himself at a military base and had celebrated with the service members.

Once he'd left the hardware store, he strolled up and down Main Street, carefully checking all the storefront windows for missing-person flyers. He saw nothing save one for a lost cat.

Though ever mindful of the frightened woman waiting at home, he stopped in at Gertie's, a coffee shop known for amazing pies. He was well aware of how much trouble he'd be in once word got out that he'd been to town if he didn't stop and see everyone who knew him.

The little coffee house was packed. He took a seat at the bar, ordered a cup of coffee and Gertie's famous peach pie. While he ate, he spoke with several other locals, all of who seemed happy to see him. No one mentioned a missing woman.

Extricating himself from the group of people wanting to discuss his last big story, he finally headed down to the sheriff's office. Though Sheriff Ray Jeffords had been at the job since Jason had been a kid, he'd shown no inclination of retiring. Since there'd been virtually no crime in Cedar ever, he didn't have much to do anyway.

"Jason Sheffield!" Springing from his chair, the sheriff rushed over and shook his hand. Once-gray hair had turned white, and his lined face bore a few more wrinkles, but the older man still had a firm grip and appeared healthy. If anything, he'd lost weight. His once-beefy frame seemed much trimmer.

They talked about the weather and the predicted snowstorm. Ray complained about the lack of tourists, and the out-of-towners who occasionally built vacation homes on newly cleared land. When Ray made no mention of a missing woman, Jason cleared his throat and asked.

"No, I haven't heard anything about that." The sheriff narrowed his eyes. "Why do you ask?"

Though Jason briefly considered filling him in on the truth, he decided against it. Until he knew exactly what Lucy might be up against, he didn't plan on letting anyone know about her.

He gave a casual shrug. "I'm working on a story," he said. "I really can't share the details."

As usual, that answer worked. Everyone knew he was a reporter.

"Let me check really quickly," Sheriff Jeffords said. He spent a moment or two typing on his computer, clearly searching some database. "Nope. We've got an Amber Alert, but unless the missing female is fourteen years old, I've got nothing."

Jason hadn't actually thought it would be that easy. He nodded. "Thank you for your time."

"No problem."

They shook hands again and Jason left. Instead of wandering the other side of Main Street, he decided to pick up a few more provisions and head back home. The food he'd bought earlier would be enough to last him a week or two, but he hadn't been factoring in feeding another person. His experience with snowstorms in the mountains had taught him it was better to be prepared.

As he shopped the small grocery-general store, this time doing some hasty meal planning inside his head, he couldn't help but wonder if Lucy would still be there when he returned home. Just in case, he purchased some generic clothing items, staying away from things like bras and shoes, where he'd need to know an actual size. Luckily, the bored teenager working the cash register didn't know him and couldn't have cared less about his purchases.

Satisfied, he found himself whistling as he drove home. He did enjoy a good mystery, especially one in as pretty of a package as Lucy.

Chapter 2

Watching as the man—Jason—drove off, she understood he'd left her with a choice. She could stay or she could go. Not really much of a decision, as far as she was concerned. She had no idea where she would go or what she would do once she got there. And how far would she get walking barefoot in the cold?

Add that to the ever-present feeling of some sort of danger lurking just around the corner, right beyond the range of her vision, and she'd take her chances with the big man and the small cabin. For now.

Lucy. Trying out the name, she decided it would work as well as anything else. Even though it didn't feel right. But then, what did?

How had this happened to her? And why? She'd actually thought things like this only happened in books or movies. Really, how awful was it to not have any sense of self, or past or present? She not only felt adrift, with nothing to anchor her, but afraid of what she might learn when her memories returned. Had she done something awful, so terrible the act had caused her mind to melt down? Or had someone done this to her? Did amnesia spontaneously occur without some sort of trigger? She didn't think so. Odd how she could know some weird, random fact, but not her own name.

Not giving in to self-pity would be a challenge. One of many, though. She didn't know much about amnesia, and if she had access to the internet, she'd do some research. Damn, she missed her phone.

Her phone. Startled, she realized if she closed her eyes, she could picture it clearly. Rose gold, the latest iPhone. Plus-size.

Excited, she jumped to her feet. Her first true memory. If she could recollect something this small, it shouldn't be too much longer before the rest came back to her.

Pacing the confines of the small cabin, she tried to clear her mind, hoping a blank slate might bring back something else. But apparently her sudden flash of insight wasn't something she could conjure up at will. No matter how hard she tried.

Trying to focus on the positive—she'd actually remembered something—she refused to let herself feel discouraged. For now, she had to believe she was safe. At least she had a roof over her head, food to eat, and someone who seemed sympathetic and kind.

She knew enough to understand that her circumstances could have been so much worse. Though she hesitated to call herself lucky, in this particular area she had been.

The sound of tires on gravel alerted her to Jason's return. At least, she hoped it was Jason. She hoped it wasn't someone else coming to visit him.

Heart pounding, she ran to the front window, lifted up one wooden blind and peered out. Yep. She exhaled in relief as she watched him climb out of a black Jeep, wearing a cowboy hat and looking larger than ever and handsome as hell. She felt a twinge of attraction, which she instantly quelled. Ridiculous, since for all she knew she could be married. Eying him again, she realized he appeared to be carrying several shopping bags.

Opening the front door, she waited, feeling oddly breathless. "I'd come out and help you, but I don't appear to have any shoes."

"We need to fix that," he said, smiling as he approached her. "I should have thought of that before I went to town. I did pick you up a couple more sweatshirts and sweatpants, though they might be too large since I don't know your size."

Grateful and touched, she thanked him. "That was kind."

"Well, you can't walk around wearing the same thing day after day. I bought a package of women's underwear too, size small, and a package of socks. I hope that will work."

"It will." For no reason, her face heated.

"I'll need to get your sizes for shoes and er, other things."

Like bras. She got it. "Thank you."

"I got some more food and stuff," he continued. "Just in case that snowstorm they're predicting turns out to be as nasty as they say."

"I didn't know about that."

"It's supposed to be a doozy."

"Oh, I hope so. I love snow."

"You do?" His gaze sharpened. "Sounds like you remembered something."

"I did. It's my second actual memory. Earlier, I remembered I have an iPhone. I could actually picture it." She shrugged. "I'm disappointed that these seem insignificant, but hopeful more and more will come in time."

"I think I remember reading that's how it works. Bits and pieces, flashes of insight. It won't be like you'll wake up one day with everything restored to you."

Which, of course, was what she impatiently wanted to happen. She decided to change the subject. "Do you get a lot of snow here?"

The glint in his eye told her he knew what she was doing. "Yeah, we get some brutal blizzards here because of our location," he said, clearly deciding to go along with her topic change. "That's why I bought all this."

As he moved past her carrying his bags, he brushed up against her, making her catch her breath. Inhaling sharply, she breathed in his scent. Man and pine and outdoors. Damn. She swallowed hard, nearly overwhelmed with desire.

Not like her at all. Or was it? She had no idea. Maybe she was the kind of woman who made love with carefree abandon. Her stomach turned, making her doubt that.

She wore no wedding ring. Nor did her ring finger show the signs of having worn one. Eying Jason's broad back, again she felt a punch of desire low in her body.

What did this sudden attraction mean? Was he her type, or were the strange feelings she'd started to experience due to the fact that they were in a sort of enforced isolation together?

Did it really matter? She had enough to worry about with her memory loss. Straightening her shoulders, she followed him into the kitchen, watching silently as he unpacked his purchases. Despite her stern internal talk to herself, she found herself aching to touch him.

"Here you go." Completely unaware of her thoughts, he tossed her a generic plastic bag of women's panties. She caught them easily. "And socks," he said, this time sliding that package across the counter. "And here, the rest of this is yours also. This bag here has the sweatshirts and stuff like that."

Still feeling overly warm, she took the bag and smiled.

"Thank you again," she told him, dropping the socks and underwear into the bag with the other clothing. "Please save the receipt. Once I have access to money, assuming I have some, I'll repay you."

"No need." Turning, he began unloading the next bag, putting things like cheese and lunch meat and eggs into the refrigerator. He left a box of quick-cooking rice and several cans of soup and various vegetables on the counter. "Those go in the cabinet right above, if you don't mind putting them up."

Of course she didn't mind. Working so close, back-to-back, it was inevitable that they'd bump into each other. Each time she did, she bit back the urge to apologize and hoped he had no idea how badly she wanted to touch him.

Frustrated, she shook her head. How was it possible that she, a blank slate, could even feel this way about a man she barely knew?

"Are you okay?" he asked, rousing her from her reverie.

"I am." Maybe if she said it firmly and often enough, she might actually believe it.

"Good." He went back to emptying the last bag of provisions.

Once everything had been neatly stowed away, he smiled at her. She felt the impact of his smile all the way to her toes, which made her grit her teeth. "Don't worry." He reached to squeeze her shoulder, and then pulled back at the last moment. "We'll get this all figured out. I did some checking in town, and there are no reports of a missing woman."

"At all?" Focusing on this rather than the urge to lean in and accept his touch, she let her dismay show.

"Nothing. I stopped in and spoke with the sheriff. He checked."

Feeling defeated, she moved away from him. Distance would help. "I'm disappointed. I really was hoping for a quick resolution to all this. As in, we'd find a report, and once I saw my face and knew my name,

I'd remember everything, just like that." She snapped her fingers. "I guess not."

This made him laugh, a deep and masculine sound. "One thing I've learned over the years in my career as a journalist is to be patient. Don't stress about it so much. Your situation is complicated—and intriguing. I'm thinking it won't be a quick fix."

Complicated and intriguing. Interesting. "I'm grateful you don't seem to mind. I don't know what I'd do without your help."

"No problem," he replied. "I remember reading something about amnesia once. I think you can't try to force things—you just have to let the memory return naturally. Even if it's in bits and pieces."

She nodded, though she once again had to struggle to hide her disappointment. She eyed him, trying to be dispassionate but failing miserably. "Still, you seem familiar to me somehow. Are you sure we didn't know each other, before?"

"I'm positive." He chuckled. "Quite honestly, I'd never have forgotten meeting you."

This made her smile.

"You probably saw me on the news, doing one of my reports from the Middle East. That's why I seem familiar."

"Maybe." Once again, she took to prowling around the cabin, more as a way to distract herself from the strength of her need to touch him. "This is very nice," she mused, running her hand over the granite kitchen countertops, enjoying the cool smoothness. "The colors are beautiful. I'm guessing either it came like this or you have mad decorating skills. I like it."

"Thanks. I did some updates after I bought the place."

Movement outside caught her eye. A small herd of deer crossed the backyard. Immediately, she went to the window and pressed her nose against the glass, watching them, enthralled.

"Deer or bear?" he asked.

"Deer." The thought of encountering a bear made her shiver. She glanced over her shoulder at him. "Do you get a lot of bears here?"

"We have all kinds of wildlife, but yes. As long as you're careful, they won't bother you."

She wanted to ask what constituted *careful*, but since she figured she wouldn't be out roaming the woods or the roads alone, she'd be fine.

Finally, the deer disappeared into the trees. Slowly, she turned around, to find Jason watching her.

Taking a deep breath, she met his gaze. "I know you checked with the sheriff and in town. But what if I'm not local? Not only do I have this ever-present sense of dread, but I almost feel as if there's something important I'm supposed to be doing."

"That's a possibility. You say you're worried. Any idea about what?"

"No. I still can't access enough memory to figure it out. It's like when you catch a glimpse of something out of the corner of your eye, but then you turn and you weren't quick enough to see it." She sighed. "It's honestly frustrating as hell." Her eyes widened at her choice of words. Another clue, maybe.

"I can only imagine. I'll tell you what. I'll scour the internet tonight, and you can look over my shoulder. We'll see what we can find."

"Thank you." She wanted to hug him. She didn't.

"You're welcome. But for now, if my satellite is still working, let's catch the news," he suggested. "I'm kind of a news junkie."

"Before we search the internet?" She struggled to hide her disappointment.

"Yes." He reached for her, stopped, and cocked his head. "Is it okay if I touch you now? I know you were frightened before, but I promise I won't hurt you."

Watching him, she slowly nodded.

"Okay." He put his hand under her chin, raising her face so that she looked at him. "But don't worry. We'll look after, OK? I don't have a DVR here, so if I miss it, it's gone. Because I'm a journalist, I like to try and keep on top of what's going on in the world."

"That makes sense." Though she didn't want to jerk herself away from him, if he kept on touching her, she just knew she would kiss him. Odd, how she could go from one extreme to the other.

Luckily, he dropped his hand. Aching, she told herself to be glad.

"What kind of journalist are you, exactly?" Changing the subject yet again. "I know you said you're on the news. What news? I'm assuming one of the national ones, right?"

"You assume correctly. I work as an overseas correspondent in the Middle East."

"I think you mentioned something about that."

"Yeah. I probably did." He busied himself with the remote. "I report mostly from war zones."

War zones. She got a quick flash of something—

danger and noise, blood and despair. It came and went too quickly for her to be able to analyze it.

The TV came on, a commercial about some local plumber.

"That sounds dangerous."

"It can be." He grinned, appearing triumphant. "I'm relieved that the television came on instantly, with a clear picture. That's not always the case. When it rains or snows, the satellite can't get a signal. That's when I read."

She looked around for books. He caught her looking and shook his head. "No room. I have an e-reader."

While she pondered that, the evening news began. They led off with a story about a coordinated suicide bombing attack in Kabul. Over seventy-five Afghans were dead, with many more wounded.

Jason swore. "That's exactly where I was reporting, a little over a week ago." He swore, again. "I'm not sure whether to feel relieved or envious that I wasn't right there in the thick of the action."

"Are you an adrenaline junkie?" she asked, her voice quivering slightly. She suddenly felt uncomfortable in her own skin. The sounds on the screen unnerved her, so much so that she wanted to ask him to turn the television off.

Too enthralled in watching and listening to the report, Jason didn't respond. Feeling as if she might throw up, Lucy jumped to her feet and fled. She wasn't sure where she was going—the cabin was small after all—but she had to get away from the news story.

Jason felt the reporter did a good job, sticking to the facts and avoiding overly opinionated commentary. He thought he might have met the guy once, a few years back, but couldn't be positive.

Finally, after a good sixty-second segment, which was long for a single story, the focus shifted to the incoming snowstorm. It was barreling through Montana and Wyoming, slated to reached northern Colorado in a matter of hours. The weatherman predicted snow would fall heavily in the entire state, with higher elevations getting the most, as usual. The ski resorts would be overjoyed, especially since they hadn't had much snow so far.

He glanced back toward Lucy, intending to comment on the weather, but she wasn't there. He found her in the bathroom with the door open and water running, though she stood motionless in front of the sink with a bowed head.

"Lucy?"

She didn't respond.

He took a step into the room and lightly touched her shoulder, about to ask her if she was all right.

She cringed, flinching away from him before he could get a single word out. Back up against the wall, she put her arms up in a defensive posture. At first, her gaze seemed wild and unfocused.

"Hey." He kept his voice quiet and soothing. "Are you OK?"

At first, she didn't respond. But awareness slowly returned. She blinked and finally lowered her arms. "Jason?" She sounded bewildered, as if she had no idea how he'd gotten there.

"You look really pale," he said carefully. "Why don't you sit down before you faint?"

"OK."

To his relief, she allowed him to lead her down the hall to the kitchen. He pulled out one of the kitchen chairs. She sat, though she moved robotically, like she'd mentally checked out.

In the den, he could hear the television playing a commercial. Lucy wiped at her eyes, even though she wasn't crying.

"What's wrong?" he asked, giving in to the urge to gently move a strand of her silky hair away from her face. To his relief, she didn't flinch away from his touch. "Do you feel sick?"

"The news…" She trailed off, clearly unable to articulate. "I'm not sure why. The clip they showed…"

"Of the bombing in Kabul?" He watched her closely, struck by the urge to take her in his arms and comfort her.

"Yes." She swallowed, hard. "It seemed…familiar. Too familiar." She shuddered.

"Familiar how? Do you think you've ever been there?"

"I don't know." Her hands shook as she twined them together. "It's possible, I guess."

Somehow, he doubted that, though he kept the thought to himself. He knew all the reporters who covered the Middle East, and Lucy wasn't one of them. And there was no other reason for an American non-military woman to be in a war zone. Unless she'd been with one of the medical-aid groups. That brought about an entirely new set of possibilities that he would have to consider later. Right now, he needed to focus on her.

"Did you have some sort of memory flash?" He

knew he shouldn't push, but the strength of her reaction to a sixty-second news story made him feel as if pushing was warranted.

"I don't know," she said again. And then she started to cry.

Jason Sheffield could deal with being shot at, running from explosions and he always maintained his cool in the midst of chaos. He considered himself tough, well trained and smart. But a crying woman turned him to putty.

Though he'd cautioned himself against touching her again, he knew she needed the healing power of touch more than anything else right now. Still, he'd be careful to make no sudden moves. Slowly, he knelt down beside her and took both her hands in his. "Hey, now. It can't be that bad."

She shook her head, attempting a watery smile at him through her tears. "Can't it?" she asked, sniffling. "I'm guessing you have no idea how terrifying it is to not have the slightest idea who you are, where you came from or what happened to you."

Grabbing a paper napkin from the holder on the table, she wiped at her eyes. "I don't know why that news segment bothered me. I don't know. I don't know anything."

"We'll find out," he assured her. "I'm a reporter. Getting answers is what I do. Let me start doing some digging. It might take a bit, but I'll do what I can, I promise."

This appeared to reassure her. She lifted her chin, still blotting at her streaming eyes. "I'm wondering if maybe I should see a doctor. Do you think it's possible there might be a medical reason why I can't remember?"

"It couldn't hurt." Squeezing her hand, he released her. "Would you feel comfortable enough to go into town with me?"

She looked down, her silky dark hair falling over her face. "I don't know."

"Once you have an appointment, we could go straight there and back." He thought for a moment, imagining the gossip if he was spotted with a mystery woman in town. "I have a better idea. One of the guys I went to high school with is a family practice doctor in Colorado Springs. It's a bit of a drive, but at least that way if you're seen and recognized, no one will know you're staying here in Cedar."

"Okay." At least she'd stopped crying. She even looked a little bit hopeful.

And beautiful, even with her swollen eyes and red nose.

"Would you like something to eat?" He'd learned while working in the Middle East that, when not in immediate danger but even if still in the center of crisis, feeding people always calmed them down. "I make a mean spaghetti with meat sauce."

"I don't eat meat," she replied, her eyes going huge as she realized what she'd said. "I'm a vegetarian." Voice full of wonder, she repeated the sentences.

He watched her closely. "So that makes three memories, right?"

"Yes. I'm positive about them too, even though they're not related. I love snow. I don't eat meat. And I wish I had my iPhone."

"I do too. Did you remember anything else?"

Her smile faded, replaced by a frown. "I don't think so. No." Her stomach growled just then, making them both smile. "And I am hungry. I'd like some of that spaghetti, if I can have mine without meat in the sauce."

"That I can do. I'll make meatballs instead, for me. And I have some frozen spinach that I can microwave if you'd like."

"What can I do to help?" she asked.

Pushing to his feet, he shook his head. "Nothing. Just keep me company while I cook. Do you like wine? I have a nice bottle of Merlot I can open."

"Wine." She considered. "Why not?"

After opening the bottle, he poured them both a glass. Carrying his over to the stove, he got busy preparing their meal.

She sipped her wine and watched him, the hunger in her gaze bringing an answering spark to life inside him. He opened his mouth to speak, but then turned around and went back to cooking. He figured she most likely hoped for another flash of memory, nothing more.

The small kitchen filled with the scent of spaghetti sauce as he brought everything to the table. He also brought them plates and silverware. He topped off their wineglasses while she filled her plate with pasta and spinach, avoiding the meatballs.

She ate with a single-minded determination. He watched her, noting her dainty manners, at odds with her complete and utter focus on her food.

Finally, she finished and pushed away her clean plate. "That was wonderful," she said. "Thank you."

He'd also eaten his fill. "You're welcome. Now I wish I'd bought something for dessert."

"Like tiramisu?" she asked, then gasped. "Another flash of memory. Tiramisu is my favorite dessert."

"See?" Leaning back in his chair, he took another drink of wine. "It's coming back, bit by bit. I bet it won't be long at all before you remember everything."

"I hope so." She twined a strand of her shoulder-length hair around her finger. "I just wish I could remember why that news story bothered me so much. You seemed so familiar with it. Tell me, did you only cover Afghanistan?" she asked, her polite and slightly shaky tone telling him she was attempting to work through her fear.

"No." Instead of listing every war-torn country and city he'd covered, he thought of his return flight home, with a layover in London. "By happenstance, I was in London last week when the terrorists attacked the Tube. I covered that story since I was right there at the time."

She shuddered. "Even though I don't remember that, I can't even imagine so much bloodshed. How do you live with it, having seen so much evil?"

"I don't know. When I first started, I drank too much. After a while, I just got used to it, I guess." He glanced over at the desk he had tucked in one corner. "I've started trying to compile some of my best photographs into a book. I have enough for more than one."

"Photographs?" She frowned. "I thought you were a reporter."

"Photojournalist."

"Are you any good?" She looked from him to his messy desk covered in books and papers.

"I've won several awards," he told her. "Plus, I sell a lot of my photos to magazines like *National Geographic*."

"Wow. That's impressive."

"Thanks. I enjoy it. It's what keeps me sane." As he spoke, he realized he meant every word. If he didn't have the ability to create beauty out of chaotic darkness, he would have given up in despair a long time ago.

She eyed his desk again, her expression doubtful. "How do you find anything?"

This made him grin. "Believe it or not, I have a system. I know exactly what's in each pile." He got up and walked over to the desk. "This pile here is typed ideas for magazine articles. And this—" He stopped, catching sight of an army-green bag in his desk chair.

"What's wrong?" she asked, getting to her feet and joining him.

"That?" He pointed, loathe to touch it for some reason. "Is that yours?"

"Mine?" She went closer, eying the bag. "How would I know? I'm assuming it's not yours, so anything is possible."

He lifted it up by the handle. "A small duffel," he commented. "Would you like me to open it and see what's inside?"

She nodded. "Please."

He carried the bag over to the kitchen then placed

it on the floor. After unzipping it, he waited for her to join him.

"Clothes!" she exclaimed, reaching inside and pulling out a pair of jeans. As she rummaged through the bag's contents, she found more jeans, some black leggings, sweaters, T-shirts and even a dress. And two coats, a down parka with a hood and a jean jacket. There were several bras, pajamas, socks and panties. "Best of all," she pointed out. "In the very bottom are shoes. I see a pair of sneakers, some boots and a pair of black high heels."

Tucked into a zippered pocket she found a cosmetics bag, filled with makeup. "I guess I wear makeup," she said. "And what's this?"

She held up a plastic bag, filled with what appeared to be a long blond wig.

"I wonder that this is for?"

"A disguise maybe?" he replied. "Looks like you have everything you could possibly need," he drawled. "Did you pack that yourself or did someone pack it for you?"

She opened her mouth to answer but closed it. "I don't know."

For the first time since he'd discovered her, he found himself wondering if she was telling the truth.

Chapter 3

Focusing on the duffel instead of Jason, Lucy closed her eyes and tried to breathe deeply. She wasn't sure what to make of the way he looked at her. As if he truly believed she might be intentionally keeping secrets. Maybe she was, but she had no way of knowing that. She couldn't even explain. If he didn't understand that her mind was a blank slate, nothing she could say or do would change that.

Finding this bag was the first thing that had happened since she'd awakened in his cabin with him staring down at her that gave her real hope. The kind that made her catch her breath. Where had it come from? She fingered the rough and sturdy material. Some sort of canvas, most likely. Its existence made her feel a lot less adrift. She couldn't even begin to express her joy at having something of her own, not just the bag, but her own belongings. Makeup and clothes that she'd worn *before*. Proof that she actually had a past. Though she knew thinking so had to be foolish, she'd begun to wonder.

Wistfully holding up a pair of well-worn jeans, she couldn't help but wish whoever had packed the bag had taken the time to write her a note, explaining who she was and what exactly had happened to her. But of course, they hadn't. For all she knew, she might have packed it herself.

After dropping her clothes back into the duffel, she left the bag on the desk chair since she had no place to store it. She felt inexplicably depressed and crossed back into the kitchen to begin clearing the table.

"What are you doing?" Jason asked, eying her curiously. "You don't have to do that."

"Why not?" Aware she needed to keep busy so she didn't drown in her emotions, she carried the plates over to the sink. "You cooked, so I should clean up. That's only fair."

He watched her for a moment and then finally shrugged. "OK. But I'm going to help. I don't have a dishwasher here, so we have to do them by hand. Would you rather wash or dry?"

"I'll wash," she said.

"Let me put up the leftovers first. Day-old spaghetti is always better than the original."

Since she had no way to know if this was true, she simply nodded. Odd how memory worked. She knew exactly how to hand wash dishes but had no idea if spaghetti tasted better the day after it had been made.

Side by side working together, she allowed herself to relax. The entire routine, washing and rinsing a plate and then handing it to Jason to dry, felt comfortable and comforting. Maybe even familiar. She could actually feel the tension leaving her.

They'd just finished up when a huge gust of wind rattled the cabin, startling her.

Drying off the last plate, Jason swore. "Sounds like the storm got here earlier than they predicted. I need to carry in some more firewood. I keep the stack covered so it will stay dry, but it can be difficult to get to once the snow comes."

"Let me help," she said immediately. "Now that I have my own parka and boots, I'll be able to dress warm enough to go outside."

"Thanks. I could use your help." He snagged his jacket off the coatrack and shrugged into it, just as another blast of wind made the cabin walls shudder. "Judging from that, the storm is coming on fast and strong. The sooner we get this done, the better."

Having pulled her boots and parka from the duffel, she stepped into the boots, pleased at how well they fit. Though why shouldn't they, since they were hers?

"Do you have gloves and any kind of wool cap?" he asked, even as he put his own on. "Check your pockets."

She did. To her relief, she had both. Jamming the knit cap on her head, she zipped up her jacket before slipping on the gloves. Once she was ready, she followed him to the door. "I'm good to go."

He yanked the door open. The second they stepped outside, a blast of icy air hit her like a slap to the face. Snow swirled around them, caught by the gusty wind. Already an inch or two covered the ground. She couldn't see more than a few feet in front of them due to all the blowing snow.

"This way," he shouted, leading the way. Doubled over against the force of the wind, she followed him.

Around the side of the cabin, he'd built a three-sided overhang, inside of which he told her he stored his firewood. A heavy tarp, already dusted with snow, covered everything.

"Just a sec," he cautioned, holding up one gloved hand. "I've secured it with bungee cords to keep it from blowing off."

Once he'd released one side of the tarp, sending it flapping in the wind, he began grabbing pieces of wood. She held out her arms and he placed three there. "Can you carry that?"

"Yes." Actually, she wanted to ask for more. But with the wind howling around them, she thought she'd play it safe, at least on her first trip back. If she didn't have trouble, she'd take more logs the second go-around.

She started for the door ahead of him, wondering at the fierceness of the sudden storm. She realized that she only thought of snow as something picturesque and peaceful, not destructive and fierce. Pretty, like a holiday card.

Another memory. Too busy to dwell on it right now, she concentrated on placing one foot in front of the other and moving forward, against the wind. The short stack of firewood felt heavier than it should have, with her having to double over to keep from getting buffeted by stinging snow and ice pellets.

When she finally reached the front of the cabin and opened the door, a gust caught it and ripped it from her hand, sending it slamming into the interior wall. Still, she made it inside, struggling to keep from dropping her load.

Jason came in right behind her, stamping off snow before kicking the door shut. He carried his stack of wood over to a metal bin and dumped it there. "Here." Taking hers from her, he placed it on top of his.

"Not enough," he said. "We've got to keep that woodstove going 24/7."

They made two more trips. By the third one, Lucy could no longer feel her hands or feet. The storm had definitely gotten worse. The blowing snow made it impossible to see even her hand held out in front of her. They hugged the external cabin wall to keep them on track.

"Wait," he shouted. After he gave her the usual three pieces of wood, he took his own from the pile and dropped them on the ground. He struggled to re-attach the tarp and motioned to her to go on and get inside. "I'll be there in a minute. I'm going to go put the plow on the front of my Jeep. I backed it into the garage for that reason. Go get warm."

Numb with cold, she turned to do exactly that. But she caught her foot on a patch of ice and her leg twisted. She let out a startled cry, which the storm ripped from her lips, and she went crashing down. Her chin hit the top log in her stack, making her see stars.

"Are you OK?" Jason hauled her up and dusted her off.

Though her eyes stung with frozen tears, she managed a nod. Ignoring her throbbing chin, she stepped away, determined to retrieve the wood she'd dropped. Somehow, she managed to pick up her logs and carry them back toward the front door.

Once they were safely back inside the warm cabin, wood stowed, she stripped off her gloves and gingerly tried to feel along her painful chin. Her first touch hurt, so she abandoned the effort for now.

"Are you all right?" he asked again, removing his coat and hanging it up. "You can put your coat up here too and let it dry."

"Thanks." She took her coat off and turned to carry it to the coatrack.

Catching sight of her face, he cursed softly. "You're bleeding."

"Am I?" She stood still while he gently lifted her chin.

"Just a little." He gave her a reassuring smile. "We need to get that cleaned up."

She allowed him to lead her into the bathroom. When she caught sight of herself in the mirror, she gasped. The impact of hitting the wood had gashed her chin. There was so much blood. And of course, now that she saw exactly how bad the cut was, it began to throb even worse.

Though it was a tight fit due to the small space, he grabbed a washcloth and gently rinsed off the blood. She kept still, willing herself not to react to the pain.

After he got her all cleaned up, he retrieved some antibiotic salve from the medicine cabinet and applied that. The touch of his finger was gentle, and she knew he was trying very hard not to hurt her. Despite this, her eyes filled and her throat ached.

"We probably need to bandage it," he said. "Though I'm not sure how we'd get a bandage to stay on. Here." He handed her a piece of tissue. "Keep this pressed against it. I'm going to look for a butterfly bandage."

"That's OK," she managed. "It'll be fine. I just need to make it stop bleeding."

He turned and bumped into her. Suddenly, the situation felt way too intimate. She might not know her own name, but she still could recognize a hot man. This one was sexy as hell. Heart in her throat, she stared. He stared back.

Finally, he cleared his throat. "Let me go get some ice."

Bemused, she followed him into the kitchen. He wet a dishcloth, wrung it out and then got ice from the ice maker in the refrigerator door. He then put all of that into a large Ziplock baggie.

"Here you go." He handed it to her. "Why don't you sit down and hold this to your chin for a few minutes. I'm going to go put another log in the woodstove."

"Thanks." She nodded, taking a seat at the table and holding the ice to her chin. Hopefully, the ice would help numb some of the pain. Feeling slightly foolish, she wondered if she'd always been clumsy or if this mishap had just been a simple accident.

Outside, the wind continued to intensify, though she didn't see how such a thing could be possible. The small cabin shook as the howling wind battered its sturdy frame. She glanced at Jason, wondering if she should be alarmed. If he wasn't worried, then she wouldn't be either.

After attending to the woodstove, Jason flashed

her one of those devastating smiles and tried pointing the remote at the flat-screen TV hanging on the wall. "Nothing. Of course, with a storm like this, the satellite would be down. I'm going to hazard a guess that there's no cell phone reception either. It's never all that good up here to begin with, so that's a safe bet." He crossed to a small table and pulled out some sort of black box. "Which is why I always keep a satellite phone around. Of course, storm equals no satellite, so that's also probably a no go."

With the ice still pressed against her chin, musing over how strongly his smile affected her, she managed a nod. The movement made her wince. "Is there someone you need to get in touch with?"

"What?" Again that flash of sexy smile. "Oh, this?" He put down the black box. "No. I just like to keep up with the weather reports. This thing can access the weather radio. I'm really curious what the snowfall prediction might be now. And how long the storm will last. I get cabin fever really bad if I'm trapped in the cabin too long."

Trapped in the cabin. She froze, her breath catching. The phrase brought a flash of some memory. Explosions and darkness and gunfire. The awful choking, claustrophobic feeling of being trapped... Horrified, she struggled to catch her breath, beginning to hyperventilate.

"Lucy." Jason's sharp voice, calling a name. Even though she knew it wasn't really hers, it was enough to snap her out of her reverie. "Lucy. Are you all right?"

"I..." Realizing she'd dropped her ice pack on the table, she picked it back up. Her hands were shaking.

She couldn't seem to find the right words, any words actually. How could she hope to explain she'd gotten lost in a mysterious scenario because of a chance remark? Even worse, that she had no idea what it meant or where it had happened, or even if it actually had.

Aware of him watching her with his steady gaze, she took a deep breath. And then she tried her best to explain, aware she probably sounded like an irrational person but also knowing she hadn't chosen this. None of it. Hopefully, he would understand that.

She watched his expression as she talked, relieved to find it unchanged. Still calm, still strong and supportive.

At first, he didn't react, his gaze remaining steady as he considered her words.

"Then it was something I said?" he teased, clearly trying to lighten the mood.

This made her smile. "Yes. As a matter of fact, it was. Even though you didn't mean to." The ice had started to sting, so she lowered it, giving her chin a break.

"Here, let me have that." He took the ice pack from her and carried it over to the sink. "It's going to be OK, I promise," he said. "All of it. Your memory will eventually come back."

"How do you know?" she asked, genuinely curious.

"I just do." Which as explanations went, wasn't really one at all. Despite that, she believed him.

Outside the storm continued to rage. She imagined the snow piling up and shivered.

He noticed. "This cabin has been in my family for

decades and has withstood all kinds of weather. This is just our first blizzard of the season."

"I understand," she replied, though she wasn't sure if she really did. While she couldn't be positive, she had a sneaking feeling she wasn't used to cold weather. "So if you don't have television or internet, what do you do to pass the time?"

"You can read," he answered promptly, pointing to a bookcase full of hardback books. "I also have a deck of cards, so we could play poker or something, if you'd like."

"Poker?" She frowned. "I'm not sure I know how."

"I can teach you." He crossed to his desk and moved her duffel to the floor then got a deck of playing cards out of the center drawer. "It can be a lot of fun."

"Sure. Why not?" While she still felt a bit hesitant, this sounded like a harmless way to pass an hour or two.

Sitting down across from a handsome, capable man in his warm and comfortable cabin while a blizzard raged outside should have made her feel secure and cozy. And part of her did. But the other part, the side of her that knew things her subconscious mind didn't know, felt uneasy and unsettled, aware that unseen danger lurked right around the corner.

At least the blizzard provided a momentary deterrent. No one would be foolish enough to trek up here in weather like this. She told herself to relax.

"Are you sure you're OK?" he asked, making her realize he'd been watching her while she grappled with her nameless fear.

She lifted her chin. "I will be. Let's play cards."

* * *

Once he shuffled the cards, Jason laid them out, explaining the different combinations and which ones ranked the highest. She watched him intently, nodding at all the right places. At least she appeared to be present, grounded by her attempt to learn to play a game she probably once had known.

He'd never seen someone as lost as the woman he'd dubbed Lucy, at least here in the States. There were many like her in Kabul, hollow-eyed empty women struggling to stay alive—or hoping to die. Most of them had already lost everything and, unlike Lucy, they had no hope of every getting any of it back.

Lucy's flashes of memory appeared to be coming more often. He supposed that was a good thing. Logically, it had to mean her memory would soon be rapidly returning. Her struggles to remember tugged at his heart.

The more time he spent with her, the more he liked her. In fact, he already knew he liked her a little too much. Sexy and sensual and beautiful and plucky—all combined to make her nearly irresistible. Even though he considered her off-limits, he couldn't help but appreciate her charms.

And the way she watched him sometimes… Almost as if she was as hungry for him as he'd begun to be for her. But then again, he would continue to keep his distance. She had to be feeling pretty mixed-up right now.

As appealing as he might find her, he'd never been the type to take advantage of a woman and wouldn't start now. But knowing that didn't make him desire her any less. He could imagine the forced proximity during the blizzard would only make it worse.

"And what is the connection? I just can't figure it out." He hadn't realized he'd spoken out loud until she answered.

"The connection to what?" she asked.

"You and me." He laid down the cards and waved his hand. "Why my cabin? Clearly, you didn't simply find your way here. Someone brought you and left you."

"Do you think so? I hadn't really thought about that. I guess I've been so consumed with trying to figure out who I am that I haven't even considered how I ended up here."

He got up and grabbed his satellite phone, then remembered.

"Once this storm lets up, I'm going to call a buddy of mine in military intelligence. He'll have access to a lot more information than the local sheriff did. Maybe he could get a lead on a missing woman who matches your description."

Though she nodded, he could tell by her frown that this bothered her. She set her hand facedown and grimaced.

"What's wrong?"

"If I'm in danger, I don't want anyone to know where to find me. Not before I regain my memory and know exactly what's going on."

Normally, as a reporter, he tended to discount conspiracy theories without proof. But over the last several years, he'd gotten inadvertently caught up in more than one covert operation. This had made him realize anything was possible.

In other words, she could be right to worry. He decided to keep his thoughts to himself. "I'll be discreet," he promised. "He's used to me working on stories, so that's what I'll tell him I'm asking for."

She still appeared doubtful, but she finally nodded. "If you think it will help."

"Couldn't hurt. But since I can't call out and we have nothing else to do, how about we go ahead and play poker?"

To his surprise, she was a natural. Either she caught on quickly, or she'd accessed some prior knowledge of how to play the game. She won the first three hands. "Beginner's luck," he told her, grinning.

"Are you letting me win?" She wrinkled her nose at him in suspicion.

Desire struck him low in the gut, rendering him momentarily speechless. Gathering his thoughts furiously—now he found her *cute* too—he spoke. "Of course not. Beginner's luck is a common phenomenon. Trust me, it won't last."

She tossed her head at that. "We'll see. Deal another hand."

He did.

They played for several hours. When he noticed her yawning, her shoulders drooping, he pronounced her the winner and called it a night. "You need to get some rest," he told her. "You're welcome to have my bed if you give me a moment to change the sheets."

"No." Her immediate and vehement response startled him. Something must have shown in his expression, as she softened her tone. "The couch will be fine. You've done enough, letting me stay here, feeding me, keeping me safe. I won't put you out of your bed."

"I really don't mind," he said, meaning it.

"I know you don't. But I'll be fine on the couch. It's comfortable and close to the woodstove. I like it."

Because she seemed so exhausted, he decided not to press the point. "Your choice," he told her. "Do you need an extra blanket, or is what you have there enough?"

"I'm good." She gestured at the mound of blankets she'd been using. "These are more than enough, thanks."

"Well, good night then."

She stared at him, her eyes glittering huge in her pale tired face. "Good night."

Hating the way she watched him, as if afraid he would take advantage of her, he checked to make sure the front door was locked and dead-bolted before he got a glass of water and carried it to his room. He debated for a moment before deciding to close his bedroom door. Figuring she'd probably feel safer with it closed, he made a quick pit stop in the bathroom. After brushing his teeth, he returned to his room and shut the door.

Lucy had already turned out all the lights. A quick glance revealed a lump under the covers on the couch. Good.

After climbing into his own bed, he clicked off the lamp and let himself drift into sleep.

A loud scream awakened him. Instantly alert, he rushed to his door, yanked it open and headed to the couch, using the soft glow of the woodstove to guide him.

She screamed again before he reached her, a shrill yet guttural sound of true terror. He reached for her, calling her name.

The instant his hand connected with her shoulder, she exploded into action. Grabbed his arm, jerked him toward her. She brought up one knee and twisted her body and threw him to the floor.

Stunned, he lay there, trying to catch his breath. At least she'd stopped screaming.

A second later, wide-eyed and shaking, she crouched down next to him. "Jason! Are you hurt? I'm so sorry. I thought…"

Still dazed, though no longer half-asleep, he rolled over and pushed himself to his feet. "What the hell was that?" he asked, his voice flat. "You started screaming like you were under attack. I rushed out here to check on you, and you take me down?"

She opened her mouth and then closed it. Her beautiful eyes shone with tears. "I had a nightmare," she said, her voice trembling. "I didn't know it was you. When you touched me, I thought you were attacking me. I'm so sorry."

Of course, then he felt like a total ass. Moving toward her to take her in his arms and offer comfort, he froze when she flinched away from him.

He cursed low, under his breath. "I wish I could get ahold of whatever son of a bitch hurt you," he said. "Please know I will never hurt you. Ever."

Slowly, she nodded. Then she launched herself at him, wrapping her arms around his waist and burying her face in his chest.

Touched, stunned and slightly alarmed, he held her,

gently stroking her silky-soft hair and desperately trying not to notice the fullness of her breasts pressing
into his naked chest through her T-shirt.

Finally, she moved away. Both relieved and disappointed, he swallowed. She clicked on the light and
climbed back onto the couch, sitting cross-legged and
pulling the blankets up to her chin. "I'm sorry," she
said.

"Where'd you learn to fight like that?" he asked,
even though he didn't expect an answer.

"Self-defense classes," she responded, and then
looked as surprised as he felt. Blinking, she mulled
over what she'd just said. "I can picture the class. There
were about fifteen people, all women. We took turns
learning the moves."

"Can you remember where it was?"

She shook her head. "No. It's gone."

"It's okay." Damn, he wanted to hold her again.
But she'd let him know quite plainly, without saying
a word, that she'd come to him if she needed comfort.
"Will you be all right now?" he asked. "Going back
to sleep, I mean."

"Sure." She waved him away. "You can go back to
bed. I'm sorry I woke you. I'm probably going to sit
here for a bit, until I feel more comfortable."

Shifting his weight from foot to foot, he finally nodded. "If you need to sleep with the light on, feel free."

Back in his room, he relived the way she'd taken
him down. So easily, and he probably had close to a
hundred pounds on her. She'd had a great instructor,
that's for sure. He'd need to be careful not to make any

unexpected moves around her. He fell asleep thinking of how good it had felt to hold her.

He woke in the morning to the kind of perfect utter silence one only experiences after a fresh snowfall. The brilliant white light streaming in his bedroom window made him squint, though he knew exactly what he'd see if he looked out. He'd always loved the way the entire world felt remade and clean, as if the blanket of snow promised a fresh start.

Corny, maybe. But after spending months in blowing sand, he truly loved the cool mountains and the winter's snow.

Checking the clock on the nightstand, he saw it was a little after seven. He stretched and felt a twinge in his arm and back. Then he remembered what had happened last night. He wondered if she'd actually gotten any sleep.

He moved quietly down the short hall to the bathroom. After a quick shower, he brushed his teeth and got dressed. Then padded into the kitchen to make a pot of coffee.

A quick glance at the couch revealed that Lucy still slept. With the light on. Gazing at her sleeping so peacefully, he felt an unfamiliar and unwanted tightness in his chest. They'd just met, but he already felt close to her. And responsible for her, as if she'd somehow become more than an acquaintance, more than a friend even. As if she'd become family.

Shaking his head at his crazy thoughts, he brewed his coffee, glad that he'd get a chance to drink it in peace and quiet. He needed some time alone to try and figure out what to do about the woman he'd named Lucy.

First up, he'd need to do some research on amnesia. He jotted some quick notes in the notebook he kept on the table. He wanted to know what could cause someone to lose their memory. He also needed to learn how to help them regain it, and to find out a time frame so he'd have an idea how long such a thing might take.

Second, he'd need to put out some discreet feelers with some of his contacts. Surely, when a woman went missing, people would notice. Somewhere, she had to have friends and family who were worried about her and missing her. He would try to find those people.

And if, as she suspected, she was in some sort of danger, he'd find out why and from whom. He hadn't spent years working as a journalist without developing some intense investigating skills. He *would* learn her identity, and soon.

He'd just finished his first cup of coffee and was contemplating getting a second, when his satellite phone rang. Answering quickly, hoping the sound hadn't awakened Lucy, he heard nothing but static at first.

Then an unfamiliar voice spoke his name. "Is this Jason Sheffield?"

Cautiously, he answered in the affirmative. "How did you get my number?"

"This is NCIS special agent Paul Groesel. We're investigating the disappearance of one of our officers, Rick Engles. I understand you spoke with him right before he went missing."

"Rick's missing?" Floored, he shook his head. "We

talked right before I flew back to the States. What happened?"

"We don't know. I was hoping you might have some insight."

He thought back to the conversation with Rick. "He didn't say anything. I'd just finished a story when a suicide bomber hit the hotel I was staying at. I grabbed my camera and got some pics, and then pitched in as best as I could helping. Rick was on his way in and we'd hoped to grab breakfast or something the next day, but with everything that happened, we couldn't."

"I see. You're saying that you didn't see him at all?"

"Exactly." A horrible thought struck him. "Was he injured in the attack?"

"Again, we're not sure," the NCIS agent said. "His body hasn't been recovered. Thanks for your help. If I have any further questions, I'll give you a call."

Stunned, Jason thanked him and said goodbye. He thought back to that night, so much chaos and bloodshed. Most of the victims had been locals instead of the foreign dignitaries and reporters the suicide bomber had wanted to kill. He'd held more than one Afghan while they died. Many had suffered horribly. Most had been women and children.

That night had been the main reason he'd decided to take some time off. He'd come to the cabin to lick his wounds and try and heal. He hadn't been able to even look at the photos he'd taken and wasn't sure when he would. Even the thought of touching his camera made him nauseous. He'd carry the scars from that night a long, long time.

Chapter 4

"Bad news?" Lucy had watched his expression change as he'd listened to the person on the other end of the phone call. He'd gone from easygoing to extremely tense. Judging by that—and hearing his side of the conversation—the news he'd received hadn't been good.

"One of my friends is missing." He shook his head, the disbelief in his eyes reflecting his shock. "Rick and I grew up together. I went to college and he went into the military. He's still there."

Heart sinking, she eyed him. "When you say *missing*, do you mean he was under attack and now no one can find him?"

"No. Or at least I hope not. He was on his way to Kabul just as I was on my way out. We'd planned to meet up for a bite to eat and to catch up. We didn't get to because of what happened." Jamming his hands into his pockets, he shook his head. "A suicide bomber got into our hotel lobby and tried to blow the place up. Rick didn't know it, but he was coming into a hellish situation. I barely got out with my life. There were some US dignitaries there, though I have no idea why. It's believed they were the targets, along with the multitude of reporters. He didn't get them."

"But he got others." Uneasy now, she swallowed hard. She didn't want to ask what had happened after. She suspected she already knew.

"Yeah." His attempt at a shrug didn't fool her. "He detonated in the lobby. Most of the people he killed were Afghani locals. Women and children. All the foreigners, including myself, were either up in our rooms or out somewhere. We weren't hurt."

His gaze was far away as he moved around the room. "I went down and tried to help the locals. I also brought my camera. Years of working as a journalist had ingrained in me the need to take photos. So I did."

Judging by his flat tone, he regretted this now.

"I've worked in war zones most of my career," he continued. "I've seen a lot of awful stuff. But nothing like this." His voice broke. Clearing his throat, he looked away. "Anyway, Rick is missing. He's military, so that was NCIS on the phone. They're trying to find him."

When he turned his back to her, she understood. He didn't want her to see him wrestle with his emotions.

Giving in to impulse, she crossed the room to him and wrapped her arms around him from behind. "I'm sure he'll turn up," she said, even though she had no idea if he would.

He froze, saying nothing. Determined to offer what little comfort she could, she held on. After all, Jason had been there for her when she needed reassurance. Returning the favor seemed the least she could do.

When he finally moved away, she let him go.

"You know, now that I actually have a working sat phone, I can make some calls." He turned to face her, his mask of cool control now firmly back in place. She admired that ability, even as she regretted the fact that he felt it necessary.

It struck her that she had begun to know him, or at least think she did. He could rearrange his facial expression all he wanted, but that didn't take away the haunted look in his gaze.

Suddenly, she wanted nothing more than for him to feel better. Foolish or not, wrong or right, she could at least try to do that for him.

"Jason."

When she called his name, he stopped. Maybe he'd begun to know her as well. She went to him again, not entirely sure of her intentions.

And then she kissed him. She might not know her own name, but the instant she covered his lips with hers, she recognized the connection. Her entire body tingled with it.

Still, he didn't move. Not a single part of him, not even his mouth. Like a statue, as if he worried he'd break. Though maybe she was taking instead of giving, she continued to kiss him, willing him to open his mouth and let her inside.

The kiss went from gentle and inquisitive, to demanding and insistent. With a groan, he crushed her to him, demanding, hungry. As if she alone could fill up the emptiness inside him. Or was it the other way around? Dizzy with longing, she gave back as good as she got.

When her knees weakened, she realized they'd backed up into a corner of the room. Her back was against the wall, trapped. Panicked, she ducked away from him, retaining enough sense not to go on the defensive. After all, she'd initiated this, not him.

"I'm sorry," she muttered, shaking both with need and fear. "I didn't mean…"

"It's OK." Surprisingly gentle, he kept his distance. "I get it. You're mixed-up. You don't know what you want. I understand." He took a deep breath. "Just please, don't do that again."

She shouldn't have felt hurt, but she did. Rejection, no matter how kind, was still rejection.

"I understand," she replied, even though she didn't.

"No, I don't think you do." Dragging his hand through his hair, he appeared to be considering his next words. "I won't take advantage of you. You aren't whole, Lucy. Hell, we don't even know your real name."

"That's not my fault," she said, feeling the need to defend herself. "I don't understand how you can hold that against me."

"I don't. I'll be brutally honest, here. I'm a man. When you kiss me like that, I want more."

"I do too," she said softly.

"You don't know what you want." He growled the words. "How can you? We just met a couple days ago. You might be married, have a husband and a family somewhere looking for you. How would you feel later, once you remembered everything, if you and I made love?"

He had a point. A damn good one. Acknowledging that with a curt nod, she wished it made her feel better. "I'll keep that in mind from now on," she promised, blinking back unwanted tears. She wouldn't cry, not over this. As far as she knew, none of this was her fault. All she had to do was try to heal herself, pick up the pieces of her life and move forward.

And if she continued to desire him, well, she'd deal with that too. She might not know a lot about herself, but she felt as if she was strong. She'd have to be, to make it through all of this.

"Friends?" he asked, holding out a hand.

Though she really didn't want to touch him again, she took it, pretending she didn't feel a tingle of connection. "Friends," she agreed. "When can we go outside and check out the snow?"

Evidently, her question took him by surprise. Releasing her hand, he blinked. "You want to go out in the snow?"

"Sure, why not?"

Eying her as if she'd said something crazy, he finally shrugged. "I'll have to shovel a path from the front. If it's really deep, we won't be able to go far. I've got skis and snowshoes, but only one pair of each."

"That's OK. I don't want to go far." She smiled. "Just into the front yard. I want to make a snowman."

After a startled look, he laughed. "Do you know how?"

"I think so." She shrugged. "If not, I'm sure you'll show me."

"Are you? Honestly, I haven't done that in years."

"Then it's time you did, don't you think?" Hands on hips, she eyed him.

Cocking his head, he eyed her back. "Is that a challenge?"

She laughed. "Maybe it is."

"Challenge accepted. Wear layers. I'll meet you at the front door in fifteen." With a wave, he disappeared into his bedroom.

A snowman. She could see an image plainly in her mind of what such a thing was supposed to look like. Whether she'd ever actually built one before or not, she had no idea. But getting out into the fresh air and snow sounded like fun.

Grabbing a few things out of her duffel, she layered on a couple of shirts, stepped into a pair of leggings and then back into her jeans. Two pairs of socks allowed her to still slip her feet into her boots. Even though they were more like hiking boots than snow boots, she figured she'd be warm enough.

Jason came out of his room a moment later, rubbing his hands together. "Are you ready?"

"Yep." She could scarcely contain her excitement. Having snagged her parka, she zipped it up and put on her hat and then her hood. Finally, she slipped on her gloves.

When she looked up, Jason met her gaze, his own intense. "Do you think you remember how to do this?" he asked, one hand on the doorknob.

"I'm not sure." She shrugged. "Let's get out there and find out."

The instant they stepped out the door, it was like

they'd entered another world. Cold and still and breath-takingly beautiful. The snow seemed to be powdery rather than wet and heavy, which made for easier movement but would make building a snowman more difficult.

How she knew all this, she had no idea. The work-ings of her mind continued to perplex her.

"Do you want to make this a team effort?" he asked, grinning. His breath made puffs of steam in the air.

"Team," she replied promptly. "I think one snow-person is enough, don't you?"

"I agree." He knelt down and began gathering snow. She chose a spot a few feet away and did the same. They each pushed their snow into the middle, piling it up. When they'd accumulated enough, Jason began shaping it into a ball.

Despite the cold, time passed quickly. They took turns rolling the bottom ball in snow and patting it down until it was large enough. Same with the mid-dle. When they finally got ready to make the head, she let him do it by himself. She went looking around for sticks to use as arms, rocks or something to use for eyes, and anything that might work for a nose.

With snow burying everything, locating anything wasn't easy. She lucked out finding two relatively similar-sized rocks to use for eyes. And a couple of broken branches for arms.

"I've got some pebbles we can use to outline a mouth," Jason said, standing back and surveying their handiwork.

After some more foraging, they managed to locate everything else they needed.

"He looks perfect," Lucy said, so happy she twirled around until she fell backward into the snow. "I'm making a snow angel," she said, moving her arms and legs. Part of her knew only children did this, but the rest of her didn't care.

He smiled and watched her, not commenting. But when she'd finished and struggled to get to her feet, he grabbed her hand and pulled her up. "Nice," he finally said, releasing her immediately and eying her handiwork.

Just like that, her joy faded. There was something familiar about this, but as usual, she couldn't quite place her finger on exactly what. And the more she tried to catch it, the more the memory danced away in the wind.

Belatedly realizing he watched her, clearly waiting for a response, she thanked him and turned away, not wanting him to see her frustration.

"Are you cold?" he asked, evidently picking up that something was wrong.

She seized on that as an excuse. "Yes. I think I'm going to go inside." Without looking at him, she hurried toward the cabin. When she stepped up onto the front porch, she stamped her feet, hoping to shake off most of the snow.

Right behind her, he did the same.

Inside, she kept busy peeling off her gloves and hat, removing her coat, and finally, her wet boots and socks. She placed the boots close to the woodstove and draped the socks over part of the stove. Crossing to her duffel in her bare feet, she grabbed a dry pair of clean socks and put them on. Since she didn't have house shoes, she decided to wear sneakers.

She blinked back tears, muttered an excuse and escaped to the bathroom. This was one of the things she hated the most about having no memory. She had not the slightest idea why she suddenly wanted to cry.

As Lucy disappeared into the bathroom, Jason divested himself of his own damp clothing. Standing close to the woodstove, he added another log and held his hands out, hoping to warm them.

He felt…happy. It had been years since he'd built a snowman. Surprisingly, he'd enjoyed the experience, mostly due to the unfettered joy Lucy had taken in it. Watching her had been more entertaining than the actual construction of their snowman.

She'd laughed and teased and worked hard. The work and the cold air had brought color to her cheeks, making her even more beautiful. If such a thing was even possible.

He'd never met another woman like her. This rattled him. He wasn't sure what it was about her, but he realized he could easily come to care for her. Which wouldn't be true, as neither of them knew exactly who she was. He'd always considered himself a realist, not one to allow himself to be duped or deluded into believing something that wasn't true. He dealt in facts, not abstracts or suppositions.

Maybe his heightened feelings were due to how badly he'd needed to find some beauty in his life, some of the lighthearted joy and innocence that seemed to come to her so easily. After bearing witness to so much hatred, so much human suffering and death, being with someone as uncomplicated as Lucy felt like a welcome breath of fresh air.

Of course, this wasn't fair to her. Like all human beings, once Lucy regained her memory, she'd be the sum of all her experiences, her wants, her needs. She might even become a completely different person.

Odd how sad thinking about that made him feel.

After warming his hands, he'd gone into the kitchen and rummaged in the cupboard until he located what he needed to make them both hot cocoa. He'd done a few internet searches on amnesia, but he felt like he'd get more accurate information from an actual physician. Time he called his friend Phil, the doctor.

Lucy emerged from the restroom, sniffing the air as she came into the kitchen. "That smells perfect," she said. "And makes me think I should be associating it with childhood memories." She frowned, clearly trying to access those.

He waited, hoping for her sake that something, even the smallest memory, would surface.

After a moment, she shook her heard. "Nothing."

Instead of commenting, he slid her mug of hot cocoa across the counter to her. Snagging it, she grinned. "What, no whipped cream?"

"Sorry, I'm all out," he responded, wondering if she realized that she'd made that connection at least. It might be small, but it was better than nothing.

While Lucy sipped her cocoa, he used the satellite phone to place the call. As usual, he had to leave a voice mail. He knew his friend would get back to him when he had a chance.

Once he left that quick voice mail, he reached for

his own cup and took a sip. Perfect, he thought, as the hot drink warmed its way down his throat.

"Thank you for today," Lucy said softly, eying him over the rim of her mug. "I truly enjoyed playing in the snow."

"No problem." Hesitating, he decided to go ahead and ask. "Something happened to you, right before we came in. What was it? Did you have another memory?"

"No." She sighed. "I kept feeling like there was something I was supposed to remember. It felt like whatever it was kept dancing right outside of the edge of my vision. Very frustrating."

"I can imagine. That call I just placed was to one of my friends who's a doctor in the Springs. I've done a fair amount of research on amnesia, but I want to hear what he thinks."

"That's great," she said, taking another sip. "This really would be so much better with whipped cream. Just so you know."

"I get the point. Next time I pick up supplies, I'll be sure and get some."

She rewarded that with a broad smile, which had him grinning at her like a fool. To cover, he drank more cocoa.

They ate leftover spaghetti for dinner. After they ate, once again they did the dishes side by side, which should have felt uncomfortably domestic, but didn't. He tried the television, pleased to note the satellite receiver was working again. Scrolling through the guide to see what choices they had, he almost asked her what she liked to watch. Luckily, he caught himself in time.

He settled on a lighthearted sitcom, deciding that since it was only thirty minutes, he could always change it if she didn't appear to like it.

She sat beside him on the couch, sticking as close to the other end as she could. They watched the show in silence, making him wish he'd asked her to play poker or even Scrabble instead.

When the show ended, he glanced over at her, meaning to ask her if she wanted to watch something else. She'd fallen asleep, her head pillowed on her arm.

His heart caught midbeat. He debated on whether to get up and pull the blanket over her, then decided to leave her alone for now. After the nightmares she'd had the night before, she probably was exhausted.

Jason watched a couple more sitcoms before the evening news came on. Once again, Kabul led off the program. Another suicide bomber had struck, this time a hospital. The loss of life had been tremendous.

He felt that same old bitter ache, aware of the futility of his need to do something, anything, to make it right. He couldn't; he'd tried. Reporting the unbiased facts had been his job, was every journalist's job, but at some point he'd come to feel he should have done more.

When that story ended, he waited to see if there would be a report on his missing friend, Rick Engles. But there was nothing, which didn't entirely surprise him. At this point, no one seemed to know if he'd gone AWOL, had been kidnapped, hurt or what. Jason knew his friend well enough to know he'd never desert, so he'd been either taken or injured.

Jason clicked off the television and got up to go to bed. Lucy hadn't stirred at all, so he quietly covered her with the blanket and went into his room to get some sleep.

* * *

When he opened his eyes in the morning, he realized Lucy must have slept through the night peacefully. Either that, or he just hadn't heard her. He hoped it was the former.

Taking care to move as silently as possible, he showered and dressed before heading into the kitchen for his normal coffee. To his surprise, she was already there, seated at the kitchen table, with a half-empty cup of coffee.

"Good morning," she said, greeting him with a hesitant smile. "Did you sleep well?"

"I sure did." He smiled back. "I'm guessing you were free of bad dreams last night."

Though her smile wavered slightly, she nodded. "I think so. Either way, I slept. Do you think the roads will be passable today?"

"It depends on if the plows made it up this way. I haven't heard them, so I'm guessing not yet. There aren't a whole lot of people who are year-round residents this far up. Since we're not anywhere near a ski resort, we don't get vacationers in the winter."

Nodding, she sipped her coffee. When his had finished brewing, he pulled out a chair opposite her and sat. "Are you hungry? I have some eggs that I can fry up with English muffins if you'd like."

"I can do that," she said. Judging by her expression, she'd surprised herself. "I think I know how to cook something like that."

This time he decided not to comment on what obviously seemed another memory. "If you don't mind, then go for it," he said.

She drained the last of her coffee and got up. "Where do you keep your skillet?"

"Cupboard next to the stove. Do you need any help?"

"Nope. I think I'm good."

Relaxing, he enjoyed his coffee while he watched her move around the kitchen. She had the kind of feminine grace that he attributed to dancers or athletes. Again, the mystery of her intrigued him. What kind of work had she done before? What kind of circles did she move in? Were her friends artsy or educated or down-to-earth types?

Did she have a lover or husband somewhere, and children?

The thought ended his fantasies quickly, as it should. He needed to try to find some objectivity where she was concerned.

"Here you go," she said, sliding a plate in front of him. She'd given him two perfectly cooked sunny-side up eggs and a toasted English muffin. She set a glass of orange juice down in front of him, plus the jar of preserves. Then she went back and fetched her own plate.

He dug in. Damn, he'd forgotten how nice it was to have someone cook for him. And there he went again. Making more of something ordinary than he should have been.

After they ate, they fell into their usual routine of doing the dishes side by side. While he had a bit of cabin fever, he didn't feel right leaving her here on her own.

She went to take her shower. While she was gone, he pondered possible activities. He had a snowmobile in the shed out back, but it hadn't been started since last winter and he wasn't even sure it would run. He could check on that, but he knew he had some snowshoes and cross-country skis around here somewhere.

Digging in the front closet for his snowshoes, he was surprised to find another pair. His old pair from childhood, worn and with a few crosspieces missing. But still serviceable. Now if only he could locate another pair of poles. After a bit more searching, he found another set of poles in his bedroom closet.

Lucy emerged from the bathroom, toweling off her hair. "What are you doing?" she asked, eying the pile of stuff he'd dug out of the closet.

"Would you like to learn how to use these?" he asked, holding up the old pair. "They're snowshoes."

She came closer, taking them from him and examining both sides. "They seem to be broken." She pointed out the areas with holes. "Will they still work?"

"I don't see why not." He eyed her feet, which were much smaller than his. "I'm thinking they might fit you well enough to work. It'll get us out of the cabin. Are you game?"

"Definitely." Her eyes sparkled with excitement. "Let me get my hair a bit dryer and put some layers on. I can't wait to do some exploring."

Bemused, he nodded and watched her go. Her enthusiasm was one of the things he liked about her.

Lucy returned a few minutes later, clearly already bundled up. "You aren't ready yet?" she chided, making him laugh.

"I will be. But you need ski pants for something

like this. I only have one pair and I know they won't fit you."

"It's OK. I have long underwear, leggings and jeans on. Layers. I promise I'll let you know if I get too cold."

He got dressed quickly and once they were both suited up, he handed her the snowshoes and poles. Grabbing his own, he opened the front door and stepped back for her to precede him. When she passed him, she glanced sideways up at him and grinned.

For a half second, he froze, caught up in her powerful beauty. Then he shook it off and followed her, closing the door behind him.

Outside, he squinted into the blinding, glittering whiteness. Cold, with the air so crisp and clear they could see their breath frost, but beautiful. Ahead, miles of undisturbed snow stretched out before them. Unblemished save for the area where they'd made the snowman.

The snowman stood, like a lonely sentinel forever trapped in ice, facing toward the driveway, as if gazing down the hill.

"We did good," she said, still smiling. "I really like him."

"I do too." Determined to continue to ignore how warm her smile made him feel, he gestured toward the driveway. "Which way do you want to go? We can go up or we can go down."

She considered for a moment. "I think up. At some point, we should have a great view of the road, right?"

"True. But like I said, I doubt it's plowed yet. Cedar is a small town and we only have one plow. A lot of people have their own plows they put on their trucks so they can take care of their own driveways, like I do. It'll probably be a day or two before the road is passable."

"What happens if someone has a medical emergency?"

"If they don't have a snowmobile, then they'll call someone who does. Most people who live up in the mountains away from the town have contingency plans."

They started the trek up the side of the peak near his house. He stayed slightly behind her, watching in case she had trouble with the snowshoes. But after a slight hesitation in the beginning, she appeared to take to them easily, her movements growing in confidence. She used the poles as if she'd been doing this for years.

"Your hips might hurt tomorrow," he said. "It's a little bit different of a cadence than regular walking, plus the snow provides resistance."

Appearing unfazed, she nodded. "Good to know." Head up, eyes sparkling, she breathed in the crisp air with relish. Looking around her, she appeared to be in her element. Some people preferred hot, others liked cold. Lucy definitely appeared to the latter. Maybe that piece of information might help narrow down what part of the country she'd come from.

"Jason, are you coming with me?" she called out. He realized she'd gone off ahead of him, moving through the tree line straight up, circumventing a safer path.

As he started forward, a gunshot rang out, the sound reverberating through the mountains.

Chapter 5

Lucy instinctively threw herself to the ground, getting a mouthful of snow in the process. The soft impact made her cheekbone and other bruises hurt again, though they were fading as she healed. She didn't know where Jason was or if he'd been hit, but she somehow knew better than to stand up to find out. No point in making herself an easy target.

"Jason?" she called out, low voiced. "Are you okay?"

"Right here," he answered, sliding on his side toward her. "I can tell where that gunshot came from. There's absolutely no reason someone would be shooting up here. It's not hunting season and this is all private property."

Heart pounding, she nodded. For a moment, she felt

dizzy. The world shifted, and she thought she might pass out. *Not. In. The. Snow.* "Are you sure?" she swallowed hard. "That it was a gunshot?"

"What else could it be?" The grim set of his jaw told her he meant it. "Don't take the snowshoes off. Despite the way they limit our movement when down like this, they're still the quickest way to get out of here."

With all the craziness that had been her life lately, she had no trouble believing they were now in danger.

Apparently, Jason did. "This makes no sense," he muttered. "Why would anyone be shooting in the mountains after such a heavy snowfall? Sounds like that could definitely cause an avalanche."

The word made her shudder. She glanced above them, hoping she wouldn't see a wall of snow heading toward them.

"You hear it before you see it," he said.

"Oh." She looked back, in the direction from which they'd come. The cabin was no longer in sight. "What now? I don't like feeling so exposed."

"I'm not sure. There's a long, open stretch between us and the cabin. If there is a shooter aiming for us, that would be the area where he'd have the best shot."

Hearing him say this out loud made her stomach swoop. "Do you really think he's aiming for us?" Her voice shook.

"I doubt it." His prompt reply made her feel slightly better. "But since we have no way to know for sure just yet, and with all the other weirdness going on, it's better to play safe than be sorry."

Other weirdness. Being her showing up in his cabin with no memory and a vague sense of danger.

"Then what do we do?" A hint of the desperation she felt had crept into her voice.

"Try to make it to the next grouping of trees," he decided. "We can shelter there until we figure out what exactly is going on."

They moved as quickly as they could to implement that plan. What had started as a fun outing had turned ominous and dark.

Another gunshot, echoing over and over. She couldn't tell if it was closer or not.

"No bullet hitting anywhere near us," he said. "That's good. For all I know, it might be someone hunting illegally. The deer take more risks when they can't find food."

Though she felt sorry for the deer, she fervently hoped that was the case. "Can we go back to the cabin?"

"Not yet," he replied. "Right now, we just need to wait. Whoever it is might just be trying to flush us out."

So wait they did, cold seeping through the soles of her boots. Though her parka kept her warm, her fingers and toes felt frozen. But she didn't want to complain—she wanted to live. "If someone is after us, they probably want me," she said. "I'm sorry."

Gaze steady, he shook his head. "You don't know that. For all we know, it might be a hunter, or some idiot trying out his new gun. If they were after you—or us—why would they fire warning shots to alert us?"

He had a point. Though still tense, she relaxed slightly. She could no longer feel her feet at all.

When it had been silent for twenty minutes, he

touched her arm. "We're going back to the cabin. I want you to stay with me and move as quickly and as quietly as you can. I'm pretty sure whatever that was had nothing to do with us, but there's no sense in being careless."

She nodded. "I understand."

"Then let's go."

Grabbing her poles, she started out after him. They kept as close to the tree lines as they could, and when they were in open spaces, she struggled to keep up with his pace. It was difficult to move quickly in such deep snow. Twice she stumbled, used her poles to right herself and kept going.

Finally, the cabin came into sight. They paused to rest near a large evergreen tree. She couldn't help but notice Jason wasn't even breathing hard, while she could barely catch her breath.

"Are you okay?" he asked.

"Yes."

"Good." His gaze drifted past her, toward the direction they'd come, before eying the cabin. "It all looks the same, at least from here. I'm going to try and stay within the same tracks we made coming up. That way we can tell if anyone else has been here."

His offhand comment kicked her heart rate up a notch. She nodded, hoping this would all turn out to be nothing.

"Keep your eyes and ears open and your head down," he ordered. "Stay right behind me and if I tell you to do something, like hit the ground, do it immediately and without question."

"Got it," she replied, her heart in her throat.

They started off. As they crossed the clearing between them and the cabin, she braced herself, almost certain she'd hear the sharp crack of a gunshot right before a bullet slammed into her back.

Another flash of memory. Rubble all around her, the sound of gunfire and sirens outside. Screaming and wailing, someone sobbing. Darkness, hidden, flinching away from the sudden flashes of light.

"Lucy." Jason shook her. "You can't zone out. Not now."

Blinking, she sucked in a great gasp of cold air. "Sorry," she managed.

"Look." He pointed. "Footsteps circling the cabin."

"I see them."

Jaw tight, he hustled her toward the door. "I didn't lock it up. I never do, since it's so isolated. Clearly, it's time I start."

At the door, he pulled her close. "Stay right behind me. If someone is inside, I'll protect you."

Fear stole away her voice, but she moved even closer.

"One, two, three." He slammed open the door. A quick glance revealed the cabin appeared to be empty.

And ransacked. Whoever had broken in had been in a rush to go through their stuff.

"Damn it all to hell," Jason cursed. He kicked the door shut behind them and turned the dead bolt.

Staring around her in stunned disbelief, Lucy shook her head. The cushions had been pulled from the couch and tossed, her duffel emptied, and her clothing scattered all around the room. Someone had rifled through all the paperwork on Jason's desk. Papers were strewn everywhere.

"I don't understand." She made a slow circle, taking in the destruction. "What on earth could they have been looking for?"

"I have no idea," he said, removing his snowshoes and tossing them aside. In short order, he peeled off his gloves and removed his jacket. After taking off his own boots, he immediately began picking up his papers, stacking them back on his desk. A moment later, she took off her snowshoes and wet boots plus her own outerwear, and then began gathering up her clothing.

Once he'd gotten his desk reorganized, he crossed to stand in front of a painting of a sunrise over the mountains. Glancing over his shoulder at her, he pulled the artwork down from the wall, revealing a wall safe. "Good. It's undisturbed. Even if they found it, there's no way they could get inside."

Though she was curious about its contents, she didn't feel it was any of her business to ask, so she didn't.

"I safeguard my photographs," he explained anyway, correctly interpreting her look. "Though most of them are digital, I'm compulsive about backing them up. I've got both the actual memory cards and the backups in there." Plus, he utilized an online storage site as well. He'd long ago come to believe he couldn't be too careful.

She looked from him to the safe and back again. "Why would anyone want to steal your photographs?"

Though he shrugged, she sensed his casual facade wasn't how he really felt.

"Tell me," she insisted. "I won't ever understand if you don't explain."

"I'm an award-winning photojournalist," he finally explained. "My photos are in high demand and I'm paid handsomely for them. In addition to that, I'm under contract for a book of war photos. Some of these might contain sensitive information. I always look through them to be sure. Since I just got back from the Middle East, I haven't had time to see what all I have."

"That still doesn't explain why someone would want them. Are you saying they'd try to pass them off as their own?"

He frowned. "That's possible. But there are those who will use damning photos to blackmail high-ranking officials. It's well-known, though no one who is a highly respected journalist would stoop to such a thing. Since I took a lot of pictures when the suicide bomber hit the hotel in Kabul, there's the possibility I captured something I should not have."

Though maybe the amnesia was making her a bit dense, she still didn't understand. "Wouldn't you know? I mean, I'd think you'd be well aware of what exactly you photographed, right?"

"Not always," he admitted. "When there's a lot going on, in the heat of the moment, I'm just moving around and taking shots. One right after the other. Sometimes out of thirty shots, I'll get one good one. Often I surprise myself with what I've inadvertently captured." Replacing the artwork on the wall, he turned to face her.

Slowly, she nodded, willing herself to relax. "That

means you think you were the target of the break-in, not me."

"Not really." His grim answer had her tensing up once more. "Since whoever did this isn't inside right now, we can't exactly ask. And I should tell you, though he or she could have used skis or snowshoes to leave, I didn't see any tracks. I'm about to go out and check in the direction of the driveway."

She watched him, suddenly nervous for his safety. "That would mean they might still be around."

"Exactly. Because with the roads still impassable, the only way to get up here would be with a snow-mobile. And we haven't heard the sound of one start-ing up."

Watching her eyes go wide, Jason didn't have the heart to tell her the rest of his concerns. While he wasn't sure if the intruder had come for his photos or was after Lucy, there remained a strong possibility that he or she was still lurking around.

"Do you know how to handle a weapon?" he asked, even though he figured she didn't.

"Like a...gun?" He wouldn't have believed it pos-sible, but her eyes got even wider.

"Never mind." He figured he had his answer. "I've got several guns here, pistols and shotguns. It would help if you knew how to use one. I'll teach you, but I don't have time to do that today."

Eying him, she blinked. "I'm familiar with guns," she said, the expression on her face indicating she'd surprised herself as much as him. "I used to go to the shooting range about once a month, just to blow off steam."

"Who taught you?" he asked quickly, hoping she might be able to capture the rest of the memory.

"I..." She shook her head. "I don't know. That wasn't like a memory, where I could actually visualize something. It seemed more like a *knowing*. You asked a question and I just knew the answer."

Not sure if he believed her, he went to the big gun safe that stood in the corner of his living room. After punching in the combination, he eyed his assortment of pistols before choosing one for her. A nice little SIG Sauer P238, one of his lighter and more compact pistols. "Have you ever shot this?" he asked, handing it to her. "It has a six-round magazine and it's easy to handle."

Taking it from him, she eyed it dubiously. "I'm not sure." Hefting it up, she sighted it at the front door. "This feels good," she said. "I'll need some ammo."

He handed her several clips and watched her as she expertly loaded one into the chamber. Maybe she really did know how to handle a weapon. That made him feel slightly better.

Turning back to the gun safe, he chose one of his favorite hand guns, his trusty Ruger .38 Magnum. He loaded it, grabbed some spare ammo, and then closed and secured the safe.

"If I go out there, are you absolutely sure you can defend yourself with that?" he asked.

She regarded him seriously. "Well, I haven't practiced with this particular gun, so I don't know how it handles, but I do know how to point it and shoot it. If someone comes for me, I won't hesitate, if that's what you're asking."

Her answer told him she really did know her way around a firearm. "Good. I want you to lock the door after me."

"Will do."

One glance at her, and his chest ached. She seemed so small, so vulnerable, even though she held his pistol with a confident grip. He didn't know what had happened to her, why she'd lost her memory or how she'd ended up in his cabin. So help him, if he ever found out someone—man or woman—had deliberately hurt her, he'd use every resource he had to make them pay.

This time, instead of snowshoes, he put on his ski boots and grabbed his skis and poles. If he happened to run into whoever was out there, this would give him more flexibility and speed.

Outside, the snow-shrouded world remained silent. Stepping down from his front porch, he clipped on his skis. He'd decided he'd follow the other tracks as far as he could.

After circling the cabin and then going inside, the intruder had gone down instead of up. Not toward the snow-covered driveway, where he or she would have been easily spotted, but perpendicular to it. The tracks kept inside the trees, providing cover. This meant most likely snowshoes rather than skis.

Jason skied the edge of his driveway, using his poles and an angled stance to keep his speed down. He even considered going back to the cabin and switching to his snowshoes, but since he didn't figure he'd be going far, he knew he could walk back up.

Sure enough, the tracks emerged from the brush at the point where his driveway met the road. Since the plow hadn't yet made it through, the snow remained pristine and untouched. Except for the unmistakable snowmobile tracks.

But how? Sound carried in these mountains and he knew for sure he hadn't heard the loud engine of an Arctic Cat. Had it been an electric snowmobile? He remembered reading about Taiga electric snowmobiles, so such a thing was entirely possible. Even though they weren't as rugged as a traditional gas-powered machine, they were less expensive and left a much smaller global footprint. He'd have to ask around in town. If someone in these parts had one, he was sure everyone in town would know about it.

At least this meant the intruder had left. Though they hadn't left any clues as to what they'd been after.

Removing his skis, he trudged back up the slope. When he reached the front door, he knocked sharply. "Lucy, it's me."

A second later, she opened the door, looking relieved.

He stamped his ski boots on the front porch and shook off the snow before stepping inside. "They're gone," he told her. "I found snowmobile tracks at the end of the driveway."

"I'm glad." She unloaded her pistol and placed it on the table. "The safety is still on."

Nodding, he shrugged out of his outerwear. "I'm going to keep mine on me for now, just in case. Do you want to do the same, or would you rather I put yours in the safe?"

Her gaze searched his. "Do you think I'll need it out?"

"No idea. If you feel better with it locked up, I can do that. It's a simple thing to get it out of the safe. I'll give you the combination."

"Okay. I sort of feel better with it safely under lock and key. Looking at it all the time will just make me feel as if I'm in constant danger."

Since he understood that, he put up both pistols and ammo and locked the gun safe. He'd just jotted down the combination and handed it to her when his phone rang. Answering, he waited for the usual static to subside. "Hello? Hello?" he said.

"It's Sheriff Jeffords. How secure are you up there at your place?"

"'Secure?'" Odd question, but he felt certain Jeffords had a reason for asking it. "Well, now that you ask, someone broke in to my cabin and went through my things. It's kind of weird since the road still hasn't been plowed. We—I was out and about on snowshoes, and I heard some gunshots."

"Gunshots?" Clearly appalled, the sheriff cursed. "Damn fool could have started an avalanche."

"I know. But there wasn't one, at least not near me. I'm unclear as to what he or she was shooting at. I hightailed it back to my place, and that's when I saw the other set of tracks. Whoever it was came inside. Went through everything. The place was a disaster."

"I'm guessing your door wasn't locked?"

"Of course not." Jason didn't bother to hide his frustration. "We've never needed to lock our doors around here. Until now. You'd better believe that's going to change. I'll be locking it now."

"Did they take anything?"

Jason shook his head, even though the other man couldn't see. "Not that I can tell."

"Do you want to file a report?"

"Not at this time," Jason replied. "There doesn't seem to be a point." He suddenly remembered the sheriff had initiated this call. "Did you know about this?"

"No. How could I?"

"True. But you called me. Is there a reason?"

"Yeah, there is." Sheriff Jeffords cleared his throat. "A couple of guys showed up here this morning, despite the town being absolutely dead with everyone staying home due to the snow. They came in from Denver, they said. They were asking a lot of questions about you."

"Were they military?" He couldn't help but wonder if this had something to do with Rick's disappearance.

"Not that I could tell. One of them claimed to be law enforcement, but not only did he not say what branch, he never showed me his badge or any ID. When I asked to see something, he growled some nonsense about top secret and left." The sheriff paused. "Jason, what exactly is going on with you?"

Glancing at Lucy, who listened to his end of the conversation with interest, he considered his words carefully. "Nothing, at least that I know of. I got a call the other day from some military type to let me know Rick is missing. But I don't know why they'd send anyone here to talk to me about that."

"Rick Engles?" The sheriff sounded stunned. "What happened to him?"

"I don't know. We were supposed to meet up when

I was in Kabul on assignment, but it fell through. I had no idea he was missing until I got that phone call." He thought for a moment. "There's no reason they would have sent anybody to talk to me personally. And if they had, they would have been in uniform or had no problem showing their credentials."

"True." Jeffords paused. "Maybe it's about something else. It must have been pretty damn important for them to head this way from Denver right after we got hit with a huge blizzard." He paused. "And, despite Rick being a local, they never once asked about him. Just about you."

"Did they leave you a card or any contact information? Maybe I can give them a call and straighten all this out."

"Nope. Like I said, the moment I asked to see credentials, they left. You don't have to be a police officer to figure out they had something to hide."

"But what?" Jason couldn't figure it out. He lived his life in the public eye, readily available, with nothing to hide. Nothing, that is, until Lucy had come into his life.

"That's the question," the sheriff agreed. "Anyway, I just wanted to let you know. If I find out anything more, I'll give you a shout."

"Thank you." Ending the call, Jason relayed to Lucy all the information the sheriff had given him.

"Wow." She fiddled with a strand of her hair. "Do you think it's possible those men were looking for me?"

He gave her the blunt truth. "Could be. I'd guess that's definitely a possibility. Until you get your memory back, we don't have any idea."

She met his gaze, her expression serious. "I don't want to be putting you in danger."

"I'm not worried."

"I am," she said doggedly. "I couldn't live with myself if anything happened to you because of me."

"You won't have to." Though he wanted to pull her into his arms and comfort her, he managed to restrain himself. "Believe me, I've been handling myself in dangerous situations for a long time. I'm not worried."

His confident tone coaxed a hesitant smile from her. "I guess I don't have a choice but to take your word for it."

"I guess you don't," he replied, crossing to the window and eying the never-ending blanket of snow. He'd never been good with confinement and always managed to find activities to delay cabin fever as long as possible. Add to that the temptation Lucy continually presented and he knew he'd be in deep trouble if they weren't able to get out and about soon.

A workout would definitely help. When he didn't work out at all, like he hadn't the last few days, he could tell a difference, both mentally and physically. Due to the size of his cabin, he had room for only a set of adjustable dumbbells, but that would be enough.

He went back into his bedroom to change, then he dragged his weights out from under his bed and carried them into the living room. The spot between the couch and his desk was where he usually did his workouts.

"What are you doing?" Lucy asked, eying his dumbbells.

Once he explained he was going to do some lifting

and body-weight exercises, she lit up. "Do you mind if I do them alongside you?"

He shrugged. "As long as you don't hurt yourself."

"I won't." Her confident reply had him remembering the way she'd taken him down. She'd claimed to have taken self-defense classes. Maybe she lifted weights too.

"Let me go change," she said. "I have a pair of leggings and a long T-shirt. I'll be right back."

"Okay." He went ahead and started warming up with push-ups and sit-ups while he waited. When she emerged from the bathroom, he couldn't help but stare. Black leggings hugged her shapely legs and her long T-shirt clung lovingly to her shape. She also put her silky hair into a jaunty ponytail.

A jolt of desire hit him, low and hard. He swallowed, going back into his push-ups, desperately trying not to think about how badly he wanted to be doing them over her.

"What?" she asked, hands on her hips. "This is the only clothing I have suitable for working out. Do I look weird or something?"

"You look fine." His curt answer might not have been reassuring, be it was the best he could do. Right now, he needed to do some heavy lifting and hopefully make him forget what he wanted to do with her body and his.

Though he preferred to break down his workouts into sections, working legs one day, upper body the next, when short on time, he'd do a more comprehensive all-body workout. Today, since he wanted to really push himself, he planned to do it all.

"Warm up first," he told her.

She frowned. "I usually do a little cardio to warm up. Since you don't have a treadmill…"

"Do jumping jacks or burpees," he advised, though he wasn't sure he could withstand watching her do burpees. He actually felt relieved when she chose to do jumping jacks.

Picking up his weights, he chose twenty pounds and began with hammer curls.

She finished her jumping jacks. Slightly winded, she came over to stand near him, watching as he lifted. Again, he felt a sizzle of wanting, which he attempted to channel into working his muscles.

"Can I jump in when you finish your set?" she asked. "I'm just going to do the same workout as you."

He eyed her. "You talk as if you've worked out before."

"I have." Her confident smile almost undid him. "And no, it's not a memory per se. Again, it's just something I know."

Sweating, he finished up his set. "What weight do you want?" he asked. "I have this set on twenty."

"Fifteen should be fine," she replied. "Though since I clearly haven't worked out in a bit, I might have to go down to twelve."

"Okay." He set the weights up at fifteen and handed them to her.

With perfect form, she easily completed three sets of twelve. Damn if he didn't find this working out together sexy as hell. He shook his head. Thinking like that only led to trouble.

"Did I do something wrong?" She frowned.

"Of course not. You clearly know what you're doing."

"Then why'd you shake your head?" she asked.

"At my own foolishness, not anything you did." No way did he plan on telling her how badly he wanted her.

Luckily, she didn't press. Instead, she handed the weights back to him.

They continued on like that for thirty minutes, going through a full repertoire of body movement. They even did fifty crunches side by side. When they finally finished, her skin gleamed with a fine sheen of perspiration. Drenched in sweat, he figured he looked worse. Her next words confirmed that.

"You can have first shower," she told him. "I think I'm going to do some yoga moves for cooldown."

Damned if he didn't want to stick around and watch that. Instead, he took himself off to the shower without another word.

Chapter 6

Once Jason had left the room, Lucy half-heartedly put herself through a few now-familiar yoga moves. Though parts of her body remained sore, the bruises had begun to fade as she healed. She wouldn't have been able to comfortably do any of the stretches and moves as recently as a few days ago.

Despite trying to clear her mind and take herself to a place of peace, all she could think about was how badly she wanted to join Jason in the shower. She could picture him naked, in mouthwatering detail, and could imagine stripping off her sweaty clothes and slipping in behind him. They could lather each other up with soap, and then...

No. This needed to stop. Instead of yoga, she put herself through an intense cardio routine of burpees, mountain climbers and push-ups. *High intensity interval training*, she remembered it was called. Exactly what she needed to try and scrub the lust from her mind.

As she was walking around the perimeter of the cabin to try and cool down, Jason emerged from the bathroom. "All yours," he called out, before disappearing into his bedroom and closing the door.

She grabbed some clean clothes and hurried into the bathroom. Stripping her damp workout gear off, she eyed herself critically in the mirror. Sad to say, she still didn't fully recognize the dark-haired woman staring back.

Hopefully, that would come soon. She really wanted to mention the possibility of her seeing Jason's doctor friend. She'd definitely feel better if she had an idea of a memory-return timeline.

Jason. A complete stranger had become her entire world, through no fault of theirs. She couldn't help but wonder what place he'd occupy in her life once she had herself back.

Stepping into the hot shower, she shivered. She felt pleasantly sore, but also aching. Working out and watching Jason had only made her crave him even more. So much so that she'd had trouble with the yoga moves. Up until today, she hadn't even known she liked to work out and do yoga, so she considered that a win.

But on the other hand, the constant push-pull of her attraction to Jason had begun to take its toll on her. When her memory finally returned, she wondered if she'd learn she was free to act on it, or if she'd learn she was married to another man. That latter thought terrified her. How could she ever forget someone she loved?

But then again, how had she managed to forget herself?

Once she finished her shower, she got dressed in the clean clothes and blow-dried her hair. Taking a deep breath, she emerged to find Jason in the kitchen, cooking them something for lunch.

"Feeling better?" he asked, without turning around. "I know I do. I'm fixing tomato soup and grilled cheese. Pull up a chair and it'll be ready soon."

"What do you want to drink?" she asked, marveling at how domestic they sounded. Was domesticity something she was used to, in her other life? Maybe that's why it felt so comfortable, so right. "I can get that," she said. "While you're cooking."

Milk for him and water for her. She carried both full glasses with her to the table and sat down, unable to keep from admiring his narrow waist, lean hips and nice backside as he moved from stove to counter.

Luckily, the sound of the snowplow came just as they were sitting down to lunch. She'd just taken a bite of her grilled cheese sandwich after dipping it in her soup.

"Listen," Jason said. "I'm going to go look. If I stand in one particular spot on the front porch, I can usually catch a glimpse of the plow through the trees." He jumped up and grabbed his coat, stepping outside.

Uncertain whether she should continue eating or wait for his return, she decided she might as well enjoy her lunch while it was still hot. She'd had three spoonfuls of soup and another couple bites of her grilled cheese by the time he returned.

"Yep, it's the plow," he said, hanging up his coat. "Just in the nick of time, if you ask me." Sitting back down, he proceeded to demolish his lunch. When he'd finished, he grinned at her. "You know what that means?"

Savoring the last bite of grilled cheese, she eyed him. "No, what?"

"We need to get the driveway cleared. Once we can get to the road, we can go into town. Actually, we can go anywhere. I'm sure all the major highways are clear."

"Will we shovel?" she asked, trying not to sound as horrified as she felt. Just the thought of trying to clear that much driveway made her feel queasy.

"Shovel?" he laughed. "That would take all day. I have a great snowblower and once I clear away the front of my garage, I have a large metal plow that I put on the front of my Jeep. Now that the big plow's been through and won't kick snow back onto my hard work, I'm going to get on plowing it."

"I'll join you once I clean this up," she replied.

He actually hesitated. "Do you want my help? We can knock out the cleanup in a few minutes."

"Nope." She waved him away. "You go ahead and get started. I've got this. Maybe if you get done today, we can go somewhere tomorrow. I would really like to get out of this cabin."

He arched one brow. "Don't tell me you've got cabin fever too?"

"Of course I do. Who wouldn't? I might not know who I am, but I wouldn't mind seeing the countryside around here."

Her comment made him laugh again. "We're on

the same page," he said, suiting up. "Feel free to join me if you feel like it. No problem if you'd rather stay here in the warm cabin."

After he'd gone outside, she remained in her seat, her cheeks burning. She felt hollow, burning from the inside out with her absurd need for him. Pressing her hands to her cheeks, she willed herself to settle down. Then she pushed to her feet and began clearing the table, knowing the simple act of moving would help. It always did.

She heard Jason start the snowblower. The thing roared to life as if eager to tackle the job. She listened as Jason began to work, clearing a path from the front porch to the driveway, before starting on the larger task. The sound seemed oddly comforting, though she couldn't say why.

Once all the dishes were clean, dry and put away, she wiped down the counters and looked around the small kitchen. Already, after only a few days here, it felt like home. Dangerous for a woman who no doubt had another home somewhere, possibly with someone else. She wondered why the thought made her so sad.

Enough of this. She grabbed her duffel, doubled up her socks, put on her boots, and then her jacket, hat and gloves.

Outside, the sun shone brilliantly, glinting off the snow so brightly she had to squint. She stood for a moment on the porch, shading her eyes with her hand, watching as the plow kicked up plumes of snow. Jason had already cleared the area directly in front of the garage. He turned the snowblower off, pushing it to one side, before opening the garage door. Spotting her, he waved her over. He'd backed his Jeep in, and there was a good-sized metal plow attached to the front end.

"Where'd you get something like that?" she asked, a little awed.

"They're pretty common up here," he replied, grinning. "Those of us who live outside town know we have to be able to take care of ourselves in an emergency."

"Can I ride along?"

"Of course."

Barely restraining herself from jumping up and down with glee, she crossed around the front of the Jeep and climbed into the passenger side. Buckling in, she waited impatiently for him to join her.

Once he had the snowblower stowed inside the garage, he joined her. "This is going to be fun," he said. "I've always enjoyed using this plow."

Men and their toys. The thought came out of nowhere, making her frown.

Of course, he picked up on that. "What's wrong?"

Instantly, she smoothed out her expression. "Nothing. Just trying for a memory. It's difficult sometimes, like they're dancing in the fog, just out of reach."

He covered her hand with his. "It'll get better. I promise."

Just like that, the atmosphere changed, becoming charged. Their gazes locked, and she swore she could hear his heart pounding just as hard as hers. Neither moved, frozen in place, and for one breathtaking second, she just knew he was about to lean forward and capture her mouth with his.

Instead, he blinked and looked away. Clumsily inserting the key into the ignition, he started the engine. "Are you ready?" he asked without looking at her, his voice rusty.

"I am." She couldn't help but feel a bit sad.

Shaking that off, she watched as he drove out of the garage onto the cleared area. Putting the Jeep in Park, he also engaged the parking brake. "Be right back," he said.

He went around to the front and lowered the plow. When he got back into the Jeep, his brown eyes sparkled. "Here we go," he said.

They made several passes, driving down and then up, before taking a trip back down. "There we go," he announced happily. "We can now get out!"

"Today?" she asked hopefully. "Maybe we could go into town and have something to eat later."

He shook his head grimly. "Not a good idea. Not yet, at least. If we do anything like that, we're going to have to go farther away, like Colorado Springs or something. I don't want anyone in town recognizing you and knowing you're with me."

Hurt stabbed her at first. But then she realized he wanted her to stay hidden for her own safety. If someone was looking for her, the less she was seen, the more difficult it would be for them to find her.

"Thanks," she said.

"Sure. We'll figure something out for tomorrow." Parking again, he went out and raised up the plow before returning to back the Jeep into the garage. Once he'd killed the engine, he turned to her and smiled. "Come on. I think we've earned a couple of mugs of hot cocoa, don't you?"

I prefer tea. Darjeeling, to be exact. Another thought from nowhere. One more tidbit of self-knowledge that she'd keep to herself for now. "Sure," she replied. "Cocoa sounds great."

The afternoon slipped by, more quickly than it should have. They played cards and she offered to cook the evening meal. He shrugged and told her to knock herself out. So she did, rummaging in the refrigerator, trying to decide what to make.

He set the table while she cooked. She decided on turkey burgers and sweet potato fries. Both were premade and frozen, but simple to make. She baked the fries while cooking the turkey burgers. She'd been pleasantly surprised at how good they tasted once fried up in a skillet. When she'd found them in the box in the freezer, they'd looked so unappetizing that she'd almost given them a hard pass. Instead, deciding to take a chance, she'd gone ahead and cooked them. And hadn't been disappointed.

Quick and easy meal. And healthy too.

After they'd cleaned up, they watched the news again, like an old married couple. As the news announcer came on, Lucy tried not to get anxious, but she couldn't help but worry that she'd see something that would set off another panic attack. Unfortunately, she wouldn't have any warning because she had no idea what might be a trigger.

Thankfully, the news ended without anything happening, though she couldn't have repeated what the program had been about. Next, a talk show came on. She tried to watch but had no idea who most of the guest were, never mind the host, so she let her mind wander.

Sitting on the comfortable sofa that also served as her bed, she must have dozed off. Because the next thing she knew, she was standing in what appeared to be a hotel room, gazing out the window. The view seemed comprised of buildings, some of them old and in various stages of deterioration. She got a sense of age, and also danger.

Behind her, someone spoke. A man, though she never turned to see his face. His cultured voice whipped into her, the thin veneer of civility undercut with a fine thread of cruelty. She couldn't quite make out the words, but knew they were full of hurt and scorn.

Once, she might have felt pain. But now she only felt tired. She regretted coming on this trip with him, regretted agreeing to give them one more chance. She glanced down at her left hand, relieved to see no ring. At least she hadn't married him. With a start, she realized she felt nothing. Not love, not anger or regret. Just…nothing. She felt split in two, observing herself from a distance, hoping something would give her a hint of something, anything. Her name. Where she was? The name of the man.

Suddenly, she couldn't stop shivering. The force of the tremors shook her awake. She blinked, wrapping her arms around herself, icy cold.

Taking deep, ragged breaths, she looked around her, gradually realizing where she was. Jason's cabin. The television on, though Jason was nowhere in sight. Not in the living room or the kitchen.

Suddenly deeply, irrationally worried, she pushed to her feet and went looking for him.

The bathroom door was open, the light out. He wasn't there. Since his bedroom was the only other space in the cabin, and the door sat half-open, she pushed it open.

Sitting cross-legged on the bed, Jason looked up in surprise when she entered. He wore no shirt, and his muscular chest gleamed in the dim light from the bed-side table. A small silver laptop rested on his thighs.

"Are you OK?" he asked, instantly concerned.

Mouth dry, she found herself at a loss for words. But instead of backing out with a murmured apology or excuse, she stood frozen in place, unable to move. "What are you doing?" she croaked.

He held up his computer. "Reviewing some of the shots I took while I was in Kabul. You were resting so peacefully that I didn't want to disturb you."

Unable to help it, she shuddered. "I had a dream. It wasn't bad, not exactly. But it wasn't good either." She gave him a brief description.

Something flickered across his expression when she mentioned the man, and smoothed out when she spoke of her relief that she hadn't married him. "That must mean I'm single, right?" she asked, her voice weak. If she'd been healthy and whole, she knew nothing on earth would have stopped her from launching herself across the room onto the bed and tackling him.

"Maybe," he replied carefully. "If you really think it was more than a dream." His steady gaze watched her. "Do you?"

Lord knew she wanted to say yes. She practically

ached with the need. "I think so," she said, which was the best she could do without telling an outright lie. Hopeful, though she had no idea why, she waited for his response.

"That's good." He looked from her to his laptop, and back again. "Do you want to help me look through these? You're welcome to hop up here, or we can go in the kitchen if you'd rather."

Her cheeks were heating and she suddenly lost her courage. "I think I'll just go to sleep." She covered her mouth, faking a yawn. "I'm really tired."

"OK. Sleep well."

"You too." Finally, she made her legs move and backed out of the room, closing the door quietly after her.

Standing by the couch, she grabbed the remote and clicked off the television. Looking down at her hands, she wasn't surprised to realize they were shaking.

Letting herself drop down into the soft cushions, she covered her face with her hands. What the hell was wrong with her? She should be confused. She should be worried. Instead, all she could think of was how badly she wanted Jason. She wanted his arms around her, to taste the salt of his skin, to feel him move deep inside, filling her up.

Her entire body burned. They'd discussed this. They both knew neither of them could complicate things, that she had enough to worry about and figure out without adding a relationship to the mix. But still...

The simple motions of making up her bed helped steady her somewhat. Once she'd finished, she clicked out the light and crawled under the comforter, hoping she would slip into sleep quickly.

For one heart-stopping moment, when Lucy had appeared in his bedroom doorway, her hair tousled, her eyes still drowsy from sleep, Jason had thought she'd come to ask him to make love to her. With his body instantly aroused, he hadn't been sure he could resist.

Damn, he knew he shouldn't touch her—he'd recited a hundred reasons a thousand times at least. But he was only a man, and he wanted her more than he'd ever wanted any woman, anywhere.

Now that she'd gone, he resisted the urge to put the laptop aside and go after her. Nothing good would come of that.

Shutting down the laptop, he turned off the light and got ready for bed. They both needed to get out of this cabin. He'd take her for a drive, maybe into Colorado Springs, and hopefully that would clear the air.

It had to.

The next morning, she clapped her hands together in delight when he told her his plans as they sat at the table enjoying their coffee. Then, she instantly sobered. "What if someone sees me?"

"We're going to a larger city, not Cedar. I'm thinking we'll drive into Colorado Springs."

Considering him, she finally nodded. "Do you think we can get in to see your doctor friend? I'm tired of not understanding what's going on with me."

"That can probably be arranged," he told her. "I left him a message the other day and he hasn't returned it, but that's not unusual. He's a busy guy. Let me call him again. It's early enough—I should be able to catch him before he goes in to work."

This time, Phil picked up on the second ring. "Sorry I didn't call you back," he said, forgoing the usual greetings. "It's been crazy around here. What's up, Jason? Where are you now?"

Jason laughed. "I'm back in Cedar."

"You are? Can you make it into the Springs for lunch or dinner?"

"I can. I'm heading that way today, as a matter of fact. And I need to ask you a favor." As simply as possible, Jason told him about Lucy.

As Jason had expected, Phil was intrigued. "I've never actually met an amnesia patient. I have no idea what my schedule at the office looks like, but I'm sure I can fit her in. Any idea as to a general time?"

Jason checked his watch. "Noon? Maybe we can go to lunch after?"

"That'd be perfect. See you then." Phil ended the call before Jason could even say goodbye.

Looking up to find Lucy watching him, Jason grinned. "You're in. He'll see you at noon today."

Her answering smile lit up her face. "Thank you so much," she said. "Maybe I can finally get some answers."

Then, before he could react, she reached up and kissed him.

No doubt the quick press of her lips on his had been an impulse. The same as the way his arms came up to keep her in place. Instinct, nothing more. And when he deepened the kiss, he told himself the same thing.

Drowning in the taste and feel of her, nothing rational or polite about it.

He drank her in as if she was essential to his survival. Lost himself in her, even as she wrapped herself around him, her soft curves molding to him.

Dangerous. He couldn't make himself break away from her. Not yet. He wanted, needed, another minute. Just. One. More.

Finally, she wrenched herself away from him, her chest heaving as she struggled to catch her breath. She stared at him, her eyes huge and vulnerable, and he felt his heart squeeze in his chest, just a little bit.

"I'll go get ready to leave," she mumbled and rushed off toward the bathroom.

Only when he heard the click of the door closing did he release the breath he hadn't even been aware he'd been holding.

"What the…" Dragging his hand through his hair, he tried to process what had just happened. He swore her taste still lingered in his mouth.

He shook his head, too bemused to be angry at himself. Because he understood the truth. He could be careful, he could avoid even the most casual contact with her, but if she touched him, or kissed him, all bets were off. When they came together, they ignited like a match to gasoline-soaked tinder. Clearly, there wasn't a damn thing either of them could do about it.

He heard the sound of the shower turning on and closed his eyes. For a second, all he could think of was how she must have looked right now, naked, with water sluicing off her smooth skin and full breasts. His body stirred and he cursed, angry at himself.

Briefly, he considered going outside, just to burn off some energy. But they still needed to eat something for breakfast, and he needed his own shower before they left. Since anywhere beside Cedar was a considerable drive, especially without knowing the road conditions, he needed to stick around.

So instead of busying himself with firewood or snow shoveling, he set about scrambling eggs and making toast. He made them both a plate and ate his standing up.

She emerged a moment later, her expression once again composed. Avoiding his gaze, she went to her duffel bag and started rummaging around in it. He took that as his signal to go get ready himself.

"I made breakfast," he said as he headed off toward the bathroom. "Your plate is on the counter. I already ate."

"Thank you." Her soft response tempted him to wait, to turn himself around and park himself in the kitchen so he could watch her eat. Instead, he gathered up his rapidly shredding willpower and marched off to take his shower.

Once the door closed behind Jason, Lucy allowed her shoulders to sag. She didn't know what the heck was wrong with her. No matter how strictly she talked to herself, no matter what she resolved, the instant her skin came into contact with Jason's, she lost her ever-loving mind.

What had she been thinking when she kissed him? The impulsive act had nearly gotten them undressed and making fierce, passionate love. Which she had to admit, in a deep, visceral way, she wanted. Even though she knew to do so was wrong. Wasn't it? It had to be. At least until she was fully herself.

Eying the scrambled eggs and toast that he'd left for her, she carried her plate to the table and ate without tasting it at all. When she'd finished, she washed it down with the rest of her cold cup of coffee and then went to her duffel bag and began rummaging through it.

Due to the ever-present, unsubstantiated feeling of being in danger, she insisted on wearing a disguise. Or as much of one as she could cobble together with what little she had.

The wig that had been tucked inside the duffel bag seemed to look relatively natural. Long blond hair didn't feel like her, but then she didn't have any real idea what she did and didn't like.

After securing the wig on her head, she eyed herself in the bathroom mirror. It felt heavy and unnatural, but she supposed if she pretended it was a hat, she'd be fine. Since she didn't have bobby pins to keep the wig in place, she borrowed one of Jason's old baseball caps and made a ponytail, pulling that through the back part of the cap.

Since she had makeup, she put on foundation and powder, a tiny bit of mascara, and then chose a lip gloss over a lipstick, using the small mirror that came with the powder compact.

When Jason emerged from the bathroom and caught sight of her, he stopped short. "Lucy?" he asked, incredulous. "You look…wow."

Not sure whether to take that as a compliment or

not, she shrugged and put her hands on her hips. "What do you really think?" she asked.

"You look great, but then you looked great before. What's with the disguise?"

Haltingly, she tried to explain. She must have done a pretty decent job, because the confusion in his face cleared.

"I get it," he said. "I just need a few minutes and I'll be ready to go."

When he returned, he held out a pair of oversize aviator sunglasses. "Here. These will protect your eyes from the brightness of the snow and help with your disguise," he told her.

Thanking him, she tried them on. "Well?"

"You look totally different," he said.

Grateful, she nodded. "I appreciate you doing all this for me," she said. "I mean letting me stay here, feeding me and trying to help me regain my memory."

"Stop." He held up one hand, his expression fierce. "Thanks are not necessary. I'm just doing what any human being with an ounce of compassion would do. Understand?"

"You have a big heart," she said. "I might not know my own name or where I came from, but I do know not everyone would be so kind." She didn't like to think of what could have happened to her if Jason had been a different kind of man.

Odd how there were certain general things she knew, while there were so many more specific recollections she didn't have. She hated not knowing how long it would be until she was herself again, whoever that might be.

Maybe this doctor would have some answers.

"Are you ready?" he asked.

"I'm ready," she said cheerfully, determined to be as upbeat as possible. "I can't wait to get some answers."

She followed him out to his Jeep and climbed in the passenger side and secured the seat belt around her.

Since she didn't remember arriving at the cabin, she studied the landscape with interest as they drove the winding road down the mountain. She didn't see another house for several minutes. "You really are isolated, aren't you?"

"Yep." He shrugged. "I own a lot of acreage up here."

"Really? How much?"

"Fifty-six acres. Most of that particular hill."

She gaped at him. "Wow."

"It's been in my family for years," he told her. "We used to come here on vacation when I was a kid. I bought it from my mom a few years ago and did some upgrades. Now, it's my home. In between traveling all over the world for my job."

"Do you miss it when you're gone?"

He didn't answer immediately, instead appearing to concentrate on the road. When he finally glanced her way, his expression seemed rueful. "You know what? I really do. Not only the cabin and the land, but the community in Cedar. It's a great little town. Small enough that everyone knows everyone. We all look out for one another. It's exactly what I need after leaving some of the hellholes I spend time in."

The bleakness in his tone moved her. Throat aching, she decided to focus more on the passing landscape than the big man beside her. When she gave in to her emotions, they only seemed to cloud the situation.

As the land grew less steep, she saw more and more houses. Most of these sat tucked back behind long drives amid towering trees. "Where's the town?" she asked. "I would have thought I could have seen it from up there."

"You'll see it soon enough," he responded. "But first we go up one more slope. When we get to the other side, it'll be spread out below. I always wished my cabin had that view."

The road curved and twisted, taking a meandering route rather than straight across the mountain. She sat up straight in her seat, eager to see the sight he'd mentioned.

And then they rounded a curve and there it was. The town glittering like a jewel below them. She caught her breath, both enamored and afraid. "Do we have to go through town to get to Colorado Springs?"

"Yes." He glanced sideways at her. "Don't worry, we're not stopping, except at stop signs or red lights. It's still a good distance after we pass through town before we reach an actual highway."

Though she nodded, she couldn't help but worry that someone would see her.

"Don't worry," he said, making her realize her concerns must have shown on her face. "Just scrunch down in the seat. With your hair up under that hat and those sunglasses on, you could easily be a guy. If you're spotted, no one will think anything of it, I promise."

Chapter 7

Lucy's heart pounded, and she waited until the last possible minute before bending over to hide, pretending to be searching for something on the floorboard. She really wanted to see what the town looked like but couldn't risk it. Small towns were usually hotbeds of gossip. Someone might notice a woman with Jason and wonder who she was. News like that might travel like wildfire, right to the man or men who represented a danger to her. Especially if everyone knew Jason. Her enemy would know right where to look for her.

Even if she didn't know his face or his name, she knew he was out there somewhere. Searching for her.

"You're worrying too much," Jason told her, eying her sideways as she bent almost in half, trying to act nonchalant.

Glancing up at him, she shrugged.

He turned out to be right. They sailed through the charming little mountain town without any problems. Another time, she would have loved to explore Main Street. From her quick glance, it had looked like the kind of place where she could roam leisurely, checking out the cute little shops and maybe having a meal at the café she'd spied on the corner.

"You can get up now," he said. "Cedar is behind us."

Slowly, she sat up, refusing to feel foolish. "Better safe than sorry," she said, her voice more flippant than she'd intended.

"I agree." He drummed his fingers on the steering wheel. "But now you can relax and try to have a little bit of fun."

Though she nodded, she felt like it might take a while before the tension left her shoulders. She wasn't even sure she knew how to have fun. Not yet anyway.

Once they'd left the town in their rearview mirror, they continued on through more winding roads, up mountains and down again. While the roads had been cleared, the landscape remained covered in snow. The scenery—beautiful, remote and somehow exotic—called to her on an elemental level. She wondered out loud what it would be like to live here full-time. "Do you become immune to it, or does seeing this always take your breath away?"

He chuckled. "Most times, there will always be something that hits you like a punch in the gut. A herd of deer silhouetted against a full moon. The sun rising over the mountains to the east and setting over the ones to the west. The way the sky darkens right before a good rain. Around here nature has a way of constantly reminding you how lucky you are."

His response made her smile. She liked the way he used words to paint a picture. No doubt that ability came with being a journalist, even if he did most of his reporting with photographs rather than words.

Finally, she saw a sign proclaiming the interstate ahead.

"Wow. We're pretty far off the main roads, aren't we?"

"Yep." He nodded. "That's why our Cedar stays so small. We're not convenient to anything. The closest towns to us already have ski resorts and tourist attractions. We get some of the spillover from them—that's how my family came to buy our place way back when—but we're pretty low on the radar as far as tourism."

"Is that good or bad?" she asked.

"There's been a long-standing debate about that," he replied. "Cedar seems pretty equally divided between those who want to do whatever it takes to bring in the tourists and their money and those who want to keep things just the way they are."

She regarded him curiously. "And which camp do you fall in?"

Instead of answering immediately, he gave her question some thought. "I really don't know," he finally admitted. "I've always sort of stood on the outside looking in, watching them argue and discuss and debate. I'm gone so much that I don't feel as if I have a say, you know?"

Though she didn't, she nodded. "Do you ever think you'll travel less, stay in one place?"

"Settle down, you mean?"

Instantly, her face heated. Still, she stuck to her question and pushed ahead. "Sort of. I don't mean like the kind of settling down with a wife, kids and the proverbial white picket fence. I just meant less traveling into dangerous places, that's all."

Another long silence. He kept his gaze straight ahead while driving. "I've been seriously thinking about it," he finally admitted. "Recently, I contracted to put together a picture book tentatively titled *War—A Special Kind of Hell*. I've got to submit the photos I've chosen and the layout I have in mind, as well as a brief write-up for each, in a little over two months. That's part of the reason why I took a ninety-day leave of absence."

"Wow. That sounds fascinating. If you'd like some help, let me know."

He glanced her way, one brow arched. "Some of the photos are...brutal. I'm not sure you'd want to see them. That's why I've got to be selective. The ones I choose will show the atrocities of war, but selectively."

Mulling over his description, she nodded. "I imagine that might be difficult to do."

"Yes, it might. But I've taken thousands of photographs over the years. The most recent are from the suicide bombing in Kabul. There are tons of others, both from Afghanistan and Iraq. I was even sent to Sudan and Libya."

"That sounds like hours and hours' worth of work," she commented.

"It is." He glanced at her again, this time one corner of his mouth curving in the beginning of a smile. "And I'd better get started."

She couldn't help but laugh. "That's an understatement," she said. "Maybe if we work an hour or two each day, you could get it done." While it felt a little awkward to say *we* rather than *you*, maybe if she helped him with this huge task, she could begin paying him back for all he'd done for her.

"Maybe so," he allowed. "One of us could use the desktop computer and the other the laptop. We'll give it a shot tonight. I warn you, though, some of what you might see will sicken you and hurt your heart. I want you to consider very carefully before you agree to help me with this."

"I will," she told him, even though she'd already made up her mind. She'd steel herself and get through it. She at the very least owed him that.

They made good time and arrived in Colorado Springs exactly when Jason had wanted to. Lucy proved to be the perfect traveling companion. She didn't talk constantly and when she did speak, her observations were astute or amusing. He felt comfortable with her. He could feel himself relaxing, letting his guard down. These days, the few women he interacted with had been either military, Afghani locals or journalists like him. It had been a long time since he'd enjoyed the company of a woman with no expectations on either side.

For the first time, he realized he was going to truly

miss her once her memory returned and she went back to her real life, whatever and wherever that might be.

He located Phil's medical office building without trouble and parked. "Are you ready?" he asked, unclipping his seat belt and turning to face her.

Expression troubled, she nodded. "I think so. But I have a question. How well do you know this doctor? Is it safe for me to tell him everything?" Her gaze searched his face. "I mean about feeling as if I'm in danger and all that."

"I trust him. I've known him for years. If we tell him that this is all private, I'm positive it will stay that way. He can't release medical info anyway, but I'll make sure he doesn't tell anyone you were with me."

"Good." She sighed and then undid her own seat belt. "I'm relieved, though still a bit apprehensive."

"Don't be." Briefly, he considered kissing her cheek, but instead settled for a quick squeeze on the shoulder. "Come on. We don't want to be late."

Though he went around to her side, intending to open her door for her, she'd already gotten out and stood waiting for him.

He took her arm. "It's going to be fine," he promised.

"I believe you." Her wry smile had him grinning back at her like an idiot. "I hope we can have lunch soon after. I'm starving."

"Phil said he'd try to make time to have lunch with us," he said. "He and I haven't seen each other in a while. We have a lot of catching up to do."

In fact, Jason was really looking forward to seeing

his old friend. It felt as if he'd lived an entire lifetime since they'd last gotten together.

Inside, they rode the elevator up to the fifth floor. Once they located the proper office, they went inside.

"Sign in, please," the young receptionist said by way of greeting. Busy entering something on her computer, she barely looked up at them.

After exchanging glances with Lucy, Jason went ahead and signed his name.

Taking the clipboard, the young woman frowned. "I'm not finding you in our system. Do you have an appointment?"

"Phil knows I'm coming," Jason said. "He's expecting me."

Still frowning, the receptionist pushed up from her chair and hurried away. Jason made a mental note to mention her attitude to Phil. Not exactly warm and welcoming. Or friendly.

A moment later, she returned. "Dr. King is currently with a patient," she said. "After that, we close for lunch."

"We'll wait," Jason shot back, deliberately cheerful. "We're his lunch date after all."

In response, she gave him a brusque nod and went back to her computer.

"Wow," Lucy murmured, as they turned to find seats in the currently empty waiting room. "I guess she's having a bad day."

"I think she is." Jason figured it was about to get worse once he spoke to her boss about her attitude.

A few minutes later, a middle-aged woman emerged,

apparently the last patient before the office closed for lunch.

"Jason!" Phil sauntered into the room, grabbing Jason up in a quick guy hug. "So good to see you."

Lucy stood too, wiping her hands on the front of her jeans nervously. When Jason introduced them, Phil took her hand and shook it. "Nice to meet you. Would you two like to go back to my office or would you rather talk at lunch?"

"Lunch," Lucy interjected before Jason could respond. "I'm starving."

"Lunch it is." When Lucy turned away, Phil looked from her to Jason and back again. When he caught Jason watching him, he grinned and winked.

"I'll drive." Outside, Phil pointed to a large SUV. "That's mine."

Once they were all inside, with Lucy taking the back seat and Jason riding shotgun, Phil asked them if they both liked Thai food. Though Jason answered in the affirmative, Lucy merely shrugged. "I guess I won't know until I try it," she said.

Phil chuckled. "That's how it happens sometimes with amnesia patients. One small thing can bring back a flood of memories, or none at all. It's a very sporadic thing."

Clearly disappointed, Lucy grimaced. "I'm guessing what you're saying is there's no one size fits all when it comes to something like this?"

"Exactly." Phil beamed. "Once Jason called me, I did quite a bit of research. The one consistent guideline that I came across is that you shouldn't try to force anything. Your memories, if they return, could come slowly or all at once. The important thing is not to cause trauma."

"She has nightmares sometimes," Jason interjected. "And we've learned there are a few things that seem to trigger her."

"Trigger you how?" Phil asked, glancing at Lucy in the rearview mirror. "In a bad way?"

"Yes."

Now Phil exchanged a quick glance with Jason, though most of his attention was, of necessity, fixed on navigating the traffic. "Surely, not everything you remember is bad? Somewhere in there, you must have had a few glimmers of good things?"

"Yes," Lucy admitted. "Though they seem to be all small. Things like something my grandmother used to say, or the fact that I own an iPhone or my favorite dessert. Nothing earth-shattering or even useful. That's what's so frustrating."

"You remembered your mad self-defense skills," Jason pointed out. "She took me down," he told Phil. "I heard her crying out while in the middle of a nightmare and made the mistake of trying to comfort her."

"I reacted instinctively," Lucy said. "You have to understand, I was still asleep."

Though Phil nodded, he didn't comment.

They pulled into a crowded parking lot alongside a restaurant called Thai Terrific. Once Phil located a space, they parked.

Jason hurried around to help Lucy out. This time, he made it to her just as she opened her door. He held out his hand, relieved when she slipped hers into it, and assisted her down. Once both of her feet were on the pavement, he took her arm.

Clearly noticing the possessive gesture, Phil eyed them thoughtfully. "How long have you two known each other?" he asked as they walked toward the front of the restaurant.

Jason sighed. "Not very long. We'll tell you the entire story once we're seated."

Once inside, the hostess greeted Phil by name and led them to a booth in the back corner. "I come here a lot," he said, sliding into a seat.

Instead of sitting down opposite, Lucy fidgeted. "Do you mind switching sides?" she finally asked. "I can't sit with my back toward the door."

Though her statement must have surprised Phil, he simply got up and moved without comment.

Jason slid in beside Lucy, wondering if she'd object to being on the inside of the booth.

"Classic self-preservation technique," Phil drawled. "Now tell me everything."

Jason started with coming home and finding Lucy asleep on his couch. Before he got too far into his story, the waitress came to take their orders, interrupting them.

"The usual?" she asked Phil. He chuckled and nodded.

"What about you two?"

Since they hadn't even had a chance to open the menu, Jason ordered a simple green curry. Lucy hurriedly perused the lunch choices and chose a yellow curry for herself.

They all ordered iced tea as well.

As soon as the waitress bustled off, Jason resumed his story. Lucy listened, but didn't interrupt, not even to give her side of things.

Phil must have noticed. "What about you?" he asked her. "What do you remember?"

"That's just it," she said. "Nothing. I have no idea how I got to the cabin. I woke up on the couch, sore and stiff. My head hurt. When I took a shower, I discovered my body was covered in cuts and bruises."

"Go on," Phil asked.

"You can't imagine how horrifying it is to wake up in a strange place with no recollection of anything, not even your name or age. Clearly, I was hurt, but whether in some sort of accident or what, I have no idea. All I knew was a vague feeling that I might be in danger. From what or whom, I have no idea."

Leaning forward, chin on his hand, Phil motioned her to continue. Once again, the waitress interrupted them by bringing their drinks.

As soon as she left, Jason turned to Lucy. "Tell him about your nightmares."

She looked down, twisting her hands together on the tabletop. "I can't remember them exactly. There was smoke, fire, a sense of danger. When you touched me on the shoulder, I thought you were part of that scenario somehow. That's why I acted without thinking."

"She threw me to the floor," Jason told Phil. "She's got skills."

"And I did remember taking self-defense classes," she added. "Though I couldn't tell you where, when or with who."

"That's all right." Expression sympathetic, Phil sat

back as their waitress brought their entrées. As she placed their meals in front of them, the scents wafting from the food had Jason's mouth watering.

"I love yellow curry," Lucy exclaimed, her eyes wide with surprise. "It's something I eat quite often, when I can."

"See." Beaming at her with a pleased smile, Phil picked up his fork. "And there you have another piece of the puzzle, just like that."

Lucy opened her mouth as if to ask another question, but apparently thought better of that. Conversation ceased for the next several moments while everyone dug in to their food.

Finally, Lucy pushed her half-empty plate away. "That was amazing. But I'm so stuffed, I can't eat another bite."

Though Phil nodded, he continued eating. Jason too, though he'd nearly finished.

Finally, with both men's plates clean, they sat back and sipped their tea. The server came and cleared the table, asking Lucy if she wanted a box. She declined due to the long drive home, but made sure to state how much she'd enjoyed her meal.

No one wanted dessert, so Jason asked for the check. Phil made a token protest, but Jason insisted. Thanking him, Phil checked his watch. "I need to be getting back," he said. "My next appointment is at 1:30."

While they waited for the check, Lucy leaned forward and touched Phil's hand. "Is there any other advice you can give me? Things to watch for, or to do that might help my memory return?"

"Unfortunately, amnesia is a tricky thing. There are some in the medical profession who actually deny its existence." He held up a hand when she started to protest. "I don't happen to be one of them. And the more we come to learn, the more we can try to help. I'm not a neurologist, so that would be my suggestion. Find one and make an appointment. They are the most likely to be able to help you."

She nodded, holding her silence while Jason paid the bill and left a tip. As they pushed to their feet to leave, she shook her head. "From what you've said, it doesn't seem like anyone can actually help me. Only time can do that."

"I'm sorry." Phil put his hand on her shoulder, removing it when Jason glared. "Hopefully, things will get better soon."

As they drove back to the medical office, Phil turned to glance at Jason. "We need to get together again soon and catch up. Don't let so much time pass without making contact, OK?"

Chagrined, Jason nodded. "I realize it's no excuse, but my job keeps me constantly hopping. However, I'm going to be up at the cabin in Cedar for the next ninety days, give or take. I'm working on a new project. If you get a chance to come up, I'd sure love to see you."

"I'll do that," Phil said easily, pulling into his Reserved parking space.

They got out and Jason shook his old friend's hand. Lucy came over and held out her hand too, but Phil pulled her in for a quick, impersonal hug instead. "Don't be a stranger," he said as he strode away. Before he went inside, he glanced back over his shoulder and waved.

Jason and Lucy walked back to his Jeep in silence. As they pulled away, he stole a quick look at her, only to find her watching him.

"Your doctor friend—while nice—wasn't very helpful," she said. "I learned nothing that I didn't already know from you looking on the internet."

"But you visited with an actual medical professional," he pointed out. "Who reassured you that everything you're experiencing is typical for someone with amnesia. I'd think that would go a long way toward helping alleviate your fears."

Considering him, she finally nodded. "You're right. Thank you for setting this up."

"How about we do some touristy stuff?" he asked, figuring a distraction would be good. "We can visit the Garden of the Gods and, if we have time, the Royal Gorge. They're much less crowded this time of year."

They spent the rest of the afternoon visiting both popular tourist attractions. Lucy finally relaxed, even though the wind tangled her long blond wig.

At five o'clock, they headed back into Colorado Springs proper to grab something to eat. "If it's okay with you, I'd like to take it with us," Jason said. "I'd prefer to make it back to Cedar before it gets too dark."

She nodded and they stopped for takeout on the way out of town. He ate his cheeseburger quickly while the roads were still mostly straight. Declaring that she wasn't all that hungry, she nibbled on her chicken wrap with a real lack of enthusiasm.

After eating, she smiled a tired smile and thanked

him for a great day. It must have exhausted her, because they were only thirty minutes into the drive when she fell asleep.

He took the opportunity to sneak glances at her, unable to keep from admiring the classic lines of her profile, her full lips and the softness of her silky dark hair. Even with her gorgeous blue eyes closed, she was still a strikingly stunning woman. Worse, the more he got to know her, the more beautiful he found her.

Not the real her, he reminded himself. The woman she was right now would only be a shell of her real self, until her memories and the rest of personality returned to her. She could end up a completely different person than this woman he was coming to love.

What? Startled, he blinked and returned his full attention to the road. He had no idea where that had come from, but it wasn't even close to being true. Not only did he not have time for romantic nonsense, how could he love a woman who didn't even know who she was?

Short answer, he couldn't. Pleased that he'd settled that, at least within his own mind, he focused on getting them back to the cabin before full darkness fell.

When he reached the outskirts of Cedar, he decided to stop by the post office and check for mail in his box. While the main lobby would be closed, the door to the PO boxes remained unlocked at all times.

Hopefully, stopping wouldn't wake Lucy.

Since Cedar basically shut down at six, the streets were empty. He parked right in front of the small post office and debated whether to leave the car running or not. As soon as he shifted into Park Lucy stirred.

Stretching, she opened her eyes, turning to look for him, though for a moment her hazy gaze seemed unfocused.

"Jason?" She pushed herself up straight in her seat and dragged her fingers through her hair. "Where are we?"

"In Cedar." When she started, glancing around her wildly, he touched her shoulder. "Don't worry. Downtown is pretty much deserted. No one will see you. I'm going to run into the post office and check on my mail. Lock the car after me. I'll be right back."

Though she still shifted around in her seat as if uncomfortable, she nodded. "Please hurry."

"I will." He forced himself not to give in to the impulse to give her a quick kiss and grabbed a canvas tote bag from the back before he got out of his Jeep. Once he closed his door, he waited until he heard the sound of her engaging the locks before turning to head inside.

The small area where people rented their boxes was brightly lit and could be seen from outside. He went to his and bent down to unlock it. Once he had, he could barely slide it open, despite the fact that he rented the largest size available. As he'd suspected, quite a bit of mail had accumulated in the last couple of months. Most of his bills he had emailed to him so he could pay online, so the majority of this stuff would be the ordinary sort of junk mail that tended to pile up if not dealt with.

As soon as he'd shoveled it all into his tote, he closed the box and locked it. As he headed outside, someone came in. A tall man wearing a dark trench coat and a hat, like someone playing a detective in a vintage movie.

Jason moved away, intending to sidestep him, but the man moved too and blocked his way out.

"Jason Sheffield?" the stranger asked.

Instantly suspicious, Jason eyed him. "Who wants to know?"

Instead of answering, the man raised his face and stared hard. "Are. You. Jason. Sheffield?"

"Again, what business is it of yours?" Jason tried once more to push past him, but again the man moved to block his way. For the first time, Jason wished he'd brought his pistol with him. He knew Lucy could see everything from the car and he didn't want her to get too alarmed.

"Look, buddy. I'm just trying to do my job. Are you Jason Sheffield or not?"

Deciding to just get this—whatever it might be— over with, Jason nodded. "I am."

"Great. Here." The other man pulled a large manila envelope from underneath his coat and shoved it at Jason. "Consider yourself served."

Chapter 8

Lucy looked up just in time to see Jason attempt to sidestep a large man in a black trench coat who appeared to be threatening him. While Jason was tall—at least six foot three—this man was not only taller, but had the build of a football linebacker.

She looked around wildly, wishing Jason had left his cell phone so she could call 911, but he must have had it with him in his pocket. Heart pounding, she could only watch as the man confronted Jason. Though she couldn't hear what they were saying, it didn't appear Jason was in actual physical danger. Yet.

A moment later, the stranger handed Jason an envelope of some sort and left. When he exited the post office, he turned right, taking himself to a large pickup he'd parked at the very end of the lot. Without even glancing her way, he started up his truck and drove away.

So engrossed was she in watching the other man that she didn't even see Jason leave the building. When he tapped on the driver's side window, it made her jump. She fumbled with the unlock button and pressed it. Opening the door, Jason slid inside. He placed his tote bag on the back seat and she saw the new envelope the man had given him sticking out of it.

"What was that?" she asked, hoping her voice didn't betray her worry.

"A process server," he answered. "I'm not sure what all that's about, but I'll take a look at it when we get home. I'll feel better once we're there."

"Me too," she breathed, trying to settle her jangled nerves. They drove the rest of the way in silence. Eying the downtown area since she'd been hunkered down when they'd driven through earlier, she saw Jason had been speaking the truth. Everything appeared locked up tight. The nicely shoveled sidewalks were deserted and there weren't many other cars driving on the plowed streets.

As they reached the edge of town, she saw one place remained open. Stella's Pub the sign proclaimed. There were at least ten cars in the parking lot.

"It's the only bar in town," Jason said. "Their food is actually good. And they have several craft beers on tap."

About to ask him to take her there, she closed her mouth. Until she knew what weirdness made up her past, she wouldn't be going anywhere in Cedar. She simply couldn't risk it.

They were nearly at the turnoff for the main road that would eventually lead up to his cabin when she noticed Jason tense.

"What's wrong?" she asked, swallowing back a residue of her earlier panic.

"There's a car coming up behind us," he said, his hands tight on the steering wheel. "From here, it appears to be going way too fast."

Due to the guardrails and the drop-offs on both sides of them, there wasn't anywhere they could pull off. Jason accelerated, but it wasn't long before the other vehicle's headlights filled the interior of his Jeep.

"He's got the damn things on bright!" Jason said, cursing. "Now he's right on my bumper."

No sooner had he said the words than the other vehicle made contact with theirs. It hit them hard and fast, the metal making a crunching sound. The Jeep shimmied, but Jason managed to keep control.

Wide-eyed, Lucy alternated between watching him and glancing over her shoulder at the truck behind them.

"Hold on," Jason ordered. "He's trying to run us off the road."

This time, instead of tapping their bumper, the pickup swerved and tried to pull up alongside them. Jason accelerated, but the truck did too.

"Brace yourself," Jason said. "I'm about to slam on my brakes."

When he did, the Jeep fishtailed, but he somehow kept it under control. Apparently taken by surprise, the truck zoomed past, red brake lights flashing as they tried to slow.

"There's a big curve ahead," Jason said, even as he swung the Jeep around. "If that guy is driving drunk, I hope he remembers it. Otherwise, he'll go over."

As soon as he'd gotten them turned in the opposite direction, Jason floored it. As soon as they reached the outskirts of town, he pulled into the parking lot of Stella's Pub, killed his lights and parked in between two other vehicles.

"If he didn't lose it on the curve, we should see him go past," he said. "Assuming he was actually chasing us. If it was just some drunk heading home, then we'll check for guardrail damage on the way to our turnoff. Other than that, I hope he made it safely."

She stared at him in disbelief. "Surely, you don't really believe that?"

"Believe what?"

"That this was just a random thing. It probably was the same guy who broke into your cabin."

Keeping his gaze on the road, Jason sighed. "Maybe. But we don't have proof. I don't want to be too paranoid, so I'd prefer to think we weren't the actual targets."

A second later, the truck came barreling past them, heading into town.

"I guess we were," Jason admitted. "Damn it. Now I've got to figure out why."

Again, she couldn't help but wonder if all this had to do with her. But then again, why? And Jason had been served with notice of something. Perhaps those two were related. It could be entirely possible none of this meant someone was after her.

In fact, the only justification she had for believing

that was the gut feeling, the niggling sense of worry and fear.

They sat there in the parking spot for a few more minutes.

"I want to make sure he doesn't come back," Jason said. "I don't want to deal with another episode like that. Ever again."

"Me neither," she agreed, still feeling a bit shaky. "Today sure has been eventful."

He laughed, though the sound had no humor. "That's one way of putting it."

After waiting several more minutes, he grimaced. "Ready?"

She nodded, unable to keep from glancing once more in the direction the other vehicle had gone.

Jason put the Jeep in Drive and turned his headlights back on as they pulled out. This time, he drove faster than he had before, continually checking his rearview mirror. Luckily, they reached their turnoff. Even then, as he drove them up the steep winding curves of the road that led to his place, he kept up a faster pace. "That SOB better not come up here," he commented, his voice full of a grim threat.

Honestly, that reassured her. Though she felt a bit better, she too kept glancing over her shoulder to check that they weren't being followed.

When they finally pulled up to the cabin, they both let out simultaneous sighs of relief. "We made it," Lucy said.

"Yes."

But when Lucy started to get out, Jason held up a hand to forestall her. "Wait here," he ordered. "I want to check everything out first. It should just take me a minute. Lock the doors until I get back."

He was out of the car before she could respond. Once again nervous, she clicked the door locks and glanced all around the vehicle. Nothing appeared out of the ordinary, but what did she know?

A moment later, Jason returned. Making the thumbs-up sign, he told her she could go ahead and get out of the car.

Once she'd unlocked the doors, he reached in the back seat and retrieved his tote bag.

Though her legs felt wobbly as the result of all that excitement, she managed to make it inside the cabin without asking for his assistance.

The instant they were both in the house, he made sure to lock the door behind them.

"That was crazy as hell," he said, dragging his hands through his hair. "That guy could have killed us."

Now that they were safely inside, she felt calmer. "I know. Thank you for not letting that happen."

Her comment made him laugh. "Yeah. I guess I'll be making another report to Sheriff Jeffords." He dumped the contents of his bag on the kitchen table and shook his head. "There sure is a lot of stuff here. It looks to be mostly junk mail."

"I see that," she replied, unable to take her gaze from the manila envelope. "Aren't you curious to find out why you were served?"

He met her gaze. "I am. But I'm also dreading opening it. I mean, how much weirdness can happen in one day? I can't help but wonder what the hell I did to piss someone off. First the break-in, and now someone tries to kill us. None of it makes sense. This is as crazy as when I'm working the war zone over in Kabul."

Again, she had the unshakable suspicion that all of this was because of her.

"Let's focus on the envelope for now," she advised, clenching her hands into fists to keep from reaching out and touching him. "Maybe whatever is inside will at least give you some sort of explanation for all the craziness."

"Maybe." But hands jammed into his pockets, he still didn't make a move toward the table or the envelope sitting in the middle of a large pile of mail.

Finally, she couldn't take the silent inaction any longer.

"Don't you want to know?" she asked, not bothering to hide her exasperation.

"Yes," he answered. "But like I said, I also dread knowing. I've only been served one other time in my life and it wasn't pleasant."

She waited for him to elaborate, but he didn't. Instead, he sighed and walked over to the kitchen table. He picked up the unmarked envelope and turned it around and around in his hands.

Seriously? "Open it already," she exclaimed.

He shot her a mildly curious glance but went and got his letter opener from his desk and slit the seam. Reaching inside, he slid a single piece of white paper out and read it silently.

"Well?"

"I've being subpoenaed," he said, his voice echoing his disbelief. "They want me to testify about the disappearance of my friend Rick Engles. But that makes no sense. I didn't even get to see him right before he vanished. I have no information to give them that would help."

Eventually, he set the letter aside, though he reread it one more time. "I'm going to have to appear in the NCIS office in Colorado Springs," he said. "It's a total waste of my time."

"Not if it helps them find your friend," she pointed out gently.

"Agreed. But it won't. I haven't heard from Rick since the explosion. He never followed up with me or responded to the message I left him. There's nothing I have to say beyond that. Not helpful. Not helpful at all."

A strong wind had begun to blow by the time they finished straightening up the kitchen.

"I bet the satellite is out again," Jason said. "It's pretty temperamental as it is. Any strong storm with wind, rain or snow knocks out the signal."

She actually didn't mind. "I guess we'll just have to play poker or Scrabble," she said, not even attempting to hide her glee.

Of course, he picked up on it. "Which do you prefer?"

"Scrabble, I think. I'd like something that would really occupy my mind."

Laughing, he went and got the game from under the television console.

They played an intense game, each challenging the other's word choices more than once, resorting to the dictionary to make certain the words were real.

Finally, Lucy stifled a yawn. "I think this day has caught up with me."

He glanced at his watch. "Wow. It's later than I realized. Time to go to bed."

Though she knew he hadn't meant anything by his innocent statement, her entire body heated. Foolish, she thought, pushing to her feet and gathering up the tiles.

Once they'd put the game back into the box, Jason stowed it away. "Give me a few minutes and then the bathroom is all yours," he said.

Tongue-tied, she managed a nod.

Later, once Jason had retreated to his bedroom and closed the door, she made up the couch and turned off the light. Despite her earlier exhaustion, she tossed and turned and couldn't get comfortable.

Maybe it was divine providence, but just as she thought she might be able to drift off, she heard something outside. A clanging sound. It might have been wildlife, but then again it might not. Holding absolutely still, she listened, waiting to see if she heard anything else.

Nothing but the relentless sound of the wind.

After a few moments, she relaxed. Plumping her pillow, she snuggled under the covers and closed her eyes.

Then she smelled smoke.

Three loud knocks on his bedroom door hopefully were enough to startle Jason awake. She pushed the door open and took a deep breath, staying in the doorway. Though the room remained dark, she could make out the shape of Jason, just now drowsily sitting up in his bed.

"I heard something outside and now I smell smoke," she said, her voice shaky.

Turning on his bedside lamp, he swung his legs over the side of the bed and into his boots, sans socks. "Are you sure?" he asked, removing a pistol from the lockbox in his nightstand and, after dialing in the combination, he checked to make sure it was loaded.

"Positive."

"Stay here." Rushing past her, he grabbed his coat, putting it on as he hit the door.

She caught her breath, wishing she could help in some way.

She looked around wildly and grabbed the metal poker from near the woodstove. This would work if she had to help in any kind of self-defense, just in case she didn't have time to look up the combination to Jason's gun safe where he kept the rest of his weapons.

"Lucy!"

She wasn't sure if it was the wind, or if Jason was calling her name. Either way, she refused to sit inside and do nothing, especially if he was out there grappling with an intruder. She stepped into her boots, glad she'd worn her socks to bed, and grabbed the sweatshirt she'd worn earlier.

Coat on, she rushed outside after him.

Jason spotted the new set of footprints first thing. The wind had already gotten to work blowing snow to obliterate them, but he was able to follow them around to the side of the cabin where he kept his firewood.

As soon as he rounded the corner, he knew they

were trouble. Someone had set the woodpile on fire, no doubt hoping the wind would fan the flames.

Yanking on his gloves, Jason got busy trying to use snow to put out the fire. Luckily for them, instead of helping the flames grow, the wind appeared to be unsuccessfully trying to put them out. Clearly, some sort of accelerant had been used on the woodpile, most likely gasoline, and the tarp he'd used to cover the logs had been yanked to one side.

His efforts barely helped. No sooner did he get one area put out when another caught. The fire burned strongest in the alcove closest to the wood siding of the house. So far, it hadn't latched on to the cabin. If it did, the cabin would most likely be a goner.

"Lucy!" Hoping she'd hear, he shouted out her name. The wind carried it away. "Lucy!"

A moment later, she appeared, still pulling on her gloves. She appraised the situation instantly, joining him in his efforts to use his hands to shovel snow.

Shovel. Remembering he'd left his snow shovel on the front porch, he jogged over to get it. When he returned, he used the large flat shovel to propel snow onto the fire as fast as he could.

Slowly but surely, he appeared to be making progress.

Lucy doggedly continued her own efforts, and they worked side by side, bent against the force of the wind. Finally, the last of the fire went out, sending up dense smoke.

"There," Lucy exclaimed. "We're victorious."

"Not yet," he cautioned. "Keep on with the snow in case there are hot spots."

Grimly, they both kept after it. Finally, with snow piled up on his ruined firewood, he called a halt.

"We're safe," he told her, putting a hand on her shoulder. "For now."

They stamped the snow off their shoes and went inside.

"Someone set that," he said, his voice as grim as he felt. "They wanted to burn us down inside our house."

She swallowed hard. "Did you see them?"

"No. But I found tracks. And gasoline or something similar was sprayed all over the firewood. If not for that wind stirring up the snow, the cabin would be totally engulfed by now."

"But why?"

"That's the million-dollar question. I have to wonder if all this has something to do with Rick disappearing."

"Or with me being here."

The misery in her expression left him no choice but to pull her in for a hug. As he did, he realized she was trembling. "Stop blaming yourself. You have no way of knowing that."

Neither of them felt inclined to move. He loved holding her, the feel of her soft curves snuggled up against him. The clean scent of her hair, and the fruity scent of the body lotion she used on her skin.

But when his body stirred and desire made his mouth go dry, he forced himself to release her and take a step back.

"Do you think you can go back to sleep?" he asked, trying to sound casual.

She grimaced. "I doubt it. But don't let me keep you

up. I'll just sit out here with the lights on and read or something."

Again, as he gazed at her trying to be strong, his chest constricted. "You take my bed," he said, swallowing tightly. "I'll spend the rest of the night out here on the couch."

"I don't know." As she stared at him, her blue eyes shadowed, he realized she'd begun shaking again.

"Lucy…"

He wasn't sure who moved first, but they wound up in each other's arms once more. Holding her close, breathing in the sexy, feminine scent of her, he realized he would do anything to make her feel better. Anything.

"Jason." She said his name, her voice broken. When he raised her chin so he could see her face, her lips parted. He couldn't do anything but cover them with his own. She returned his kiss with abandon, reckless and demanding. Shocked and more aroused than he'd ever been, his senses went on overload, taking her mouth with a soul-deep passion.

When her tongue met his, mating and dancing, he tried to hold himself back, but that battle had already been lost.

Tangled together, they ended up in his bedroom. "Lucy," he began, trying to protest, aware he needed to remind her that they shouldn't, couldn't, but she shushed him and pulled him in for another searing kiss, and he forgot what he'd been about to say.

She pulled off his shirt, her hands still unsteady, and then, with her gaze locked on his, her own. He couldn't move or tear his gaze away as she unhooked her bra and let it fall to the floor. Her breasts were all he'd imagined, full and ripe and sweet. He swallowed as he reverently reached for them, loving how they perfectly filled up his hands.

Unable to resist, he left the lure of her mouth to taste her nipple. The feel of his tongue made her moan and arch her back for more, even as she writhed against him.

On fire, nearly lost, he regained enough of his mind to attempt a second rationalization, to let her, make her, say no and deny that she wanted this as badly as he did.

"Lucy?" he rasped, a question in his voice. Instead of answering him with words, she replied with a sexy, seductive smile and a deep, sensuous kiss.

But when she reached for his zipper and unzipped it slowly, and his body surged against her hand, he was lost. Past the point of no return.

They managed to hastily shed the rest of their clothes, mouths still locked together, and stumbled toward his bed. Just before, he reached in his nightstand and retrieved a condom, slipping it over his arousal. She pulled him down with her, on top of her, arching her back so that all he had to do was shudder to push himself inside her.

Pleasure exploded the instant she sheathed him in her warmth. He struggled to maintain control, holding himself still, hoping if he didn't move, he wouldn't lose all restraint.

Lucy clearly had other ideas. She pushed herself against him, urging him on, her body clenching around his as if feverish with need.

He reared back, withdrawing slightly, muttering a request that she be still. Eyes wild, pupils dark, she shook her head defiantly, sending her hair whipping around her on the comforter. Arching up, she kissed him, deep and wanton, as if she couldn't possibly get enough.

His hastily erected wall didn't stand a chance. Giving in to the wave of desire, he began to move. Fast and furious, deep and hard. She matched him, stroke for stroke. And when she began to shudder as she reached her climax, he followed right behind.

They held each other as their heartbeats slowed, sweat-slickened bodies still fitting together as if neither could bear to break apart.

As she curled against him, her eyes drifting closed, he couldn't help but wonder at the bitter irony of fate, sending him this woman now, under such crazy circumstances.

None of that mattered now, though he knew it should. He stroked her hair, realizing he was forever changed. He knew deep inside himself that he'd never be able to feel the same way about another woman. He wasn't sure if this would turn out to be a blessing or a curse. Only time would tell.

As for her, perhaps when her memory finally returned, she'd look back on her time with him fondly. Or not at all. He had no way of knowing.

"You didn't take advantage of me," she said, before he could manage to summon up the question. "I wanted you as badly as you wanted me."

Though technically she was right, the knowledge did little to appease his guilt. He should have been stronger, but damn if they hadn't fit together as if they were made for each other.

"This changes things," she continued, her words mirroring his private thoughts. "I should let you know, I don't want to go back to the way we were before."

Bemused, he wasn't sure how to respond.

Apparently, she took his silence for dissent. "Jason. What's done is done. Nothing we can do or say will undo that. We might as well go forward with this change. Who knows how long this will last?"

And that, he thought silently, was the point. How long until she remembered herself, her life, and left him behind with a thanks and a carefree smile? He'd be left shattered, alone to try and pick up the pieces.

Of course, he said none of this. Instead, he managed to smile and nod. "Come on," he said, patting the spare pillow next to him. "Let's try and get some sleep. I'll give the sheriff a call first thing in the morning."

She smiled back and curled up into him. His heart full and aching, he turned out the light and hoped for sleep.

He must have fallen asleep. When he next opened his eyes, the other side of his bed was empty and the scents of coffee and bacon made his mouth water.

Getting up, he pulled on a pair of sweatpants and a shirt and padded barefoot into the kitchen.

"Morning," Lucy said, her smile warm. "I don't know about you, but I worked up an appetite."

As if on cue, his stomach rumbled. They both laughed. He ambled over to the coffeemaker and brewed a cup, then carried that back to the kitchen table. Sipping it, he watched her work, enthralled by the graceful way she moved around the kitchen.

"Here you go." She placed a plate with two fried eggs, toast and four slices of perfectly cooked bacon in front of him.

"Thanks."

Once she took a seat across from him with her own plate of food, they both dug in.

After they'd finished eating, he eyed her across the table.

"I'm going to call the sheriff in a few minutes," he said. "This time, he's going to have to come up here. Unless you want me to tell him about you, you'll have to stay in my bedroom with the door closed."

Alarm briefly flashed in her eyes, smoothing out just as quickly as it had come. "I'll hide," she answered. "I'm sorry, but I don't trust anyone yet. With the exception of you, of course."

"Of course." He smiled, still trying to get his unruly libido under control. Unbelievable that he could still want her so intensely after a night of making love.

He got up and helped her with the dishes. Once everything had been neatly placed in the rack next to the sink to dry, he turned and went to his satellite phone. Picking it up, he punched in the number for the Cedar Sheriff's Department.

The regular dispatcher, Wilma, put him right through to Sheriff Jeffords. Once Jason explained what had happened, the sheriff told him he'd leave immediately and would be there in a few minutes.

Ending the call, Jason relayed this information to Lucy.

"Wow, that's quick."

He shrugged. "Cedar is a small, peaceful town. We don't usually get a lot of crime here."

"That's nice." Was that a touch of wistfulness in her voice?

"It is," he agreed, checking his watch. "Since I don't know how long you'll have to stay in my room—Sheriff Jeffords likes to talk—why don't you grab something to drink and a snack before he gets here?"

"Good idea." She did exactly that, carrying those items to his bedroom before making a stop in the restroom. When they heard the sound of a vehicle pulling up in front, she lifted her hand in a quick wave before disappearing and closing the door behind her.

Jason stepped out onto the front porch, greeting the sheriff at his vehicle. Here in the mountains, the two sheriff's department vehicles were four-wheel drive SUVs instead of squad cars.

Lifting his hand in greeting, Jason led the other man over to the woodpile area. There, the flames and smoke had made singe marks on the wood.

"Damn." Getting out a camera, Sheriff Jeffords began snapping photos. "You're lucky your place didn't burn down."

"I know." Jason gestured at the snow. "The wind was blowing pretty hard and swirling around all this snow. I think that's the only thing that saved us."

"'Us?'" The sheriff looked at him, one brow raised in question.

"Figure of speech," Jason said, managing a sheepish grin. "Me, myself and I."

"Okay." Back to snapping photos.

"I could have taken those myself." Jason felt compelled to add. "I don't know why I didn't realize you would need them."

"It's all good. Just doing my job. After all, it's not like there's a whole hell of a lot going on back in town." He chuckled.

Once he'd finished taking his snapshots, the sheriff stowed the camera back in his bag. "Now I'll need to take your report. Do you mind if we go inside and get out of the cold?"

Since he'd been expecting this, Jason gestured toward the door. "Not at all. After you."

As he stepped into his living room, he couldn't help but glance at his closed bedroom door. Luckily, Sheriff Jeffords appeared preoccupied with getting out his pad and pen and didn't notice.

"Ready? Go ahead," the sheriff said.

Leaving out any mention of Lucy, Jason recounted the events of the previous evening while the other man took notes. When Jason finished, the sheriff closed his notepad and nodded grimly.

"Are you sure you don't have any idea why someone might be targeting you?" he asked.

Jason started to shake his head no, but then he remembered the subpoena. "My military buddy Rick Engles is missing," he recounted. "I've gotten one phone call asking questions, and now I've been subpoenaed to testify at a hearing. I'm not sure why. Rick and I were supposed to meet up in Kabul, but there was a terrorist attack and we never did. I headed back to the States and assumed he stayed there, doing his job. I didn't even know he'd gone missing."

If possible, the sheriff's brow furrowed even more. "I agree, that's mighty interesting," he allowed. "But targeting you doesn't seem to fit with that. Anything else?"

His pictures. And Lucy, though of course he couldn't discuss her. Deciding whether or not to mention the photos, Jason figured why not. As he'd mentioned to Lucy earlier, there were many reasons someone could want those. He went ahead and filled in the sheriff, taking care to touch on all angles.

Chapter 9

Until today, Lucy had never really spent time in Jason's bedroom. She'd always felt she owed him that amount of privacy at least.

Now, with a closed door and a stranger outside keeping her in the small room, she allowed herself to really look around.

Her first impression reinforced her notion that Jason preferred organization and order. He apparently made his bed every morning, smoothing out any wrinkles or folds in the beige and black comforter. She perched on the edge of the mattress for a moment, breathing in the intangible scent of him that somehow managed to linger in the air.

Pushing to her feet, she wandered over to his dresser, eying herself in the mirror. As usual these days, the sight of her caused a brief jolt of shock. In her mind at least, she looked completely different. More polished, more poised, with an easy confidence shining from her blue eyes and apparent in the way she carried herself.

Stunned, she realized she'd just experienced another memory revelation. Letting herself absorb and digest this, she tried tentatively to see if she could remember her name.

Nothing. A big fat blank. Nothing beyond the fact that she knew she usually looked different.

Eying Jason's dresser, she picked up the lone bottle of men's cologne and smelled it. Musky, masculine and something she'd yet to smell on him. Part of her felt glad—she loved the natural, outdoorsy way he smelled. The other part of her felt a bit piqued. Clearly, he only used the cologne for special occasions, or special people.

Ridiculous to feel that way. They were together every single day. Why would she even expect or want him to wear cologne around her? Answer, she didn't.

Replacing the stopper, she put the bottle back where she'd found it. On one corner of the dresser, he had a display that linked to a wireless weather station he must have set up outside. Wind direction, speed, temperature, all were displayed.

Next to that sat a polished wood storage box. A men's jewelry box, she thought. But since Jason wore no jewelry that she'd seen, she couldn't help but wonder what he kept inside.

She glanced back at the closed door, full of misgivings. It would be wrong to snoop, but she told herself she wouldn't touch anything, even as she slowly raised the lid.

A diamond ring sat in solitary splendor inside. It appeared old, the gold tarnished and the large marquise-cut diamond dulled with age. She couldn't help but wonder at the story behind it, who had it belonged to and what it might mean.

Knowing she couldn't ask, she closed the lid and continued her exploration of the room. On the nightstand, he had a lamp and a beat-up alarm clock, nothing else. His sliding closet door was closed, and she left it that way, already feeling bad about snooping.

Outside, she could hear voices, Jason's and another man's, who must be the sheriff, though she couldn't make out the words. When they came inside, she tensed up, but knew there was no way Jason would let him see her.

They continued talking, Jason clearly filling him in on all the possibilities that might make someone want to stalk and harm him. All of them except her. True to his word, Jason never mentioned her, and finally the sheriff left. She waited until she heard his vehicle drive away before opening the bedroom door and peeking out.

Jason stood near his desk, apparently lost in thought. When he caught sight of her, he smiled. "Hey there. I was about to come get you."

Come get you. The phrase triggered a memory. She walked out onto a stage alongside a man, though she couldn't see his face. Thunderous applause greeted them—actually, *him*. She was there in a supportive role, while he…

Just like that, the memory vanished.

Disoriented and disappointed, she blinked.

"Are you all right?" Jason asked, crossing the room and taking her arm. "You looked like you were about to faint."

"I don't faint." Her automatic response made her blink again. "I'm just trying to process another random memory." She told him what she'd seen, triggered by his simple phrase.

"This man," he asked, his casual tone fooling neither of them. "Was he famous?"

"I don't know," she said, but then realized she might. "Not movie-star or musician famous, but maybe well-known. CEO or philanthropist, maybe? Or politician?"

"That's great!" He actually rubbed his hands together in glee. "That will make it much easier to search for a missing girlfriend or wife."

"Or relative," she pointed out. "I didn't get a feeling of love when that memory came to me. More of obligation. Duty. That man might even have been my brother."

"Are you just guessing or is that your gut feeling?"

She sighed. "Guessing. Whenever I have these flashes of memory, any time I try to expand them, everything shuts down. It's frustrating."

Pulling her close, he gave her a quick hug, though he released her before she gave in to the temptation to linger. "It sounds like your flashes of memory are coming more frequently. That's got to be good."

"I guess." Try as she might, she couldn't summon up any enthusiasm. "I need more, though. For example, it'd be really nice if I could remember my name."

He laughed. "Patience. Eventually, you will."

She liked the certainty in his voice. "I know. Impatience is one of my greatest faults."

"See?" Grinning, he repeated what she'd said. "Bit by bit, it's all coming back to you."

His optimism was infectious. She nodded, her heart skipping a beat, and grinned back.

They spent the next several hours poring over his photographs. He'd had her set up three folders on the computer, labeling one No for the photos that were too graphic or simply bad shots. Another folder called Maybe for all the ones she wasn't sure about. And the last folder was titled Yes for those rare photographs that were clearly above par.

Though she knew he'd have to go over everything she'd done later, he'd told her that the simple beginning to sorting would help tremendously.

Since he'd warned her, she braced herself before clicking on the first set of images.

Many of them were disturbing, some gut-wrenchingly so. Some seemed routine, matter-of-fact, while others carried an exotic flavor. All of them, the banal and the horrifying, were starkly beautiful.

"You're really talented," she mused, no doubt telling him something he already knew.

Peering at her over the top of his laptop, he smiled. "Thank you. Remember, if looking at these gets to be a bit too much, you can stop."

"I'll remember," she said, already clicking to open the next file. She had no idea where these were taken; however, the degree of wretchedness of life appeared to have increased. Here, terror and pain and grief shone from people's eyes. In one particularly disturbing shot, a mother cradled her wounded or dead child. In another, Jason had captured resignation in the ancient gaze of an old man who sat cross-legged on the street littered with rubble, his bony back against a crumbling wall.

Reminding herself that she had a job, she carefully sorted the pictures, moving them to one file or another. She lost track of time, so engrossed had she become in her task.

"Let's take a break," Jason said, standing and stretching. "We've been going at this long enough."

Pushing to her feet, she nodded. "I'd really like to get some fresh air."

Hearing this, he grinned. "It's a balmy thirty-seven out there. I'm thinking with that temperature and the sunshine, a lot of the snow should have melted."

She eyed him steadily. "Does that mean we can go for a walk without needing snowshoes?"

"I guess we won't know until we go outside and check it out."

It took a few minutes for each of them to get bundled up in layers. She felt a level of anticipation that seemed out of line with merely going outside for a walk, but didn't care.

Once they stepped outside, the crisp air made her inhale deeply and stand up straighter. "It's beautiful out here," she exclaimed, instantly invigorated. Jason had been right, the snow had mostly melted, except for a few spots that remained in the shadows.

She walked down the porch steps, into the yard, twirling around and taking in the patches of muddy earth. Remembering the path, she walked around the back side of the cabin, passing the still-blackened firewood.

Instead of stopping to look at it once more, she refused to allow her exuberance to dim and continued on. Laughing, Jason followed.

"There." Stopping, she pointed at the path, mostly clear of snow, winding up through the trees. "Let's go. I love a good hike, even though I don't have my hiking boots."

"See." Jason caught up to her and prodded her with his elbow. "Another one. Seems like those memories are coming closer together. I predict it won't be long until you know everything."

Though she nodded, she didn't want to dwell on that right now. She wanted to live in the moment, rejoice in the clean mountain air and snowless path. And of course, the amazing man at her side.

Together they hiked up the path, managing to avoid most of the muddy puddles, though they hit their fair share. It felt great to stretch her legs, and she could feel her lower back loosening up. Slightly out of breath, she inhaled great gulps of cold air. "What a perfect day," she told him, taking his hand and swinging their arms in the air.

He glanced sideways at her, a smile quirking the edges of his mouth. "You're sure happy."

One brow arched, she grinned at him. "I am. I think I must be an outdoorsy type of person."

This time, they made it to the top of the hill, overlooking the cabin. "Look," he pointed. "There's the road that leads to our driveway."

The words had no sooner left his mouth when a caravan of vehicles came into view. One, two, three and then four vehicles, mostly pickup trucks with one SUV.

"What the…" Jason scratched his head. "They're coming from town. I wonder where they're heading. There's not much else up that road but a couple more houses."

She froze. "What if…"

His expression changed as he realized what she'd been about to say. "Damn it." Tugging her hand, he started back down the trail. "Maybe if we hurry, we can get to the cabin before they get here."

Due to a combination of the steep slope, the mud and rocks, they couldn't run. Hand in hand, the two of them climbed back down as quickly as they could. She slipped and stumbled a couple of times, and only his grip on her hand kept her from falling on her behind in a puddle of mud.

They'd barely rounded the last corner when she heard the unmistakable sound of tires on gravel. Skidding to a halt, she stepped back, hoping no one had seen her.

Multiple car doors closing rang out as loud as gunshots.

"You go," she said, jerking her hand free. "I'll stay up here until they leave."

"Don't be ridiculous. I have no idea how long they'll stay."

"I don't care. I can wait them out." Lifting her chin stubbornly, she tried to hide her very real terror. Meeting people meant she'd once again be exposed. Vulnerable.

"You can't. Once it gets dark, you'll freeze."

"Not if you get rid of them quickly. What do you think they want?"

He thought for a moment before cursing again. "I imagine the sheriff told someone in town about the fire and the stalker. Cedar is a good town, full of great neighbors. They're most likely here to help me clean up, cut new firewood and help in any way I need." He took a deep breath. "I can't just run them off when they went through all the trouble to drive up here. Just come out with me and I'll introduce you as a friend who's visiting. It won't be a big deal."

Maybe not to him. She shook her head. "The idea of even doing that terrifies me. What if one of these people turn out to be the one who's after me?"

From his blank expression, she could tell the thought had never occurred to him. Holding her gaze, he shook his head. "Lucy, I know these people. I've known them for years."

Lifting her chin stubbornly, she refused to look away. "That may be true, but what if one of them brings their new friend, who just happened to arrive in town around the same time I did? You have no way of controlling what happens."

He glanced down at his cabin. "You know everyone is congregating on my front porch, knocking on the door."

"Probably," she agreed, nodding.

"Wait here," he started to say. But just then, two of Jason's visitors came around the back of the cabin and spotted them.

"Hey!" one of them shouted, waving. "Jason."

Lucy swallowed her panic, looking from Jason to the two men below. A moment later, several others joined them.

"Too late," Jason told her. "Might as well go on down."

When he took her arm, she didn't resist. Side by side, they headed down to meet their visitors.

Judging by the tightly rigid way Lucy held herself, Jason knew if she kept it up for too long, her entire body was going to hurt like hell tomorrow.

"It's okay," he murmured, figuring nothing he could say would reassure her, but aware he had to try anyway.

She shot him a look full of disbelief but didn't comment.

As they picked their way down the last of the trail, several more people joined the small crowd waiting. He quickly scanned their faces, recognizing each and every one of them.

"No strangers," he told Lucy, right before they reached them. Big Earl stepped forward, his beard not able to hide his huge grin.

"Hey there, Jason," he boomed. "Now we know why we haven't seen much of you in town." Transferring his light blue gaze to Lucy, he chuckled appreciatively.

"Lucy, this is Earl. Earl, Lucy." Jason performed the introductions quickly. There were seven others, and he took care to name them one by one.

To her credit, Lucy gave every impression of being at ease. She shook Earl's huge hand, kept a friendly smile plastered on her pretty face and gave no evidence of her earlier fear.

They followed him around to the side of the cabin so he could show them the woodpile and the singe marks. Lucy came too, though she hung out on the outskirts of the small group and didn't speak. While he understood she was trying to make herself invisible, he figured she didn't realize that no red-blooded male would fail to notice a woman as beautiful as she.

In fact, several of his friends glanced sideways at her, then at him, as if trying to understand the situation.

Jason didn't elaborate and he knew no one would be pushy enough to ask.

Once they finished inspecting and commenting on the burned area, Jason led everyone inside. Judging by the grim set of Lucy's mouth, she wasn't happy about this, but he didn't really see what else he could do. It would be rude to make everyone stand around outside.

Everyone crowded into his small living room, some sitting, but most standing since he didn't have enough chairs. Jason went into the kitchen and brought out all four chairs. A few more men took a seat on these. An older man named Joe who owned the local hardware store handed Jason a box. "Security cameras," he said. "I figured we might put them up around the perimeter of the cabin. Next time, you'll have the SOB's face on film."

Next time. While Jason appreciated the sentiment, he really hoped there wouldn't be a next time. "Thanks," he said. "Are they complicated to install?"

"Nah, not at all. In fact, we can knock this out in half an hour, especially since we have so much help."

At his direction, everyone trouped back outside, with the exception of Lucy, who chose to stay inside. A quick glance at her revealed she wished the earth would swallow her up.

Unable to help himself, Jason went over and squeezed her shoulder. "It's going to be all right," he told her. "Stay in here and keep warm."

Relief shone in her blue eyes. She nodded, standing ramrod straight and watching him as he followed the others outside.

Joe clearly knew what he was doing. He directed the installation of four cameras, one at each corner of the cabin. To Jason's surprise, they were up and running within thirty minutes. "Let's set you up with an account," Joe said. "I'm assuming you have a computer and Wi-Fi."

"I do." With Joe leading the way, they all went back inside. Jason booted up his laptop and signed in before handing the computer over to the older man.

Joe typed for a few minutes and then passed it back to Jason. "Here you go. I created a shortcut and everything. Your sign-in is *JSheffield* and right now your password is *JS*. You'll want to change that. Anything recorded will be stored in the cloud and can be accessed on that website. You have a free thirty-day trial. After that, you'll have to pay."

"Thank you," Jason said, truly grateful. "I appreciate you. If there's any way I can repay you, please don't hesitate to call."

Joe shook his head. "No repayment necessary. We look after each other here in Cedar."

Which was one of the things he loved about the small town.

"I brought a cooler of beer," one of the younger guys exclaimed. "It's in my truck. Let me go get it." He hurried out, returning a moment later pulling a good-sized Coleman cooler on wheels.

Canned Coors Light was passed around. Even Lucy accepted one, popping the top and taking an experimental sip. Jason watched her face from across the room, trying to ascertain whether or not she liked it.

"Earth to Jason." One of the older men, a grizzled former mine worker named Dustin, elbowed him. "I've seen that look before, my friend. How long have you and Lucy been together?"

Though everyone had been talking, the room immediately got quiet. No one bothered to hide their interest, eying Jason as they waited for him to answer.

Not sure how to respond, when Lucy came over and slipped her hand into his, he struggled not to show his surprise.

"Not long enough," she replied for him. "We're at the stage in our relationship where we're constantly learning something new about each other."

The cleverness of her response made him chuckle. "That's for sure," he said, turning and giving her a kiss on her cheek.

Most of the men laughed. Only one guy, Tad Gibbins, sipped his beer in silence. The intense way he gazed at Lucy made Jason slightly uncomfortable. He could only imagine how she must feel.

About to ask Tad to knock it off, Jason cleared his throat first, hoping the other man would get the hint. Instead, Tad moved closer until he stood a few feet in front of Lucy. He chugged down some beer as if he needed liquid courage before speaking.

"You look familiar," he said. "Have we met?"

Lucy stared back, making Jason admire the way she held her ground. "I don't think so," she replied. "I haven't really been into town much."

"You're not from around here, are you?" Tad persisted. "Even so, I can't shake the feeling that we've met."

"We haven't." Her tone sounded positive, even though Jason knew there was no way she could be. Not unless her memory had suddenly and miraculously returned, which he doubted.

Finally, Tad shrugged. "If you say so," he mumbled, moving back to the other side of the room.

The group stayed another forty-five minutes, filling Jason in on everything that had happened in Cedar since his last visit home. Several times, Jason caught Lucy eying one of the men while he repeated the latest gossip, her expression skeptical.

Later, after everyone had said their goodbyes and driven off, Jason went back inside to find Lucy with her back to him, rummaging in the refrigerator. When she straightened up, she turned and made a face at him. "Those men gossip more than a bunch of real housewives," she said.

Laughing, he agreed. "But they're good guys. I told you there was nothing to worry about."

"Maybe not." But then her expression sobered. "Except that Tad guy kind of freaked me out. I don't understand why he kept insisting we'd met before."

"I wouldn't take him too seriously," he said. "He's probably thinking of some actress or model he's seen on TV."

"Right," she snorted. "Because I look like I could possibly be a model. An actress, maybe. But not a model."

Once again, he realized she truly had no idea of the power of her own beauty.

"Anyway," she continued. "He worried me. He was so…intense. Do you think it's possible he might be the one who's been causing all the trouble? I followed everyone outside so I could check out their vehicles, but none of the trucks looked like the one that tried to run us off the road."

"Tad?" Jason shook his head. "He's relatively new to Cedar, but he's been here long enough for me to know he's a good guy."

Though her expression registered her disbelief, she finally nodded, accepting his words.

The phone rang. Landline again. When Jason answered, the caller identified himself. "Paul Groesel with NCIS."

"Why'd you subpoena me?" Jason asked, keeping his voice level. "I've already told you I don't have any idea where Rick went. I'm as worried about him as you are. Forcing me to come in for questioning is just a waste of everyone's time."

"I apologize," Groesel said. "But that subpoena was out of my hands. Actually, Rick Engles is just a small part in a very large puzzle. We sent you a subpoena because we need to see all the photographs you took in Kabul at the hotel, before and after the explosion."

Confused, Jason dragged his hand through his hair. "You don't seriously believe Rick had something to do with that, do you?"

"We need to see your photos," Groesel repeated.

"But why?"

"Right now, we can't give you an explanation. That's classified."

Jason bit back an automatic retort. By now, he should be used to dealing with the military. "I'm reviewing the photographs myself."

"No need to do that. Just bring them all."

This rubbed Jason the wrong way. "They're *mine*. I'm contracted for a book of my best shots. Believe me, I'm going to be taking a look at them."

Silence, then Groesel cleared his throat. "This may be a matter of national security," he declared.

Though Jason didn't say so, he didn't believe a word of that. If this, whatever *this* might be, truly was a matter of national security, agents would have already been at his cabin, confiscating the work he'd spent months on.

Luckily, he'd backed everything up, both in the cloud and on thumb drives.

Just to be certain, he checked the subpoena again. His presence was required, nothing more. "I won't be bringing any photographs," he finally said, wondering if he should reveal his hand so early on. "If you need them that bad, you'll have to get another subpoena."

The other man cursed, a particularly virulent string

of words that would have been mildly shocking had Jason not heard them all before.

"Come on," Groesel finally pleaded. "Help me out here. We won't keep them. We just need to take a look."

Nope, nope and nope. Still, Jason decided to hedge his bets a bit. "Is there any particular location or time period you're interested in?" he asked, hoping for a clue. "I mean, there are thousands of photos. All taken over the last two and a half years, in various hot spots and war zones."

The other man hesitated. "The last six months would probably work."

As specifics went, that wasn't much to go on, though it was better than nothing.

"I'm sorry," Jason finally replied. "Get another subpoena. Then I'll know this is legit."

Again, silence on the other end of the line.

"Is there anything else I can help you with?" Jason asked.

Groesel cleared his throat. "Actually, there is. I just wanted to check on you. Has anything unusual happened lately? Like death threats or hate emails?"

Like almost being run off the road? Like having someone try to set your house on fire? That kind of unusual?

"No, not really," Jason lied, wondering if Groesel was threatening him. "Why do you ask?"

"Again, I'm afraid I'm not at liberty to discuss. Please, write down my number and call if you remember anything or if anything strange should occur."

Jason almost asked the other man if that had been a

veiled threat, but once again held his tongue. Instead, he thanked the other man and ended the call.

"Something's going on," he said, telling Lucy what Groesel had wanted. "None of this adds up. What do my photos have to do with national security? They were taken out of country. All of them. The last ones were of the terrorist attack on the hotel. In addition to that, I never met up with Rick. Sure, I tried to reach him, but I was unsuccessful. I've tried a few times since I left Afghanistan, but haven't been successful."

Expression serious, she shook her head. "That's really weird."

"Yes, it is." He decided to go ahead and mention the rest of it. "On top of that, he asked if anything unusual had happened lately. Specifically, death threats or hate emails."

She gasped. "Was he threatening you?"

"Not specifically, but yeah. I think he was."

The phone rang again, startling them both. Wary, he answered.

"Listen to me," Groesel said. "You don't understand what's going on, or how serious it is. The fire was no accident, nor was the truck trying to run you off the road. Either you turn over the photos, or your life could be in danger." He hung up without giving Jason a chance to speak.

Stunned, Jason slowly replaced the phone in its base. "That was him again. This time, he most definitely threatened me. He told me either I turn over the photos or my life will be in danger."

Lucy swallowed hard. "What are you going to do?"

"I don't know," he answered, though he did. He'd

never been the type to give in to threats and he didn't figure he'd start now.

Except he now had someone else to consider. Blinking, he realized Lucy watched him, her eyes huge in her pale face.

"Hey," he said, crossing the room to cup her chin and press a lingering kiss on her lips. "Look at the positive side. At least we know for a fact that they're not aware of your existence. Groesel never mentioned you, not once. So none of this is targeted at you."

Though she nodded, the shadow never left her gaze.

Suddenly, he knew what they needed to do. "We need to go through the last six months of photos as quickly as possible. We need to figure out what they're after. And what they don't want us to see."

Chapter 10

Lucy admired Jason's determination, though privately she wondered at how he'd come by his rock-solid fearlessness. It would make sense that bravery and a reckless disregard for danger would be a by-product of being a photojournalist in war zones. She imagined one would eventually become inured to the concept of death waiting just around the corner.

Just thinking about something happening to Jason made a black aching rock settle in the pit of her stomach. She was glad he'd shown her how to handle a pistol, even though she suspected she'd already learned her way around a firearm sometime in her still-too-shadowy past.

"Let's get to work," he declared, grabbing the laptop and motioning at the desktop computer. "I've already booted it up and signed you in."

Glad to have a distraction from her tumultuous thoughts, she took a seat and, after following his directions, pulled up the photo files. He'd labeled them by the month and year in which they'd been taken. "Which ones should I look at?" she asked. "I don't want to duplicate your efforts."

"I think it'll be good if we have time to cross-check each other," he said. "Don't worry about what I have or haven't seen. They're all filed by date. Examine the ones from the last six months. You start in April and go forward. I'll start with this month and work backward. Look for anything that seems out of place."

"Can you be more specific?" she asked, not really clear on what would constitute out of place.

His rueful smile made her mouth go dry. "Not really. The best I can explain is if you have the slightest thought that you see something out of place in a photo—a face, a vehicle, a situation that doesn't belong—move that file to a new folder. Don't overthink it, just move it and go on to the next pic. OK?"

"OK." Sounded easy enough. She clicked on the file folder marked April and got to work. A few files in, she found herself captivated. The photos were fascinating—many brutal and stark, dark and dismal testaments to the cruelty of life. But there were others so beautiful they made her ache. A child's expectant smile, the love shining in a woman's eyes as she gazed up at her man. A colorful and exotic flower, blooming in between stacks of rubble. Jason had a talent, she realized. With his photographs, he made her see the world in a completely different light.

About an hour later, he got up to get something to

drink and brought her a bottle of water. She thanked him without looking up from the computer monitor.

They were both so focused on the task at hand that when the weather radio bleated its alert tone, they both jumped in tandem. A moment later, the metallic voice issued a severe weather alert—blizzard warning. Twelve to eighteen inches accumulation.

Muttering under his breath, Jason rushed to the door and peered outside. Lucy followed. Heavy snow had already begun to fall, huge fat flakes making lazy spirals on their way to the ground. Right now, it looked beautiful, though she suspected so much might be dangerous.

"I guess we should have caught the news," Jason said, shaking his head. "We'll likely be stuck here a few days, which is normal. These winter storms blow up quickly in this region. Luckily, we're still well stocked with provisions. I think we'll be all right, as long as you can stand the cabin fever."

His disgruntled tone made her laugh. "Hey, I can't think of anyone I'd rather be stuck in a cabin with."

"Of course you can't," he shot back, one corner of his mouth twitching in a clear attempt not to smile. "You can't remember anyone else."

Staring at him, for one second she wasn't quite sure how to react. Maybe another time the truth would have hurt, but for now, she had to see the humor. She laughed again. "Good point," she said dryly. "But for now, I stand by what I said."

"I'll ask you again once your memory is back." Just like that, he managed to kill her good mood. Sometimes, when she let herself relax, she felt normal. Not like a freak who didn't even know her own name. The pressure to remember could zap all her strength if she let it. And she suspected Jason wouldn't understand. How could he? What he'd said had only been the unvarnished truth. She had no idea what she'd be like when she knew everything about herself.

She took a minute to ponder that, since it made no sense for the simple truth to make her feel bad. Why the feeling of pressure? More than anything, she wanted herself back. All of herself. Flaws, faults, the bad along with the good. Whoever she might be, she wanted to know that person.

Yet she wanted Jason too, with every fiber of her being. Just thinking of a world without him in it made her feel sick.

Staring at the photo on the computer monitor blindly, she couldn't help but wonder what she would do once her memory returned. If she would turn out to be romantically unencumbered, would she still want to stay with him? Right now, she couldn't help but feel as if their paths were destined to forever intertwine. Except she actually had no idea whether Jason felt the same way. And right now, with only a tiny portion of her memory returning, she didn't have the right to ask him.

Frustrated, she wondered if she ever would. Blinking, she looked around to see that Jason had already returned to his laptop. He caught her looking and smiled. "Might as well get back to work," he said. "We aren't going anywhere tonight. And I'm betting the satellite is out, so there won't even be TV."

He was right. She took her seat in front of the desktop and clicked on the next file.

An hour later, she yawned and stretched. She'd

moved several files to the folder she'd designated as Questionable, though she had to admit she hadn't seen anything earth-shattering.

"Do you want to take a break?" Jason asked, raising his arms above his head as he performed his own stretch. "Maybe we should think about making something to eat."

She glanced at the clock. To her surprise, it was long past time for dinner. "I'll fix something," she said. "If you want to keep working, go ahead."

Already immersed in his work, he gave an absent nod.

In the kitchen, she checked the fridge to see what meat had been thawed. A packet of ground hamburger sat on the shelf and she remembered she'd taken it out yesterday. They had onions, kidney beans, canned tomatoes, even some canned jalapeño pepper—in short, everything she needed to make a big pot of chili. How she remembered the recipe, she didn't know. Instinct, maybe. Or perhaps she'd often made this in her murky past. Either way, she knew how.

Humming under her breath, she got to work. Once she'd browned the meat and chopped the onion, she mixed together the other ingredients in a Dutch oven and let it simmer while she returned to the computer.

"That smells good," he said, glancing over the laptop to grin at her.

"Thanks. It needs to simmer a bit and then it'll be ready to eat. That'll give us time to get through a few more of these files."

He nodded absently, already immersed in his task. With a quiet sigh, she sat herself down and got back to work. The starkness and horror of some of the photos was in direct contrast with the occasional shots of beauty. Jason had managed somehow to find the shining amid the despair. An old woman sharing a loaf of bread with a child, a ragged-looking dog sleeping on a rock in the sun.

If not for those, she didn't think she could continue viewing. The reality of war and what people could do to each other sat like a black pit in her stomach. She couldn't imagine what Jason must have felt like, actually being right there, seeing all of this firsthand.

Tears stinging her eyes, she looked away from the computer, pushing to her feet and going to stir the chili.

He got up and followed her. "What's wrong?" he asked, almost as if she'd expressed her conflicting emotions out loud.

She started to shrug and say nothing, but then decided to tell the truth. After all, he'd taken the photos. He had to be intimately familiar with the way viewing them would make her feel.

Haltingly, she tried to explain. He listened, his expression tender, and then pulled her in for a long hug. "You don't have to look at them anymore if it's bothering you. I can do the rest of them myself."

She snorted, relishing the way she felt in his strong embrace. "I wouldn't do that to you," she said into his chest. "It's just sad. I'm sure I'll survive."

One kiss on top of her head and he let her go, watching as she stirred the chili. "That looks really good. Just the smell of it is making me hungry."

She turned off the burner and nodded. "Me too. I think it simmered long enough. Let's eat."

Just then, the power went out, plunging them into

darkness. The glow of the woodstove provided the only light. Jason got up and rummaged in one of the kitchen drawers and extracted a box of matches. "I've got a backup generator we can use if we need to. But for now, let's eat by candlelight."

"OK." She nodded. "Do you think the power will be out long?"

"Probably until the storm is over. This high up, when the power goes out, it's usually a downed power line. They won't be able to get out here to fix it until the storm abates."

She didn't like that. For whatever reason, no electricity made her feel less safe.

"Which means we won't be able to go through any more photos, at least on the desktop" he continued. "Though my laptop is fully charged, so I can use that at least."

Partly relieved and partly disappointed, she nodded and began ladling the chili into bowls. Jason went to the pantry and returned with a bag of corn chips. He also got shredded cheddar cheese from the fridge. "Now I'm ready to eat chili," he said.

She watched, bemused as he mixed the corn chips in with his chili and topped everything with cheese.

"What?" he asked, noticing her watching. "This is the best way to eat chili, hands down. You ought to try it."

Sitting down across from him, she shrugged and grabbed the bag of chips, pouring several on her chili.

"You need more than that," he told her. "Usually, I put them in first and then pour the chili over. It's like a Frito pie."

"A what?" she asked.

"Frito pie. Haven't you ever been to a high school football game? They're one of the concession stand staples."

She thought for a moment. "I don't know," she finally said. "I'm tired of not knowing anything."

"It'll come." Taking another spoonful of chili, he swallowed and made an appreciative sound. "This is really good."

"Thank you. I always used to make chili when it snowed."

Dumbstruck, she stared at him. "Another memory."

"Yep. I told you, it'll come. Remember what Phil said. You've got to be patient."

Nodding, she finally picked up her spoon and dug in. He was right, the chili tasted exactly as it should. She liked the addition of the corn chips. They added a salty crunch that felt pleasing on her tongue.

After they'd eaten, they did the dishes side by side. "We'll eat this again tomorrow," Jason said. "Let's let it cool somewhat before we store it in the fridge."

He sat down on the couch, grabbing his laptop. "You're welcome to sit with me and help me look at the next few files," he said. "I've decided to go through the most recent next. The ones from the hotel bombing in Kabul."

She nodded, taking a seat next to him on the couch, careful to keep a few inches between them. While he booted up the laptop, which had gone to sleep mode, she amused herself by imagining all the things she'd rather be doing with him right now instead of going through photographs. But since a blizzard would have them snowed in again, she figured they'd have lots of time. Plus, she reminded herself that he had a deadline.

"Stop." Finger shaking, she pointed to the photo on his screen. "Who's that man?"

He shrugged. "Someone who was traveling with the vice president. The VP and a good-sized entourage made an unannounced and unscheduled stop in Kabul. Word had it that he was meeting with some high-ranking Afghan official, though it was so classified no one knows for sure. They were staying at the same hotel." He took a deep breath. "The one that was bombed."

For whatever reason, she had to force herself to look back at the photo. Once she could stare at it without wanting to puke, she nodded at him to go ahead and click the next one.

The same man and several others. This time, she focused on a tall man standing with his back to the camera. "Him," she exclaimed.

"What? Do you recognize him?"

Staring, she knew she did. His name hovered right out of reach, not quite at the tip of her tongue. "I know him," she breathed. "I think. It's hard to tell without seeing his face."

"Let's keep going through the pics," Jason advised. "Sooner or later I'm reasonably sure he turned around."

Ignoring the trepidation that made her stomach ache, she nodded and tried to breathe as he kept clicking. The same man in several frames. Back to the camera, still his back and finally, his profile. Pausing, Jason eyed her as she studied the clean aristocratic lines. "Anything?" he asked.

"Not yet. Maybe in the next one I'll be able to see his full face."

Sure enough, in the next photo, the unknown man completed the turn. Facing the camera, he stood out from all the other men. Handsome, yes. Arrogant too, judging by the disdainful look on his face as he eyed the camera. But again, she knew there was more. Unfortunately, she had no idea what.

Jason watched her closely, waiting while she stared at the photo.

"I know him." She swallowed hard, tasting bile. "Though I'm not sure how or in what way. But there's something familiar about him. And though I can't give you a definite answer why, I know that whatever it is, it isn't good."

"Just relax," Jason said. "Look at the picture and see if anything else comes to you."

Taking a deep breath, she tried to do as he asked. Carefully, she blanked her mind, emptying it of all thoughts while she focused on the photograph of the handsome man's face.

Flashes of violence, staccato and unconnected, she thought. The man shouting, cursing. Movement, everything a blur. She closed her eyes, letting the images wash over her. More angry shouting. A small group of women, huddled together under a dirty blanket, weeping and crying in fear. Trying to comfort them and when she did, a fist smashed into her face. Crumpling and falling, but still conscious enough to feel the kicks and the punches. All from one man, the one with the aristocratic features. Pain, such pain. She cried out, lost in the horror of the memory.

"Lucy." Jason's voice, calm and reassuring, in her ear. "It's all right. I'm here. You're safe." He put his strong arms around her, offering comfort. *Jason.* She let herself sag against him, shaken and still not quite certain what the memories actually meant.

"Lucy," he said again, moving the hair away from her face with gentle fingers. "Are you all right?"

Was she? She took a deep shuddering breath. Now, with him holding her close, she guessed she was. "I'm okay," she managed, haltingly trying to explain what she'd seen. "But I have no idea what any of that means."

He glanced from her to the photo still up on the computer screen. "Clearly, it's somehow tied to this man."

"I don't know. Maybe." Yet she knew deep within herself that it was. All of it. "Who is he?"

"I don't know. But I plan to find out." Keeping one arm still around her, he moved the photo to the special file. "If you're up to it, would you mind helping me look through the rest of the shots I took this day? There might be something else that looks familiar or triggers a memory."

Though that was the absolute last thing she felt like doing, she gave a slow nod. "I'll do the best I can."

He kissed her on the mouth then, a quick, reassuring press of his lips that left her wanting more. "That's all anyone can do."

Amazingly, he'd managed to make her feel better. She sat next to him, hips touching, arms too, and eyed the photos as he brought each up. When she realized there weren't any more of the one particular man, she began to relax.

He'd taken several shots of the rubble, but in them he'd managed to capture the reactions of hotel employees and others, probably customers. Shock, horror and dismay were a few of the emotions on their faces. Seeing them, she felt each and every emotion too.

Tears pricking her eyes, she said nothing, just continued watching the screen as Jason clicked from photograph to photograph.

In some of them, there were bodies. Dead bodies, twisted up among the rubble, many covered with sheets, but many more not. Swallowing hard, she looked away. "I hope you're moving those to the file of unacceptable ones."

With a quick sideways glance, he nodded. "I am. You don't have to look anymore if that upsets you. I'm not callous—I'm just so used to documenting whatever I see that I keep shooting pics."

"I know," she commented softly. "I saw the ones from Yemen earlier. I had to close one entire file when I saw the school bus that was hit by a mortar attack. I left that one for you to go through. I'm sorry, but I was afraid I might have nightmares."

Gaze locked on hers, he nodded. "You know what, Lucy? I think I did you a disservice when I asked you to help me with this." He shut down the laptop, waiting a moment before closing it. "I'm done for the day anyway. How about we play a game of poker? Or Scrabble, if you'd rather."

Instead of answering, she got up and walked to the door, opening it and peering out at the thick veil of falling snow. "I think I'll need a little bit of time to collect myself."

With that, she closed the door and took herself off to the bathroom. She felt like she needed a hot shower. Maybe then she could wash the sick feeling of horror away.

When he heard the sound of the shower turning on, Jason felt even worse. He hadn't even given a single thought to how viewing candid photos of the horrors of war might affect someone who wasn't used to seeing the atrocities mankind visited on each other.

In addition to that, she'd recognized someone who'd been there the day of the bombing. How was such a thing possible? Had she been there too? Even if she hadn't, he had to wonder what the connection might be.

Pacing the confines of the small room, he wondered if this might be why NCIS wanted to see his photographs. This man, the one who'd inspired such a powerful reaction in Lucy, who was he?

Finding out would be first on his list of priorities.

Walking past the subpoena he'd dropped on the kitchen table, he glanced at the date he was supposed to appear. Though it wasn't for another ten days, he couldn't help but hope there'd be another blizzard right before then, making the roads impassable.

The shower cut off, letting him know Lucy would be emerging soon. Picturing her toweling off, a rush of pure desire hit him, so powerful he staggered.

Telling himself he needed to cool off, he went to the front door and stepped outside onto the porch without a jacket. The porch light illuminated a wintry wonderland. Though the full force of the blizzard hadn't yet arrived, the snow continued to fall thick and heavy. It appeared to be the kind of powdery snow beloved of skiers everywhere.

He stood and watched it, loving the absolute silence, until the cold began to penetrate his clothes. Shaking his head, he turned and went back inside the warm cabin.

Lucy stood near her duffel bag, wearing a pair of flannel pajamas that she'd buttoned up all the way to the top. A pair of fuzzy slippers completed her look.

He froze, struck dumb with wanting. She looked cute and sexy, in a way that made him ache to slowly take those pajamas off her. "Where'd those come from?" he asked, his voice like rusted nails. "I haven't seen you wear them before."

"I haven't." She smiled at him, clearly having put her previous issues to rest for now. "I was looking for something other than a pair of thick socks to keep my feet warmer and I found these slippers." She lifted one foot. "When I noticed they went with these pj's, I had no choice but to put them on. Do they look too silly?" She peered at him, her smile slipping.

"Not silly at all." He could no more have kept himself from going to her than he could have stopped his heart from beating. "In fact, you look amazing."

She frowned, as if she couldn't tell if he meant it or not. "Thanks," she began.

He kissed her then, cutting off what else she might have been about to say. They lingered over the kiss, neither in a rush to take it any further. Not yet. The night was, as the saying went, still young.

When they finally broke apart, breathing heavily, she shook her head. "Wow."

Her one-word comment made him grin. "I told you those pajamas are sexy."

"Only to you," she said, laughing. The sparkle had come back to her eyes. "Listen, I know we talked about playing Poker or Scrabble," she said, her mouth swollen from his kisses. "But I really think we should go through some more of the Kabul photos."

"Are you sure? I don't want to put you in another bad place again."

She lifted her chin. "I'm positive. Right now, the not knowing is driving me nuts. I have to see the rest of the pictures. There might be something in them that will trigger my memory."

The determination in her voice told him she meant what she said. While going through more photographs didn't sound particularly appealing, it had to be done sooner or later.

"Fine," he said. "We'll spend another hour or so on the photos and then we'll call it a day and do something fun."

"Sounds good." The wicked gleam in her gaze told him exactly what she thought would be fun.

Smiling back at her, he marveled at the rush of affection he felt in addition to the bone-deep feelings of desire. In his life, he'd known many women, some of them beautiful, some of them fascinating, but no one had ever affected him the way this woman did. And neither he nor Lucy knew her real name or much about her past.

Would the truth change things between them? He couldn't see how it wouldn't.

Settling back on the couch with his laptop, he waited until she'd taken a seat beside him to open it and turn it on.

"Start where we left off," she ordered. "Actually, if we could go back to where that man faces the camera. I want to see him again."

Though he had his doubts about the wisdom of this, he was also intrigued. The reporter in him wanted to get to the mystery and find out the truth. But part of him also wanted to prolong their idyllic paradise just a little bit longer.

He scrolled through the thumbnails until he located the one she'd requested and clicked on the file. When the other man's chiseled features filled the screen, he too felt a small shock of recognition. "I know who that is," he mused. "Though I can't remember his name right now. I swear, we were introduced at some point. He was part of the vice president's entourage."

Studying the photo silently, she finally nodded. "Nothing else came to me. Let's continue."

"I took a lot of shots there," he warned her. "Some of them might be...gruesome."

"I'll survive." Her dry tone had him glancing at her. "I really want to see every single one. I don't know why, but I'm sure there's a valid reason. I'm hoping it becomes obvious by the time we've finished with that file."

Nodding, he clicked on the next shot.

They went through forty or fifty photos, most of people, some of the rubble the explosion had caused, without anything causing Lucy to react. Swallowing hard at the next shot, he warned her from this point on, she might find the images difficult to look at. "They'd started bringing people out of the rubble."

Though she gave a grim jerk of her head, he knew nothing he could say would prepare her, so he simply brought up the next photo.

For the next several moments, they reviewed the pictures in silence. Death and injury, bodies coated in the gray powder of destroyed concrete, limbs missing or twisted in impossible fashion. Grief and pain all came through with a violence that couldn't begin to match the horror of the act that had done this.

He glanced sideways at her, worried. When he noticed the tears sliding silently down her cheeks, he wondered if she was even aware of them. Unable to help himself, he reached over and gently wiped them away with his finger.

"It's OK," she told him, sounding husky. "I'm fine. Continue."

Marveling at the steel inside her, he did as she asked.

"Wait." Shock rang in her voice. "There. The woman on the stretcher. Do you have more of her?"

"I'm not sure. There were so many people being brought out of the rubble. There's only one way to find out." On to the next shot.

Her again. Close up. As he stared at the woman's battered features, a sort of horrified recognition came over him. "She... That woman looks like..."

"Me," she said flatly, knowing the truth deep in her heart. "That's me. Apparently, I was also there when the hotel in Kabul exploded."

Chapter 11

For a second or two, Lucy couldn't catch her breath as she stared at the image of herself immortalized by Jason's camera. Bloody and unconscious, she was almost unrecognizable. Her eyes were swollen, and a huge bruise purpled her face. She looked…dead. Or at least seriously injured. Clearly, she'd been hurt in the bombing of the same hotel where Jason had also been staying. There was the connection, albeit a fragile one. Still, this had to be the reason why someone had taken her to him.

Which would only make sense if they knew each other. And while she had no way of knowing whether they did, judging by Jason's reactions from the moment he'd walked into his home and found her there, they did not.

For the first time since her arrival, she felt a frisson on doubt. What if Jason was pretending not to know her? What if all along he'd been aware of every single thing that had happened to her?

Hyperventilating, she told herself to calm down. She might not have known Jason long, but he wouldn't do something like that. He'd made it clear that he considered them in this—whatever *this* might be—together. And he'd been just as shocked as she when her picture had popped up on that screen. She'd bet her life on it. For the first time she realized she might literally be doing exactly that.

"Are you okay?" Jason asked, putting his arm around her. "This has to be a big shock."

"Did you know?" she heard herself ask him. "Did you remember taking a picture of me?"

He didn't drop his arm, as she supposed a guilty man would have. Instead, he pulled her closer, holding her tight. "Of course not," he murmured. "I take so many shots, I can't possibly remember them all. To be honest, I kind of shut myself off in a disaster of this magnitude. I focus on capturing the images without even thinking. I make snap judgments about the light and the subject and keep clicking away. I had no idea you were there. No idea at all."

She believed him. "I had no idea either," she said, trying for a small joke.

Her attempt at humor made him chuckle. "No, I'm guessing you didn't. This is all very convoluted and strange. It's got to be tied together somehow. Even if we don't know all the particulars."

"I agree." Still, gazing at her photograph, she

couldn't help but chastise herself. How could she have forgotten such an awful and life-altering event? But then again, how could she have forgotten her entire existence, everything that made her who she was? And then she wondered, had the bombing and her subsequent injuries been the reason she couldn't remember?

Gingerly, she reached up and touched her face, still staring at the photo. The swelling had gone down by the time she'd awakened inside Jason's cabin. And the bruising had faded day by day, until only the faintest shadow remained. She hardly felt them at all now.

Jason touched her shoulder, startling her. "What do you remember?" he asked. The urgency in his voice made her feel worse. Logically, the jarring sight of herself should have triggered at least a few flashbacks.

Slowly, without looking at him, she shook her head.

"Surely, you must remember something. One of those flashback things you've been having. Maybe what you were doing the moment the bomb detonated, something like that?"

"No," she cried. "That's just it. I remember nothing. I'm sitting here looking at my own face and I have no recollection of what happened. Why I was there, how I got hurt or how I ended up thousands of miles from Kabul in your remote mountain cabin."

He nodded, his steady gaze not reflecting even the slightest disappointment, though she knew he had to be feeling it.

"I know Phil said we can't force your memory to come back," Jason said. "But surely seeing yourself in a photo, during a particular time and place, must jog something loose."

"No." The more he prodded her, the more miserable she felt. "If anything, having concrete evidence like that without any logical connection makes me feel even worse."

He hugged her then, a quick embrace along with a kiss on the forehead. "Don't stress. I'm sure the memories will return eventually."

"Will they?" She didn't bother to keep the bitterness from her voice. "I'm beginning to have my doubts. I don't even know what I was doing in Afghanistan."

Though he reached for her again, she pushed to her feet, avoiding him. Instead, she chose to pace back and forth from the kitchen to the front door, making several passes in front of the couch and the woodstove.

"You're right about one thing, though. There's the connection," she told him. "You and I were both in the same place at the same time."

"Maybe so," he shot back. "But I didn't know you or you me. How'd you end up here, thousands of miles away?"

"That's an answer I'd really like to have." She stopped, spun around to face him. "Along with my name and other basic info. Is there a way to get a list of the injured? Maybe if I see my name on a list, it'll help."

His gaze dark, he considered. "I don't know, but I can check. Be aware that there were hundreds of people injured, as well as hundreds killed. I'll start with requesting a list of any injured Americans, which I'm going to assume you are, judging by your accent."

She nodded. "Thank you." Pushing back her hair with her fingers, she tried to calm her agitation. No matter how she looked at it, seeing herself in a photo Jason had taken after a hotel bombing was a big freaking deal.

When she voiced these thoughts out loud, Jason agreed. "Of course it is. It's a huge step toward finding out your name at least. And with that, we might also learn why you were in Kabul in the first place. It's not exactly a tourist destination."

"I must have been part of that diplomatic delegation you mentioned. Somehow, I honestly feel some sort of tie to that man. The one with the cruel eyes," she said. "Of course, I don't know for sure, but I have a gut feeling. If possible, can you also find out the names of everyone who was there with the vice president?"

He eyed her for a moment, his expression inscrutable. "I'm planning to, as soon as I possibly can. That's the only thing that would make sense, the only reason an American woman would be there. Unless..." He narrowed his gaze, studying her. "You're also a reporter."

"If I was, I'd think you'd know it, wouldn't you?"

"Probably." He didn't miss a beat.

"I think it's much more likely I was part of the VP's entourage. So can you find out those names too?"

"I can definitely try," he promised. "It shouldn't be classified or anything. And since I'm a reporter, getting that information shouldn't be too difficult."

"Thank you," she told him, her insides still churning. She felt slightly dizzy, as if the magnitude of today's discovery had made the earth shift on its axis.

"Do you want to look at the rest of the photos?" he asked her. "There might be more of you."

Though that possibility made her feel queasy, how could she resist? "OK," she said, trying to steel herself.

He clicked on the next image. A small child, tears running down his dirt-streaked face, stood among the rubble, clutching the hand of a badly wounded Afghani man. The next several shots were all of other wounded people, most of them appearing local. Jason moved several of them into the folder for those he hoped to consider for his book.

After clicking through another twenty-five photos, it seemed clear there weren't any more of her.

"There are still several hundred more," he said, correctly interpreting the disappointment that must have shown on her face.

Stretching, she shook her head. "I think I've had enough for tonight. Are you still up for playing a quick game of Scrabble?"

Closing his laptop and setting it on the coffee table, he shrugged, appearing less than enthusiastic. "I have another idea," he drawled, the heat in his gaze leaving no doubt of his meaning. "Might help clear your head."

This made her laugh. "To say the least," she replied, leaning in for a long, wet kiss.

They shed their clothes right there, each helping the other, neither in a big hurry. Not yet.

Instead of moving into his bedroom, they fell together on the couch. His touch, his kiss, the hardness of his muscular body, all ignited the familiar spark, burning her up from the inside out, clearing her mind, leaving room for nothing but the touch of his hands, his body against hers.

With him like this, she wasn't alone, no matter that

she didn't know her own name. With him, skin to skin, soul to soul, the possibilities of what they could be to each other if and when everything returned to normal brought tears to her eyes. And when he finally entered her, with a fierceness and a passion that made her convulse with pleasure, she cried out with relief and joy.

They made love with a furious sort of passion, and she poured all of her frustration and fear into loving Jason. He met her increasingly frenzied movements with a roughness of his own, bringing her to climax with a power that shook her to her very core.

I love him.

Damn it. She loved him.

How such a thing could be possible for a woman who was still a blank slate, she couldn't say. However, she might not know a lot of things yet, but she knew this with an absolute rock-solid certainty. She loved Jason Sheffield. And she didn't even know if she had the right to love anyone.

He'd held himself still while her body pulsed around his. Then slowly, he began to move again. Still tingling, she met him stroke for stroke, urging him toward his own release. When he found it, she held him while he shuddered with the power of his climax, amazed anew at how much she loved him. Sated and satisfied, she realized another thing. She didn't care about the possible ramifications of her love for him. No matter what the future brought, she could no more stop loving him than she could make her heart stop beating.

After his world shattered around him, Jason held on to Lucy until his heart rate and breathing slowed. For a moment, as he breathed in her scent, he struggled to make sense of what had just happened.

She'd rocked his world. Sappy as it might sound, she'd made him feel things he hadn't even realized were real. This had been more than sexual, more than a physical expression of the attraction they felt for each other. This had been on an entirely different level. They'd made love as if they'd both thought this might be their last time. Not if he could help it, but he knew the real world would soon come crashing in on the idyllic life they'd begun to carve out here in his remote mountain cabin.

Life together. While he knew it couldn't last because it wasn't real, he wanted to allow himself to enjoy it while he could. As soon as Lucy's memory returned, the wheels would start spinning. Though he'd spent many years vacationing alone in his cabin, he realized with a sharp pang of grief that he didn't know how he would face it once she was gone.

Which might be sooner than he thought.

Kissing her cheek, he urged her up so they could move into his much more comfortable bed. Keeping his body intertwined with hers, he shuffled her there. Once she'd settled into her usual spot, he crawled in next to her so he could hold her as she dozed off to sleep.

As for him, he knew he wouldn't be slumbering any time soon. There was simply too much to think about.

Earlier, he'd managed not to show his reaction to finding Lucy's photograph among his Kabul hotel bombing snapshots. He'd been shocked and stunned and, to be honest, uneasy. The randomness of finding a beautiful woman with no memory in his cabin was no longer so random. Now, determining her identity would not only help her realize who she was, but might give him a clue as to why she'd been brought to him in the first place.

Unfortunately, he knew none of that would come without a price. While he wasn't sure how, he had to believe that everything was tied together with intricate threads. The bombing, the vice president and his group, NCIS, Rick's disappearance, Lucy being in Kabul and now here in Colorado. Jason felt a bit like a pawn in a cosmic game of chess, being moved about without the slightest idea of what was going on.

He intended to find out, and soon.

Though he had to be careful, with the military breathing down his neck wanting to see his pictures, it wouldn't be a difficult task to get the names of all the Americans who'd been staying at the hotel. There wouldn't be that many. Lucy's real name, along with biographical information, was sure to be among them.

From there, he had no idea. Her Facebook profile, her Twitter account, Instagram, Snapchat and any other social media page she might have would be accessible for them to view. It wouldn't be long at all before they had all the information on her. These recent revelations had been disconcerting to him. He could only imagine how she must have felt. Hopefully, each new piece of information they retrieved would bring her one step closer to remembering her past.

This was a good thing, he knew. A great thing. Then why did he feel such a strong sense of loss? As if something precious would be taken away forever.

He shook his head and told himself not to be maudlin. Instead, he focused on NCIS. Why were they even involved? Sure, he could understand them investigating Rick's disappearance, but why were they focusing on a photojournalist who hadn't even seen Rick the day he went missing? What did they know that he didn't? What was the real reason they wanted to review his photos? While they'd stated it was because of Rick Engles, which had to be patently false, Jason couldn't help but suspect that the real reason had something to do with the vice president and his entourage. Of which Lucy might have been a part.

Stroking her hair while she slept, he gazed down at her and wished for his camera, aching to memorialize this exact moment in time forever. But he knew if he slid his arm out from under her, she'd wake or move, so he stayed where he was. Never before had he been so acutely aware of the passage of time, nor had he felt it moved far too fast.

Jason had always been a man of forward momentum. He'd always believed in moving forward, not looking back toward the past. But right now, holding the most beautiful woman he'd ever known in his arms, he wished he could make time stand still.

Selfish, he knew. Lucy deserved to have her memory and her sense of self back. He didn't believe any of what had happened to her had been her own fault, though he could be wrong.

Outside, with the winter wind howling and causing his cabin walls to shake, he allowed himself the luxury of basking in the moment, all too aware he might never have another like it.

Tomorrow, he'd begin the investigation into learning Lucy's name. Assuming, he amended silently, that he had internet service. If not, he'd simply have to wait until the storm blew over. Then, he'd pour himself into getting the necessary information, no matter what it took.

Whatever the truth might be, they were about to find out. He just wanted to stay one step ahead of the feds. He needed to figure things out before his court date and before NCIS got a new subpoena requesting his photos. There had to be something incriminating he'd inadvertently managed to capture. Something they didn't want anyone to see. It seemed most likely to be something to do with the vice president. Whatever it might be, Jason only hoped he could spot it quickly.

Lucy stirred, rolling over to her other side, and he relaxed his embrace. Now that they knew she'd been in Kabul during the hotel bombing, he felt safe to guess that singular mutual connection had been at least part of the reason why she'd been brought here to his cabin. But why and by whom?

He couldn't shake the feeling that there was some clue he'd missed. First up, he needed to get a list of Americans who'd been staying at the hotel. Second, he wanted those who'd been part of the vice president's entourage to be highlighted. Once he had those, he could narrow down the names to show only females. One of those would have to be Lucy.

But with the blizzard raging outside, his hands were temporarily tied. Both the internet and satellite would likely be down, limiting his access to the outside world. He felt as if there was an endless loop of thought swirling around inside his head.

Finally, he must have fallen asleep.

He woke fully aroused, still spooning Lucy. She turned, her blue eyes wide open, and grinned. "Well, good morning to you too," she said. "I'm glad you're so happy to see me."

They made love again, this time without the previous night's urgency. Slow and languid, relishing each other's body. As they held each other, basking in the afterglow, the power came back on, startling them and make them both laugh.

Lucy sprang up first and called dibs on the shower. He watched her go before pushing himself out of bed and following her, tapping on the door to ask her if he could have a minute to clean himself off.

She opened the door, clad in only a towel, and sashayed out. "Go right ahead," she told him.

He took a few minutes and when he reemerged, she brushed past him with a smile. Chest aching, he stood like a love-struck teenager, watching until she closed the door. Still, he stood, rooted to the same spot, until he heard the shower come on.

While she showered, he made himself a cup of coffee and then began to prepare breakfast, deciding this time to make biscuits and sausage gravy.

When she finally emerged, wearing a soft flannel shirt and jeans, her hair still damp, she sniffed the air and grinned. "That smells amazing."

The timer dinged, and he turned long enough to return her smile before removing the biscuits from the oven. She got a cup of coffee and waited while he brought everything to the table.

Then they dug in, as companionable as an old married couple.

After eating, they washed and dried the dishes. Jason checked the snowfall—sixteen inches and still falling—before taking his own shower. When he returned, Lucy had already booted up the desktop computer and had started going through more photos. He grabbed his laptop and began doing the same.

When the answering machine chirped, indicating someone had left a message, even though the phone hadn't even rung, Jason couldn't believe it at first. But then he knew the thing would usually work, even in horrible weather. Which is the main reason he kept it. When calls didn't make it through, they'd go to the built-in voice mail system.

Curious, he played the message back. "Jason, it's me. I need to talk to you, ASAP. I can't leave my number and I'm calling from a burner phone that I plan to destroy immediately. Will try again with a new one. I hope to hell I can reach you. You're in danger, man. We all are." The call ended with an audible click.

Stunned, Jason stared at the machine. That had been his friend Rick. Rick Engles, who purportedly had gone missing. Heart pounding, Jason played the message again.

"Who is that?" Lucy asked, coming up behind him and putting her hand casually on his shoulder.

For half a second, he actually wondered if he should tell her, then realized they were in this together, whatever *this* might be. "My friend Rick. The one who was supposed to meet me right before the bombing and went missing." He took a deep breath and swallowed. "The one NCIS is looking for."

"That means he's alive," she said, her gaze searching his. "A good thing, right?"

"Yes. Alive is always good. Disappearing—not so much. Especially since Rick is one of the most upstanding, dependable, straight-arrow guys I've ever known. If he's in hiding, then something truly awful is going down."

Now her frown matched his. "From what he said, you can't call him back, right?"

"Exactly. Which also concerns me." He shook his head. "He mentioned a burner phone. There's no reason to have a burner phone unless you're worried about being tracked."

She nodded. "I'm getting the feeling that all of this—the bombing, the photos, your not-so-missing friend Rick and NCIS—are all connected. I just wish we could figure out how."

"Good point. I had the same feeling." Again, the niggling sense that he was missing something important. Something right underneath his nose.

They spent the next several hours poring over photographs, finding nothing out of the ordinary. Jason couldn't help but continually glance at the damn phone, willing it to ring.

But as the storm continued to rage, the phone sat silent. There were no more messages. Jason didn't know if Rick might be trying to call and couldn't get through, or if his friend was too busy staying on the run to try and reach him again.

They had soup for lunch and went back to work. Lucy had to be bored by now, but she continued to go through snapshots without complaining. He couldn't help but admire that.

They finished with their evening meal, when the snow began to taper off. "Looks like the worst of it is over," Jason said, trying out the television, relieved to find that his satellite was up and running. Which meant the phone would work too, should Rick decide to call.

Finally, as Jason and Lucy cuddled under a blanket on the couch watching a movie, the phone rang. Jason leaped to answer it.

"It's me," Rick said. "I don't have much time. Tell me, is the woman still there?" The crack in his voice belayed his exhaustion. "I just need to know if she's all right."

"The woman?" Jason glanced at Lucy, trying to connect the dots. "How do you know about her?"

"I can't believe you haven't figured it out." Rick snorted. "I left her in your cabin. I had to get her out of Kabul before they killed her."

Though he had a thousand questions, Jason forced himself to stay on track. "Define *they*."

"No time. Not yet. Just tell me she's okay. You didn't let anyone take her, right?"

Jason glanced over at Lucy, still wrapped in the blanket, now sitting up and watching him intently. "She's fine. Who is she?"

"What?" The line crackled, and for a second Jason feared they'd lost the connection.

But then Rick spoke again. "What do you mean, 'who is she?' Didn't she tell you?"

"No. She lost her memory."

"All of it?" Rick asked. "Maybe that's a blessing in disguise. After the beating she got… I'm surprised it didn't kill her. They wanted her dead, I'm pretty sure. She was in the wrong place at the wrong time."

Which meant they—whoever they were—might be after her.

"Explain. To begin with, who is she?" Across the room, Lucy stiffened, and then got up and came over to stand near him. Jason reached out and pulled her close, keeping his arm around her waist.

"She's—" Static blotted out whatever his friend had to say.

Jason waited impatiently for the static to subside. When it did, he waited a few seconds. "Rick? Are you there?"

But only silence greeted him. The connection had been lost.

Muttering a curse, Jason hurriedly hit Redial. As he'd suspected, redial didn't work on blocked numbers and the call would not go through, and he finally re-placed the phone in the cradle. "We lost him before he told me anything, other than he was the one who got you out of Kabul and brought you here. I'm not clear why, but he mentioned you were beaten, nearly killed."

"Which means my injuries were not the result of the bombing," Lucy said.

"Right. I asked him for your name, but never got it. I'm sorry."

Disappointment flashed across her face. "But he does know, right? He knows who I am?"

"Apparently."

"Do you trust him?" she asked. "How well do you know him?"

"Rick and I grew up together. That's how he not only knew about this cabin, but knew how to get in. He's one of the few people who knows where I hide my spare key."

Her lovely blue eyes widened at this. "Where is he now? Is it safe to meet with him? I'd really like to find out everything he knows."

"Me too. But it's clear he doesn't feel safe and that he thinks someone is after him. I'm sure he'll contact me again when he can."

She nodded. "The subpoena," she said. "They're going to be asking you questions about him. What if they find out he's contacted you?"

Damn. She was right. "I'll have to stall. Somehow."

"What happens if you don't show up?"

"I imagine they'll put out a warrant for my arrest. I'm not sure. I'd have to look it up." Mind spinning, he sat down. "I need to let Rick know what's going on. Except I have no way to contact him."

He pulled her close, kissing her just below her jawbone. "Right now, we might as well get some sleep. The snowstorm is letting up, and hopefully will stop completely by morning. I'll try and get some answers then."

"Sleep?" Her voice echoed disbelief. "How can you possibly sleep now, having just learned news like this?"

Her question made him smile. "It's better than sitting around and worrying about something we can't change."

Slowly, she nodded, the darkness in her gaze reflecting her disappointment. He could tell she realized he spoke only truth, even if she didn't like it. He couldn't blame her. Had their positions been reversed, he'd have been impatient to get his answers too.

"Give me a few minutes to freshen up," she said. "And then I'll join you. I can't help but wish that, at the very least, we'd been able to learn my real name."

Chapter 12

Once inside the restroom, Lucy eyed herself in the mirror. She felt on edge, jangly and restless and nervous. She was so close to learning who she was and what had happened to her. Oddly enough, she had mixed feelings about that.

In actuality, while it sounded great to finally know her real name and why she'd ended up in Jason's cabin, she realized she sort of wanted to figure it all out herself. Selfish, maybe. But she wasn't sure how'd she'd feel if this Rick person gave Jason all the information about her and she still didn't remember any of it. She suspected that would make her feel even worse.

But, she reminded herself, this wasn't all about her. Rick had involved Jason in whatever this was. Jason had stepped up, taking care of a woman he'd never even met.

He'd been a true friend—more than a friend. In a short period of time, he'd become her everything. She couldn't bear if something happened to him because of her.

Her knees nearly buckled. If she had any decency, she'd leave. Put as much distance between herself and Jason as possible. She couldn't endanger him if she wasn't around him.

But she couldn't. The thought of never seeing him again felt like a hard punch to the stomach, robbing her of her breath. She owed him more than she could ever repay, but she couldn't leave him. Not now, while she was only half a woman. Maybe she'd be strong enough to do so after she'd regained her sense of self. Maybe. And then again, maybe not.

After washing up, she brushed her teeth, lingering in the bathroom as long as she could. Not because she wanted to avoid Jason, but because she needed to get herself together before facing him. The last thing she wanted to do would be to have a total meltdown.

Finally, she felt composed enough to open the door. So much had happened in the last several hours, she wondered if she would be able to relax enough to eventually fall asleep. Maybe she could distract the both of them. A vigorous bout of lovemaking might help.

Yet she wasn't sure she had her act together enough for that. One touch, and she might simply shatter into a million pieces.

Instead of heading into the bedroom, she went to the kitchen and got a glass of water from the fridge, turning out the lights before carrying it over to the sink so she could look out the window. The porch light provided just enough illumination for her to watch the fat, lazy snowflakes drift down. Beautiful. She felt at peace, warm and snug in the quiet cabin.

Judging by the snow piled on the railing, they'd gotten well over a foot, which seemed like a lot for so early in the year. But then again, they were deep in the mountains, and she truly had no idea what might be normal for a place like this.

That thought made her chuckle under her breath. Right now with no memory, she had no actual idea what might be normal for anywhere.

Knowing Jason would be waiting, she finished her water and put the glass in the sink. Now that she'd steadied herself, she felt better. Sexy even. Just the thought of making love with Jason had her pulse quickening. Finally, she headed for his room, already planning exactly what she wanted to do to arouse him.

But when she slipped through the doorway, she realized she'd clearly delayed too long. Jason lay on his back, eyes closed and softly snoring. He'd fallen asleep while waiting for her.

Instead of climbing into bed, she stood and studied him for a moment. So damn handsome. Though a big man, he moved with a quick-limbed kind of grace that she found attractive. Heck, even asleep, he managed to radiate self-confidence, though she didn't understand how. More entranced than disappointed, she studied his chiseled profile, relaxed and unaware.

Briefly, she toyed with the idea of waking him up with kisses, but since she knew he must need his rest, she decided she'd make more use of this alone time. Still carrying her half-full glass of water, she returned to the living room, added a couple more pieces of wood to the woodstove and sat down on the couch. Alone with the flickering light of the fire, she half closed her eyes and tried to empty her mind and hope some sort of memory, no matter how brief, would come to her.

Instead, she must have fallen asleep, sitting cross-legged on the couch. She woke with her legs asleep and her back aching. Not sure how much time had passed, she sheepishly untangled herself, got up and tried to shake the circulation back into her now-tingling limbs.

Moving around the room, she yawned, realizing that she must have been more tired than she'd realized. Even though the woodstove fire still put out good heat, she went ahead and added a few more pieces of tinder to keep it going strong for a few more hours.

Eying the comfortable sofa, she briefly hesitated. She debated whether to try and sleep on the couch or get back into bed with Jason. The lure of Jason's body heat pulled her down the short hall and into his room.

Moving carefully, she lifted the sheet and blankets and managed to slip into the bed next to him without disturbing him. With her heart full, she propped herself up on one elbow and gazed down at him, watching him sleep again. She wanted to imprint the image into her memory before she slumbered.

Then finally, she settled into place, closed her eyes and let herself drift off to sleep.

She'd already been injured when the bomb went off. She saw what had happened from a distance, as if watching someone else. She'd gone looking for Russell and blundered into a scene straight out of a nightmare.

Following in the direction she'd seen him going when she'd looked out her window, she'd turned into one of the narrow alleyways that wound like a warren in the neighborhood near the hotel. Several wooden doors, spaced at regular intervals, led to what she supposed were private residences along the way. Most of them were closed.

But one was not. Slightly cracked, just enough for her to hear Russell's voice.

About to push open the door and greet him, something in his tone made her pause. He sounded angry, on the verge of violence, which seemed impossible because Russell was the most self-contained man she knew.

For a split second, she wondered if she'd made a mistake and the voice she heard was someone else. But no, he continued to talk, practically snarling, and as the words he used began to register, she recoiled in horror.

Wanting to see—needing to see—she pushed the door all the way open and stood, staring in shock. Three women, all naked, their hands tied behind their backs, knelt in front of her fiancé. Also naked, Russell held some sort of whip, and judging by the size of his erection, he quite enjoyed hitting the women with it. Purpling bruises, welts and even blood decorated their dusky skin.

Though stunned, she had enough of her wits about her to notice the women were clearly terrified. They were locals, and she realized they'd wanted no part of this at all. They were his...prisoners. Unwilling sex slaves.

She must have made a sound of horror, because Russell spun around, whip cracking, catching her on the shoulder. Realizing who he'd hit, he made an effort to check himself, but it was too late.

Pain exploded through her, and she screamed. Rus-

sell grabbed her, clapping his hand over her mouth. "Calm down," he ordered, holding on so tightly she grew afraid he might decide to strangle her next. She let her eyes blaze her contempt for him, struggling to get away.

Instead of releasing her, he shoved her, so hard that she slammed into one of the stone walls. When her head hit, her sight momentarily went black, stars appearing in her peripheral vision. She cried out again, unable to fathom how this was happening. How could the man she'd actually believed she would marry act this way?

Who was he, really?

As she struggled to remain standing, he came at her. He hit her, again and again and again. Belatedly, she remembered her self-defense class and tried to fight back, but her responses came too late. He continued beating her, until the pain became too much and she blacked out.

Gasping, Lucy flailed wildly, fought off the blankets and sat up in the bed. A dream. It had been a dream. No, more than that. Her memory had come searching for her in the quiet of sleep.

Blearily, Jason reached for her, most likely intending to comfort her, but all she saw was Russell's fist coming at her again and again and again.

Instead of lashing out, she shot backward, away, rocketing to her feet, drenched in sweat and too terrified to even try to pretend she was okay. Because she wasn't. Far from it.

"Lucy?" Fully awake now, Jason sat up too and clicked on the bedside lamp. "What happened? Are you okay?"

Shuddering, shaking, she struggled to draw breath. This was Jason, she told herself. He would never hurt her.

"Lucy?" he repeated, clearly understanding not to try and get too close. "Talk to me. Please. Did you have a bad dream?"

"I saw," she managed to say. "I saw exactly what happened to me in Kabul. And the man, the one I pointed out, he was my fiancé."

Words tumbling over one another, she told him everything she'd seen. His expression darkened as she relayed how Russell had beat her to nearly an inch of her life.

"Russell who?" he asked, snapping out the words. Judging from the rigid set of his jaw, he wanted to make Russell pay.

Oddly enough, the quiet fury in his voice calmed her. Thinking for a moment, she finally shook her head. "I don't know. I probably should, but right now it's not coming to me. But I heard him say my name, so I know that now at least." She tried to summon a shaky smile, but failed. "My name isn't Lucy. He called me Abby."

"Abby." Jason regarded her for a moment before slowly nodding. "It suits you."

"Does it?" She didn't know. Privately, she thought she much preferred Lucy.

"Yes." He no doubt meant his warm smile to reassure her. "Is that what you'd like me to use from now on?"

Her real name. Abby. Though she still had no idea of the rest of it—middle or last. Torn, she hesitated. She'd feel foolish insisting he continue to use Lucy now that she knew her real name. "Sure," she replied. "It might take a little bit, but I'll eventually get used to it."

He laughed at that. "You will. How about I call you Abby Lou until you do?"

Shaking her head, she couldn't help but smile. "We can try that. Eventually. But if you don't mind, for now let's keep Lucy. I don't feel like an Abby. Not yet. I promise to let you know when I do."

He nodded. "Sounds good."

Her smile faded as she considered the enormity of the news Rick had imparted earlier. This, along with her dream, went a good way toward filling in the blanks. "I can't help but wonder what else your friend Rick knows," she mused. At least, with all this discussion, she'd managed to stop trembling. Though she suspected it would be a long time before the horror of that memory left her.

Gaze steady, he nodded. "I'm sure we'll find out next time he's able to get through. Some of what you learn might be upsetting. Are you okay with that?"

Deciding to answer honestly, she shrugged. "I'm not sure. Part of me would prefer to remember it all on my own. But since I don't know how long that will take…"

He patted the bed beside him. "Come here," he said. "If you don't mind, I'd like to hold you."

Raising a brow, she tried to find the right words.

Something in her expression must have revealed her thoughts. "No hanky-panky," he promised, his soft smile touching her. "It's three in the morning and you just went through an ordeal that clearly shook you. I want to offer comfort and support. If you don't want me to, that's fine. Come back to bed and let's try to get some more rest."

Still, she hesitated. Her skin still crawled and she wondered if Jason's touch could erase the memory of what had been done to her.

He didn't push her or repeat his request. Instead, he simply watched her, letting her make her own decision.

"I'm not sure I can sleep," she said. Despite that, she went to him, drawn to the reassuring warmth of his muscular body. Once she'd gotten in to the covers, he curled his body around hers, holding her close with his arm. Amazingly, she managed to drift off into a deep, dreamless sleep.

She woke hours later to bright sunshine and an empty bed. The nightstand clock read 9:00 a.m. Stretching lazily, she had a few seconds of blissful quiet before the memories came rushing back.

Abby, not Lucy. Attacked by a man named Russell and beaten within an inch of her life. Brought here by Jason's friend Rick, someone she wasn't sure she even knew. And clearly in some sort of danger, though she still didn't know why or from whom.

Getting up, she hurried to the bathroom for her shower. After drying her hair and brushing her teeth, she got dressed and made her way into the brightly lit kitchen. Seated at the table with his laptop open before him, Jason greeted her by lifting his half empty cup of coffee. "There's a pan of oatmeal still warm on the stove," he said.

"Coffee first," she replied. "Have you been up awhile?"

"A few hours. I've been combing through more photos. I'm still trying to see what NCIS could possibly want to keep quiet. I know it's got to have something to do with the vice president, but damned if I can figure out what."

Punching the button to start her coffee brewing, she took a deep breath. "I think it might have to do with Russell, the man I pointed out to you earlier."

His expression darkened. "The one who beat you?"

"Yes." Swallowing hard, she waited for her cup to finish brewing. When it had, she added cream and sweetener and carried it over to the table. "What I saw in my dream last night… Well, I'm pretty sure it was a memory."

"Go on."

"I followed Russell. I wasn't sure why he'd disappeared for so long, and I'd seen him leave when I was looking out the window." She took a sip of her coffee, trying to calm her suddenly racing heart. "I ended up in an alley. You know how those are in Kabul. Tall and narrow, with a bunch of doorways leading who knows where."

He nodded.

"One door was open. Just the smallest bit, but enough for me to hear Russell on the other side. He…" Voice breaking, she struggled to continue. "He was abusing women." Without mincing words, she told him the rest of what she'd seen, and then what had happened afterwards.

His mouth tightened into a grim line and she could see a muscle working in his jaw. He didn't speak, not for several seconds after she finished relaying the facts.

Blinking back unwanted tears, she busied herself with sipping her coffee, concentrating on the taste and the way the warm liquid felt going down her throat.

While she pondered, something else occurred to her. "That's why I think your friend Rick got me out of there. My life is in danger because I saw. Whoever this Russell person is, he must be high up in the government."

"Which would explain why NCIS wants my pictures." He shook his head. "Still no internet, though the blizzard has slowed way down. As soon as I have access, I'll try to find out who Russell is."

She nodded. "I don't understand how I could get involved with someone like that. I can only assume that I didn't know."

"Of course you didn't know." He defended her without hesitation. "I hope we hear from Rick again soon. I have a feeling he can fill in a lot of the missing pieces."

Rick didn't call again the rest of the day, though the snow finally stopped. Since he hadn't left a number for Jason to call him and had used something to block his number from the phone log, they had no way of reaching him.

Tired of sitting around waiting for the phone to ring, Lucy put on her parka and gloves and went outside. The sky had cleared to that particularly bright shade of brilliant blue and the sun made the pristine white world sparkle. Across the field, she caught sight of a small herd of deer foraging for food. Delighted, she watched until they vanished into the trees.

The beauty of her surroundings made her catch her breath.

Her breath made plumes in the icy air as she contemplated leaving the porch and trying to trudge through the deep snow. The snowman they'd made during the last storm had turned to ice and wind and the second storm had made it an uneven mound of snow, barely recognizable as a snowman. She'd love to make another, but not without Jason. It wouldn't be as much fun unless she shared the carefree activity with him.

Still, she stood on the porch, gazing off into the distance, until the chill seeped up through the soles of her boots and into her bones. Only then did she turn and go inside.

Jason watched as Lucy grew increasingly restless. He knew an outing would help disperse some of her nervous energy, but he didn't want to take a chance of missing Rick's call. When she grabbed her parka off the coatrack and stamped out onto the front porch, he stayed put, continuing his perusal of what seemed like endless photographs.

He'd always loved his job. Getting the perfect shot took a lot of work and some luck. A lot depended on the lighting and the angle and the subject. In the horrible aftermath of the bombing in Kabul, he'd gone on autopilot, trusting his instincts and knowing that out of a hundred shots, one of two of them might be "the one."

He'd never imagined he'd find himself in the middle of some sort of conflict made worse by the fact that he still had no idea what was going on. For all he knew, he might be sitting on the story of the decade.

The thought gave him pause. Once a journalist, always a journalist. Though he might usually only report with photos, he'd done a few written and oral pieces in his time. With the photo book due soon, a story of this magnitude might be a gift from the gods.

Except for Lucy. Until he knew more about the truth of her involvement in all of this, he'd have to be careful. Right now, the only thing he knew for certain was that he'd protect Lucy no matter what. Even if it cost him the story.

Despite being watched intently, the phone didn't ring. When it finally did, late in the afternoon, Jason leaped for it.

"Hello?"

"Jason, this is Sheriff Jeffords."

Squashing a ton of disappointment, Jason greeted the other man. "What's up?"

"I just wanted to give you a heads-up that our secondary plow is broken down. It's going to take longer than usual to make it up your way. Do you have enough provisions to last a couple more days?"

"Yes, I do. How long are you estimating?" Not that Jason really cared. He didn't have a pressing need to go down into town.

"I'm not sure. At least three or four. We're working on getting it fixed, but right now the other one is all we have. Nothing's going to be able to make it up your way for a while, except for a snowmobile."

The subtle warning wasn't lost on Jason.

"I'll keep an eye out," he said. "Thanks for letting me know."

The phone rang again an hour later. This time, Jason refused to get his hopes up when he answered it. And of course, it was Rick.

"Where are you?" Jason asked as soon as he heard his friend's voice.

"Someplace safe," Rick replied. "Trust me, the less you know, the better."

Unable to find fault with that logic, Jason sighed. "Can you at least tell me why you're in hiding? I admit, I'm a little lost in all this. NCIS has subpoenaed me, wanting to look at my photos, though they're claiming you're the entire reason."

"That's a bunch of bull."

"Is it? Then why'd you go AWOL?"

Rick made a sound of disbelief. "To stay alive. Didn't Abby tell you?"

"She still hasn't regained her memory. Tell me what?"

"There was a huge scandal with the vice president's son. Since the VP is planning to run for president, they're taking out anyone who knows about it. That's why I had to get Abby out and why I'm staying hidden."

"The VP's son." Jason asked, "Is his name Russell? Sorry, but we still don't have internet so I haven't been able to check."

"Yes. You never were much for keeping up with the news," Rick chided. "Abby is—was—engaged to him. Apparently, she saw something she wasn't supposed to see."

"She did. She just remembered what."

"Did it involve local women being held prisoner and tortured and raped?" Rick's matter-of-fact tone seemed at odds with the awfulness of his statement.

Jason glanced at Lucy/Abby before responding.

"Yes. She just remembered. She also remembered being beaten."

"To within an inch of her life. Russell used the bombing to cover for how badly he hurt her. I think he intended to kill her and would have, if a couple of the search-and-rescue guys hadn't heard her crying out."

Jason's jaw had begun to ache from his clenching it. "How did you get involved?" he asked.

"I was there when they brought her out. Russell and his security detail were trying to interfere, to keep her from being taken to a hospital. I'd heard rumors from a few of the locals about Russell's, er, sadistic tendencies, and I put two and two together. One of Russell's men waited for me and told me if I didn't hide her, she would end up dead. He must have had an attack of conscience, though I imagine it would have cost him his life if Russell found out."

Though a slow burn of fury had begun in his chest, Jason kept his tone steady. "How'd you get her out? I would have thought the US delegation would have been notified of her departure, at the very least."

"Probably. And then they would have stopped her. That's where it pays to have contacts. I put her in a military uniform and shipped her out with several other wounded service members. I hopped a ride with them too. They flew us to Ramstein Air Base. From there, I spirited her out on a charter flight another friend was piloting. No one even noticed she was missing."

"But they did notice when you didn't show up," Jason pointed out. "Do you think they realized what you'd done?"

"Probably." Rick sounded unconcerned. "But without proof, I can't do anything. They're wanting to make sure and tie up all loose ends."

"Which is why they want my photos," Jason mused. "Quite honestly, we've been going through them. So far, we haven't found anything the slightest bit incriminating."

"That's weird." Rick went silent for a moment. "Wait, do you have any with the VP in them? Or Russell?"

"Yes. Also I somehow managed to get one of Lucy, I mean Abby, as they wheeled her out on a stretcher."

"Damn. All three of those things are probably what they're wanting to erase. What are you going to do?" Rick asked.

"I'm setting up separate files," Jason answered. "They aren't aware that I have the slightest idea what they're after. They have no way of knowing if I keep certain photos and subjects out of what I turn over to them. It's not much of a plan, but it's all I've got right now."

"Just be careful," Rick advised. "They're pretty desperate. Your life might be in danger. Abby's definitely is."

Hearing the verbal confirmation of what he already knew made Jason wish he could do like Rick had—find a private plane and spirit her away. "I won't let anything happen to her," he promised, his voice as fierce as his intentions. "Believe me."

"Good." If Jason had surprised his friend, Rick hid it well. "You two must have hit it off."

"I'll let that one slide."

Rick responded to that with a bark of laughter. "I've got to go. I'll try to check in with you when I can."

"Okay. And man, stay safe."

"You too." Rick ended the call.

Replacing the phone in its cradle, Jason paused for the space of a few heartbeats before turning to face Lucy. He took a deep breath and then told her everything Rick had said.

When he finished speaking, she nodded. "That's pretty much what I figured. I need to get out of your hair."

"No. You don't." He went to her and wrapped his arms around her, unable to keep from showing her how much she meant to him. Though he ached to tell her, to say the words, he didn't want to muddle up anything until she was 100 percent herself again.

"We're in this together," he murmured instead, stroking her hair. "No matter what."

Without looking at him, she nodded. "Are you sure? Because it seems to me that your life would go a lot more smoothly if I didn't involve you in any of this."

"I'm already involved," he chuckled. "Too late."

Despite his attempt to display a light-hearted attitude, inside he churned with a sort of frustrated anger. As a journalist, he lived to take down corrupt people like the VP and his son, Russell. Right now, neither he nor Rick, or for that matter, Lucy, had actual proof, but that didn't matter. He'd figure out a way. Until then, they all had to stay safe.

They stood for a few minutes in silence, holding each other. Finally, Jason reluctantly released her. When she murmured something unintelligible and escaped to the bathroom, he didn't follow. He eyed the television, tempted to see if the satellite signal had returned, but decided to wait in case Lucy wanted to talk later.

Walking into his bedroom, Jason stopped. The subpoena sat on his dresser, the date circled in red. Jason picked it up and stared at it, as he did at least once a day, wondering what they possibly expected to learn from him once they'd taken possession of his photographs.

And then he realized he might have a problem. According to NCIS Special Agent Paul Groesel, they were concerned with locating Rick. Now that Rick had called, once Jason had been put under oath, he'd have no choice but to reveal that he'd heard from him. Which, until he knew the entire story of what had happened in Kabul, wouldn't be a good thing.

Right then and there, he decided he'd ignore the subpoena. Sure, a warrant would be issued for his arrest, but at least this would buy him—them—some much-needed time.

As he wandered back into the living room, he saw Lucy had gone into the kitchen. With her back to him, she rummaged through the pantry, clearly looking for something, though he didn't know what. He took a moment to admire her shapely figure, marveling at the circumstances that had brought her into his life. He'd never before considered himself a particularly lucky guy, but he did now. If he could just get them through this rough patch, then he could talk to her about the possibility of them having a future together.

Now that the snow had stopped falling, he knew

they could go outside and snowshoe or ski. But even though cabin fever had begun to set in, he hated to travel too far from the phone. Twice he almost suggested to Lucy that they go out on snowshoes but didn't. He wasn't sure what or who exactly he was waiting for to call, but he'd long ago learned to go with his gut instincts.

"I thought you already talked to Rick," Lucy said, catching him eying the damn phone again.

"I did. I'm not expecting him to phone again, at least not for a while."

"Then who?" she asked.

"I'm not sure," he admitted. "Maybe the sheriff, letting me know someone is in town looking for me. Or calling with news about when we can expect the plow to make it out this way."

"Or NCIS to call and hassle you one more time." She put a casual hand on his shoulder and squeezed. "How about we take a break and go outside for a little bit? We can rebuild that snowman or just head up the mountain a little way."

He had to grin. "I've been thinking that exact same thing myself." Checking his watch, he made a quick decision. "Let's do it. We can take an hour or two and get the heck out of this cabin."

She grinned back. "Great. Let me go put on some layers. And Jason, you know what they say?"

"No, what?"

"A watched phone never rings." She grabbed her duffel bag and escaped to the bathroom, giggling.

Chapter 13

Getting dressed in the small bathroom in front of the mirror, Lucy found herself thinking back on that day in Kabul. The small bit of memory she'd dreamed had expanded, and she now remembered many more details, including the emotions she'd experienced.

She'd realized she could no longer be with Russell. Not only did she not love him, but she'd come to realize he was a cruel, emotionless man. He treated her as if she was his possession, nothing more. Trying to conform to the mold he'd made for her had changed her, and not for the better. The vibrant, cheerful woman she'd been had slowly faded away, until she felt like a mere shell of herself.

She'd actually followed Russell that last day, hoping she'd find him in a quiet, peaceful place so she could tell him she wanted out. Though they'd traveled to Afghanistan via military aircraft, she was hoping Russell would let her take another, earlier flight.

In a million years, she'd never expected what had happened after that. None of it.

Pushing the awful memories from her mind, she finished layering her clothes and emerged to find Jason already suited up and waiting for her. She snagged her parka, put on her hat and gloves, and grabbed the snowshoes she'd used before.

Outside, the icy purity of the air made taking a breath feel like a rebirth of sorts. She found herself grinning at Jason, so relieved to be out of the cabin she didn't bother to hide it.

"You must be an outdoorsy type," Jason commented, grinning back.

Blinking, she gave a slow nod. "I am." And just like that, she knew. Everything. All of her life, her childhood, her teenage years, where she'd gone to college and what kind of work she did. She remembered the gut-wrenching loss of her parents, gone twelve years now, how she and Russell had met. She hadn't wanted to date him—something about him had made her uneasy—but he'd refused to give up and had finally worn her down. He'd tried to keep secret the fact that the vice president of the United States was his father, but she'd learned it on the news and confronted him.

That had been their first major fight. She'd broken up with him, unable to abide with a man who'd lied to her. He'd been contrite, sent dozens and dozens of flowers, shown up at her job so often she'd gotten a warning, and somehow she hadn't processed the reality that his behavior had crossed over to stalking.

She'd even gotten back together with him. The knowledge made her wince.

"Lucy—I mean, Abby Lou? Are you all right?"

Jason's voice, which seemed as if it was coming from a great distance. Focusing on the here and now, she slowly nodded. "I'm…yes. I'm fine."

She needed to process everything before she told him what had happened. She wasn't ready for a barrage of questions, not yet, not until she sat down and took stock of what had happened in the past. Only once she'd done this would she be able to make a decision as to where she needed to go in the future.

One thing she did know now. A man like Russell would never let her go. If he wanted her dead, he'd stop at nothing until she'd been killed.

More than anything, she felt grateful to Jason's friend Rick. She wouldn't be alive right now if he hadn't gotten her out of Kabul. Russell would have made it look as if she'd perished in the bombing.

Which explained why Rick had gone into hiding. He knew the truth and Russell was aware of that, which meant Rick was another loose end that needed to be tied up.

"Are you sure?" Jason asked, taking her arm. "You seem a million miles away."

"I had another memory," she told him, keeping her tone light and upbeat. "I'll tell you about it once we're back in the cabin. For now, let's enjoy this day and our hike."

Though his gaze searched hers, he finally nodded. "Let's do it."

They'd made it halfway up the mountain when they heard the sound of a snowmobile. Due to the way sound echoed off the peaks, it was difficult to pinpoint the location.

Jason turned a full circle, listening intently. "I can't tell where it is, but either way, it's too damn close."

"Should we head back to the cabin?" she asked, as a chill that had nothing to do with the snow snaked up her spine.

"No. I brought my pistol this time." The grim set of his jaw told her he meant business. "I've about had it with this guy, whoever he is. Let's get back to that group of trees where we can see the cabin. As long as we stay hidden, we should be able to take him by surprise."

Moving as fast as they could in snowshoes, they headed toward the trees. Though Lucy's legs ached and burned, she managed to keep up.

Meanwhile, the snowmobile engine continued to roar. They'd barely made it inside the sheltering group of trees when it cut off.

"Just as I thought," Jason muttered. "He's killing the motor so we won't hear him as he approaches the cabin. If we were inside, we most likely wouldn't have been able to hear him at all."

Heart pounding, she nodded. "Just so you know, this person is most likely after me."

"Explain," he demanded.

"Not now." She kept her gaze trained on the cabin.

"Yes, now." The hardness to his voice was new. "Give me enough information to help me help us."

Turning, she finally looked at him. "Russell wants me dead. That's why Rick got me out of the country."

"We already know this. What's new?"

"I mean, Russell won't stop searching for me until he can view my cold, dead body. Rick too. He'll want to clean up all loose ends. Anyone who knows what he did will have a target painted on their back."

Jason nodded. "Agreed. But even so, Russell has no idea you're here. How would he even find you?"

Since he had a valid point, she didn't have a fact-based response. "I don't know," she said. "It's a gut feeling I have."

Instead of immediately discounting that, Jason nodded. "Okay. I've learned to trust gut instincts. Let's see what happens and we'll go from there."

They waited, the absolute silence both beautiful and nerve-racking.

"There." Jason pointed. "About three hundred or so yards from the house. Headed toward where we built that snowman. He's wearing all white, so he blends in with the snow."

Squinting, she struggled to locate the man. "I don't see him."

"Watch for movement. The only thing visible is his sunglasses. They're even white, though the lenses are black."

Finally, she saw him. Wearing snowshoes, the stranger moved with purpose toward the cabin.

"I can safely bet he's not going to knock on the front door," Jason declared darkly. "And since it's probably the same guy who tried to set the cabin on fire, I imagine he's going to try something else."

She watched with bated breath as the man approached the cabin. He went directly to the front porch, stepping up and removing his snowshoes before knocking on the door.

Jason pulled out his pistol. "No matter what happens," he ordered. "You stay here. Understand?"

Slowly, she nodded.

"Promise me."

Though she had a feeling she'd regret it, she promised.

When no one answered the door, the man stepped back. For one second, Lucy thought he'd turn around and leave, but he didn't. Instead, he went back, knocked again and waited. Then he tried the door handle.

"I locked it," Jason murmured. "Though it's fairly easy to pick a lock like that. The dead bolt will be only a little more difficult. I'm thinking next time I go into town, I'll buy a second dead bolt."

Sure enough, the man got something out of his pocket and worked on the lock. It didn't take him long at all before he'd picked it. He then went to work on the dead bolt. A few minutes later, he'd succeeded.

Jason cursed as the man pulled out a pistol and opened the door. Looking left and then right, he slipped into the cabin and closed the door behind him.

"Wait here." Jason took off for the cabin. Lucy watched, terrified as he cut across the broad expanse of snow, totally exposed in his dark blue parka. Luckily for him, the intruder must have been busy going through the cabin, because Jason made it to the side of the house unscathed and undetected.

Forcing herself to breathe, she waited to see what he'd do next. She figured he'd go crashing into the cabin, which scared the hell out of her. She wasn't sure what she'd do if Jason got shot.

Instead, he hunkered down on the porch, hugging the wall in between the door and the window. Then he whistled, not a warning sound, rather the noise made by a man without a care in the world. Lucy thought he somehow managed to make it sound as if it were farther away.

Jason's plan worked. The intruder busted through the front door, moving fast. Jason jumped him the instant he appeared on the porch.

A shot rang out, the sharp report echoing into the distance. Lucy's blood ran cold. She squinted, eying the two men rolling around in the snow on the porch, looking for blood.

Only her promise to Jason kept her from going closer. Heart pounding, she stayed in the shadows of the trees, hoping she'd soon see a sign that Jason had gotten the upper hand.

Finally, Jason stood while the intruder remained motionless at his feet. He squinted up in Lucy's direction, but gave no signal that it was safe for her to come down. Instead, he disappeared inside the house and then returned with a length of rope. He tied up the stranger's hands and feet before lifting him under the arms and dragging him inside.

When he'd finished, Jason came outside and motioned to her to join him.

She hurried down the slope as fast as she could in snowshoes, using her poles to keep from losing her balance. As soon as she reached the front porch, she undid the latches and stepped out of her gear.

Rushing inside, she went straight to Jason. "Were you shot?"

"It's nothing," he replied, despite the wet circle of blood on his jeans. "Flesh wound, nothing more."

"How do you know?" she demanded. "You haven't had time to check it. Let me see it." As if she knew anything at all about gunshot wounds. Still, damned if she was going to let him bleed to death if she could do something to help.

"It's fine."

Aware how stubborn men could be, she couldn't take his word for it. "Let me see."

The intruder snickered. "Yeah, let's make sure I didn't nick an artery or something."

"Shut up," both Lucy and Jason said at the same time.

"Is he secure?" Lucy asked. When Jason nodded, she gestured toward the bathroom. "Please let me take a look at your leg."

Shaking his head, Jason did as she asked. Once in the well-lit bathroom, he undid his belt and gingerly attempted to lower his jeans. But when he reached his wound, the bloody material stuck to his skin, making him wince.

"Let me," she said, gently moving his hands away. Grasping the material, she concentrated on working it away from the wound. Jason sucked in his breath, but didn't say a word as she finally separated his blood-stained jeans from his wound.

Once she did, she helped him step out of his jeans and then grabbed a washcloth. Wetting it down and wringing it out, she began to gently clean the blood from his leg. Now that she was closer and could see it better, she realized Jason was right. The bullet had grazed the outside of his thigh, cutting him, but even that didn't appear to be too deep.

"Told you," he said, grinning. "I think I'll survive."

She nodded, continuing washing the blood off. "Where do you keep your disinfectant, antibiotic ointment and bandages?"

"Under the sink."

She retrieved everything she needed. Pouring a little hydrogen peroxide into the bottle cap, she prepared to use it to clean the wound. "This might sting a little."

"Okay." He held himself perfectly still while she got the sore cleaned up, put ointment on it and then used the largest bandage she could find to cover it up. "There you are. Good to go. You'll just need to get a clean pair of jeans. I'll soak these in cold water to see if we can get the blood out."

"Thank you." Pressing a quick kiss to her lips, he took himself off to his bedroom to change.

After she placed the bloody part of the jeans in the sink, she ran cold water and left them there to soak. Then she took a deep breath and returned to the living room, where their captive waited.

Either the intruder had been hurt worse than they'd realized and was unconscious or he'd somehow managed to fall asleep. Jason's heart skipped a beat when he saw that the other man wasn't responsive.

A moment later, Lucy joined him in the living room. "Is he okay?" she whispered. "Or did he get shot too?"

Jason admitted he wasn't sure. "He didn't complain of any pain. Plus, there's no blood."

Hearing them, the other man's eyes slowly opened. They were an unusual light blue-gray color. He glared at them, first at Jason, and then included Lucy in his stare.

"If you're going to kill me," he drawled, "hurry up and get it over with. If not, then cut me loose. I've got better things to do than sit around all trussed up like a pig going to slaughter."

"Start talking and we'll see. First up, tell me why you're after her." Jason demanded.

"Her?" the stranger asked, his expression as blank as his voice. His gaze drifted to Lucy before landing back on Jason. "I don't even know who she is. I came here for you."

Stunned, Jason managed to hide his shock. "I don't believe you."

"And I don't care." A hint of exhaustion mingled with pain had crept into the other man's tone.

"Explain why." Jason knew their captive might refuse to answer. Still, he needed some sort of logical explanation for any of this to make sense.

"I've been told you witnessed something you shouldn't have over in Kabul and that you have photographic evidence. My job is to make sure none of that ever sees the light of day." He sighed. "Clearly,

I've failed. Unless you want to untie me and let me finish the job."

Jason ignored that. "Are you working for NCIS?" he asked, letting his expression reveal his disbelief that the military agency would openly attempt something like hiring a hit man. Of course, who knew. Maybe stuff like this went on behind the scenes all the time.

"NCIS?" A short, bitter laugh accompanied a shake of his head. "The military? Not hardly. I'm a private contractor."

"In other words, an assassin," Lucy put in. "Why not just call a spade a spade?"

"A private contractor," he insisted. "I don't go around killing people for money unless I have to. Mostly what I do is retrieve information. In this case, I wasn't given a choice."

"NCIS sent me a subpoena," Jason said, just to see the other man's reaction. "Clearly they're aware of whatever the people who hired you are trying to cover up."

The intruder simply stared, his expression revealing nothing.

"Which means," Jason continued, "they'll eventually have their hands on the information you were sent to eliminate."

"Not if I destroy it first." Considering he'd been tied up, he seemed surprisingly confident. This made Jason feel slightly uneasy. Maybe there were reinforcements expected any minute. Just in case, he kept one hand on his pistol as he told Lucy to arm herself. Once she had, he continued baiting the captive.

"I'm assuming you're here to get my photography

files," Jason continued. "Do you seriously believe that I wouldn't have backed them up? Even if you killed me and then you burned this entire cabin down—that was you, wasn't it?—the information is still out there in the cloud. For all you know, I could have an automatic fail-safe that sends it out to someone if I don't check in."

"But you don't, do you? People like you are far too innocent and trusting. It would never occur to you that someone like me would come after you."

That statement brought a flash of anger. Jason took a moment to get himself back under control. "You don't know anything about me," he said, his voice tight. "I'm a photojournalist who specializes in war zones. I've spent the last eight years of my life learning up close and in person about the atrocities of which people are capable. Don't try to characterize me with that kind of BS."

The stranger blinked and then inclined his head in acknowledgment. "Look, I was just hired to do a job. I'm to take you out and then destroy everything you own. I didn't know about the woman and I don't care if you backed up whatever it is they're so worried about. I only get paid if I accomplish what I was hired to do. If I don't, they'll send someone after me too."

They. Jason pounced. "Who's *they*?"

Clearly realizing he'd already said too much, the other man kept his mouth closed. Once again, his eyes narrowed, the hostility palpable.

"You know I should kill you," Jason threatened. Behind him, he heard Lucy gasp. She didn't understand that he was bluffing. "But instead, I'm going to call the sheriff and have him come get you."

"Go ahead." Though relief flashed in his gaze, the intruder kept his tone bland.

"Won't the people who hired you come looking for you?" Lucy interjected, her eyes worried. "I mean, earlier you made it sound like you were pretty much dead if you didn't complete your job."

He shrugged. "I don't know. I've never been in this situation before."

"Maybe if you cut a deal, they'll give you protection," Lucy continued.

"You watch too much TV," the captive said, though some of the hardness in his expression had softened. Lucy had that effect on people.

Jason went to her and kissed her on the cheek before he went to the phone to make the call.

After phoning Sheriff Jeffords and letting him know he'd caught the man who'd attempted to burn down his cabin, Jason kept his pistol out while he waited for law enforcement to arrive. While he hadn't mentioned on the phone the man's declaration that he'd been hired to kill Jason and why, he would. Hopefully, bond would be set high enough that this clown wouldn't get out any time soon. Especially since he'd made it clear he'd continue to try and finish his job. Jason would inform the sheriff of that and if he needed to testify before the judge, he'd get himself into town and do that too.

Since the roads still weren't plowed, the sheriff would have to use the large snowmobile he owned personally. He'd warned Jason it might take a little bit for him to get home and retrieve it, and then he'd need to pick up one of his deputies on the way. He'd hook up the sled trailer and use that to transport the

prisoner. Jason had explained he completely understood and, since he wasn't going anywhere, he'd wait.

Her gaze flitting between their captive and Jason,
Lucy appeared nervous. Jason went to her and, without taking his weapon off the intruder, pulled her in
for a hug. She whispered in his ear that she planned to
hide in the bedroom as soon as the sheriff got there.
He kissed her cheek again, letting her know it would
be a little while and why.

She nodded. "Part of me hates that I still feel like I
need to keep myself hidden," she said.

"Then don't," he told her. "He made it perfectly
clear he's after me, not you."

"That's because the people who hired him don't
know I exist," she whispered. "Or assuming they've
guessed I'm alive somewhere, at least they don't know
that I'm with you."

"Don't worry," he said with more confidence than
he felt. "We'll get to the bottom of this. I promise. No
matter how long it takes."

The intruder must have heard Jason's last few statements. He snorted. "Good luck with that," he sneered.
"You have no idea what kind of people you're up
against. And you, lady." His gaze landed on Lucy,
sweeping over her in such a way as to infuriate Jason.
"I'm not sure what your story is, or why you're with
pretty boy here, but if you want to stay safe, I sug-
gest you get as far away from him and his trouble as
you can."

To Jason's surprise, Lucy lifted her chin and met
the other man's gaze directly. "I'm not running," she
said simply. "So before you crawl back under what-

ever rock you came out from, you should know that goodness always prevails."

This made the intruder laugh out loud. "Not always, pretty lady. Such naivety will get you killed."

"Which is why I'm here to protect her," Jason declared, mildly annoyed that he'd let the other man rile him. Even if protecting her meant that Lucy had to stay hidden for a little longer, an idea which he despised.

Why? Holding her close, he realized part of the reason he hated having to keep her hidden was that he wanted to show her off to the world. As his. He wanted to take her into town and walk into Gertie's with Lucy on his arm. He wanted to go grocery shopping with her, buy flowers at the florist for her, and let everyone in Cedar know that she and he were a couple.

A couple. It had been a long, long time since he'd cared enough about a woman to want more than a casual relationship. Lucy/Abby made him want much more than that. He could even picture himself spending the rest of his life with her, which shocked the tar out of him.

Pretty sappy, he supposed. Especially since he had no idea if she even felt the same way. But truth. In a relatively short period of time, he'd fallen for her. He couldn't even really ask how she felt until he knew her memory had returned 100 percent.

Still, he continued to hold her close to his side, with his pistol trained on the captive man who'd once again fallen into a doze.

A roar of a snowmobile engine alerted him to the sheriff's arrival. Eyes wide, Lucy took herself off to the bedroom, closing the door with a decisive click.

A second snowmobile followed the first. There were three officers in total, including the sheriff, all to take custody of the one prisoner.

Backing toward the door as soon as he heard boots hit his porch, Jason immediately holstered his pistol, aware he didn't need to add to an already-tense situation.

Once they were inside, Sheriff Jeffords took Jason's statement while his men cuffed the prisoner. His prominent jaw tightened as he listened to Jason's account, from the first sound of the snowmobile to the shot grazing Jason's thigh. Jason carefully omitted any mention of Lucy, not sure what he'd do if the intruder brought her up.

The captive sat stone-faced through all of that, staring straight ahead and avoiding eye contact with anyone. He shifted his weight a little when one of the deputies cut off the crude rope tie Jason had used. The metal handcuffs were definitely a lot more secure.

A quick pat-down revealed a switchblade knife, which was bagged for evidence. "No wallet or ID," the deputy announced.

"His weapon is over there." Jason pointed to where he'd kicked the other pistol.

Using gloves and a plastic baggie, another deputy retrieved the gun.

"We'll have to hold him until the judge gets back in town," Sheriff Jeffords drawled.

"That's good," Jason replied. "Especially since he told me once he got out, he'd come back and finish the job."

"Damn." The sheriff gave the other man a squint-eyed look that had made many a man quake in his boots. This guy didn't even react.

"What's your name, son?" Sheriff Jeffords asked.

Instead of answering, the stranger continued to stare straight ahead, which made the sheriff sigh.

"You know we're going to fingerprint you once we're back at the station."

Still no reaction.

"Let's get him loaded up, boys." Zipping up his jacket, Sheriff Jeffords turned to Jason. "I'll keep you posted."

"Please do."

With two men flanking him, one on each side, the intruder managed to struggle up to his feet. Judging by the way he leaned slightly to one side, Jason realized he'd been hurt.

He pointed this out to the sheriff.

"Hang on to him," the sheriff told his men. He pulled up the intruder's shirt. A huge purplish bruise decorated the prisoner's right abdomen. "He'll live," Jeffords declared. "We'll have one of the EMTs take a look at that when we're back in town." He gestured toward the door and the deputies began to move the three of them forward.

Right when they reached the doorway, the prisoner dug in his heels. He glanced back at Jason over his shoulder, one side of his mouth lifted in a smirk.

"What about the woman?" he asked, deliberately looking toward the closed bedroom door. "Are you all going to protect her too?"

And then the deputies prodded him outside. Jason followed, refusing, at least yet, to acknowledge the bombshell the intruder had let drop. Part of him hoped against hope that the sheriff wouldn't comment on it, but he knew better.

Watching as they loaded the man onto a sled-like trailer and then secured his ankles, Jason stiffened when the sheriff came and joined him on the front porch. Side by side, they stood eying the others.

As his men and the prisoner drove away, Sheriff Jeffords turned to Jason. "You know how people in town talk. Should I ask?"

Chapter 14

When the door handle turned and the bedroom door opened, Lucy took a step back. She almost took a flying leap into the closet, mainly because she hadn't heard the second snowmobile start up. Which meant the sheriff or one of his men was still there.

When Jason appeared in the doorway, she caught her breath in relief. "I thought…" she began.

"It's OK." He held out his hand. "I told the sheriff about you. Actually, the intruder did."

Her stomach sinking, she searched his gaze. "Do you trust him?"

"I do. Come out and help me explain to him what we know."

Nodding at this, she took his hand. "If you're sure."

"I am."

The sheriff waited in the living room. A tall lean man with a close-trimmed head of white hair and a weathered face, he took off his ski cap when he saw her. After Jason performed the introductions, calling her Lucy instead of her real name, the sheriff shook her hand. His grasp felt firm, but not overly so. She remembered she'd always put a lot of stake on a man's handshake. She'd especially hated the limp, weak ones that seemed as if the man was afraid he'd break her hand.

"You look familiar," the sheriff said. "Where have I seen you before?" He took a moment, and then snapped his fingers. "On TV. I've seen you on television. Are you a reporter?"

"No," she replied softly. "I'm not. My name is actually Abby. Abby Tomblin. Though Jason calls me Lucy, which is fine." She couldn't help but notice the way Jason's jaw tightened, and she hoped she hadn't somehow hurt him. In fact, she hadn't actually known her last name until that exact moment.

Though his brow furrowed in concentration, the sheriff finally shrugged. "Doesn't sound familiar. I guess I was mistaken."

"I guess so," Jason interjected, shooting her a quick warning look. "She's got quite a story to tell, but only if she feels comfortable doing so."

She grimaced, torn.

"It's OK." Jason put his arm around her and pulled her close. "You can trust him."

Though she nodded, she still felt conflicted. Instead of pressuring her, both men waited silently for her to reach her own decision. As she studied the grizzled face of the sheriff, the compassion and kindness she saw in his dark brown eyes helped her.

"I was in Kabul with Russell Stovall," she said simply.

"The vice president's son?" Sheriff Jeffords's white brows rose.

Beside her, Jason stiffened with surprise. Slowly, Abby nodded. "I just remembered," she told Jason. "It's really weird, but a lot of things have come back to me, piece by piece."

He nodded, keeping his arm around her. "Are you overwhelmed?" he asked, his voice gentle.

Though the tenderness in Jason's gaze made her melt, she straightened her shoulders instead and shook her head. "Maybe we all better sit down. Sheriff, if you want to hear my story, this is going to take a while."

Once they were all seated, she and Jason on the couch and the sheriff in the armchair, she started talking. Through it all, Jason stayed close, holding her hand.

When she'd finally finished, she exhaled and sat quietly, waiting. Some of what she'd said had been recently remembered and she hadn't had time to tell Jason yet, so it was news to him also.

"Wow," the sheriff finally commented. "You've been through hell and back." He directed his next question at Jason. "Why the hell were you keeping this hidden from me?"

Jason shrugged. "We were being careful. And since Lucy, I mean Abby, didn't have her memory back, we thought it best to keep to ourselves."

"Well, I'm glad you filled me in," Jeffords said.

"First thing, I'm going to get in touch with NCIS. I've written down the name of the special agent who's been contacting you. Mind letting me take a picture of that subpoena?"

"Not at all." Pushing to his feet, Jason went into his room to retrieve it. When he returned, he smoothed the document out on the coffee table so the sheriff could take several snapshots with his phone.

Abby watched quietly, wondering if Jason would tell the sheriff the rest of the story involving his friend Rick. She had only mentioned Rick in passing, as the man who'd spirited her out of Afghanistan and to Colorado and safety.

But he didn't bring him up. Instead, he cautioned Jeffords not to mention Abby in any talks with NCIS or anyone else. Jeffords agreed, as long as he wasn't under oath.

Finally, the sheriff left. Once his snowmobile had roared away, Jason went into the kitchen and made them both hot chocolate.

"I didn't bring up Rick because I can't have Jeffords mentioning him to Special Agent Groesel," he finally said, handing her a mug before heading toward the couch.

"How'd you know I was wondering that?" she asked, following and taking a seat beside him. "And thanks for the whipped cream on top."

Her question made him laugh. "It's written all over your face. You couldn't decide whether or not to feel betrayed because you'd told Jeffords everything about you. Believe me, if Rick's life wasn't in danger, I wouldn't hesitate. I trust our sheriff."

She squirmed, her hip bumping his. "I mentioned his name, at least his first one when I told my story. I hope I didn't put him in any danger."

"No. Since I made sure that Jeffords understands not to mention you at all when he talks to NCIS, he has no reason to mention the name Rick. He's a smart man."

"I'll have to take your word for it," she said wryly, taking a sip of her cocoa. "The more my memory returns, the weirder my past seems."

His expression went serious. Drinking deeply from his own mug, he watched her. "Tell me about you," he asked.

She frowned at him. "I'm not sure what you mean."

"I'm guessing you've remembered almost everything, right?" At her nod, he continued, "Then tell me, before all this crazy stuff happened in Kabul, what did you do? I mean, you had a job, right? Hobbies, friends? Where did you live, and was it an apartment or a house, or maybe a modern condo?"

"Oh." She blinked. "Nothing glamorous, I'm afraid. I live in DC and work for a luxury car dealership as a salesperson. I'm really good at it." She let a hint of pride creep into her voice. "Though honestly, those vehicles tend to sell themselves. That's where I met Russell. He came in to buy a new Maserati coupe. He ended up buying the one on the showroom floor. Paid full price, I guess to impress me."

"Did it work?"

"No. I enjoy my job, but I'd prefer someone at least try to negotiate."

"How long were you two together?"

She had to think about that for a moment. "Not long. Six or seven months. When his father decided to do a PR visit to the troops in Kabul and Russell invited me along, I almost didn't go. I mean, who goes to the middle of a war zone?" She swallowed, remembering as a journalist, Jason did exactly that.

"What convinced you?"

"In retrospect, lies. Russell convinced me I'd be part of something good, beneficial to the military personnel stationed there." Her mouth twisted. "In reality, the entire thing was planned as a quick photo op for the VP's presidential campaign. We were supposed to be in and out, with just one evening as an overnight stay."

"But then the bomb happened?" Jason supplied. "And Russell got caught abusing local women."

"Right. Except in the reverse order. I don't know how he found them, or how much he paid the man who brought them to that room for him. I do think they might have been expecting just sex, or something different." Her unease had her gulping her cocoa. "I could tell they weren't expecting the violence."

She waited for him to ask another question about that night. The truth was, after finding Russell with the local women, he'd taken out his rage on her. She remembered the first part of the beating, but nothing after.

"In DC, what did you do for fun?" Jason asked instead. "I mean, surely you must have had some hobbies or something. Things you enjoyed doing in your spare time."

"I volunteered for the local animal shelter. I went up there once a week and walked the dogs." She said this in a quiet voice, remembering how Russell had disparaged one of her favorite things. "I also like to read. And work out. I lift weights several times a week."

"And take self-defense classes," he reminded her with a smile.

"Yes. Though none of that helped me defend myself against Russell's attack. He caught me by surprise."

Jason nodded. "I can well imagine. No one expects their boyfriend to start whaling on them. Especially if he's never done it before."

She took a moment to consider his words. "You're right," she finally admitted. "He'd never so much as raised a hand to me. I always thought his eyes were a bit cold, but…"

"What else?" he asked, his expression eager. "What kind of music do you like? What's your favorite food?"

"Why so many questions? I don't even know enough about you to know how you would answer those questions."

"Fair enough." Setting his empty mug down, he leaned back, arms behind his head. "I also like to read. My favorite music is classic rock, though I like anything with good lyrics and a decent beat. My favorite food is seafood, specifically Dungeness crab. Your turn."

She eyed him, so self-assured and masculine, and briefly considered simply climbing on top of him and kissing him until he forgot about all of his questions. But they had the entire night for that, so she decided to go ahead and answer.

"I like country music," she admitted, bracing herself to hear the same sounds of derision Russell had made. Instead, Jason nodded encouragingly, motioning her to continue. "And my favorite food would have to be Mexican cuisine."

"Aah. That's my second favorite." Grinning now, he tilted his head and considered her. "You say you lift weights. I run."

"You run?" She hated running. While she might do a little jogging on a treadmill, and only when she needed to add cardio to her workout, that was it.

"Yep. What about you?"

"If you ever see me running, it'll mean someone is chasing me," she replied wryly. "I'm not a fan."

Hands still behind his head, he stretched, reminding her of a big cat. "If you ever run with me, you might learn to like it."

"Doubtful." She smiled at him to ease the sting. "Why do you want to know all of this anyway?"

He didn't immediately answer. Instead, he lowered his arms to his sides and sat up straight, his expression serious. "Abby Lou, have you had time to consider the future at all?"

The future. "You mean after all this insanity is over and I can return to my regular life?" In DC. Without him. The thought made her feel empty inside.

Was that a flicker of sadness in his eyes? She couldn't be sure.

"What about you?" she asked, answering his question with one of her own. "Are you going back into the thick of things?"

"I've been thinking long and hard about that," he answered. "And I'm considering retiring. I want to get this book of photographs published, and then maybe follow it up with one that's much more lighthearted. You know, landscapes and animals and an interesting cloud formation in a dawning sky. I've seen too much ugliness in the past few years. I need to do something to help remove the stain from my soul."

He had a knack for words. "I like that," she said softly. "Will you live here?" As she spoke, she realized that it pained her to think of him living alone in this cabin.

"I'm not sure." He shrugged, still holding her gaze. "Probably. At least for now."

Nodding, she had to look down, to keep him from seeing the need in her eyes. She remembered how, even after she'd met Russell, she felt as if she'd never find the kind of love she could build a life around. Now she knew she had. She just wasn't absolutely positive Jason felt the same way.

When all this crazy covert government stuff was over, she hoped she'd find out.

For one heart-stopping moment, Jason had been certain Abby was about to discuss the possibility of a future together. He'd replied cautiously to her questions about his plan, leaving a wide-open chance for her to say she'd like to be a part of it.

But she hadn't. Though pain knifed through his heart, he'd kept a bland expression on his face. He couldn't really blame her. Not only had she just regained her memory after her former boyfriend had beaten her to within an inch of her life, but she'd learned a high-ranking member of the US government had put out a hit on them.

Asking her about her feelings for him or even hinting at any kind of commitment seemed like it would be a bit much for her to handle just now. On top of that, he wasn't sure he was good enough for her. He might be respected in his field and, false modesty aside, talented with a camera, but deep inside he knew he wasn't the kind of man she deserved.

He'd spent his life as a nomad, roaming the world. He'd never, not once, felt the urge to settle down. And while he kept his family's old cabin as a home base, he'd never stayed here for longer than a month at a time. Most times not even that. This time, he'd deliberately planned for a ninety day stay, figuring he might get itchy feet before that.

Yet the notion of retiring had been something he'd been considering for a good while, even before he'd met her. Seeing nothing but death and brutality did something to a man, twisting up his insides and making him wake in the night with cold sweats.

He'd had enough.

And though he'd spent a lot of time trying to figure out what he wanted to do next, now he knew. The future stretched out bright and shiny before him. As long as Abby was in it, that is.

They had a quick lunch, vegetable soup and crackers, and then he started cleaning up the kitchen. After refusing her offer to help, he set Abby to work cleaning the bathroom. Might as well get the place all tidy.

A few hours later, long enough for their intruder to have been fingerprinted and booked, Sheriff Jeffords called with a name. "Stephen Colter. Though he has several aliases. This guy has a rap sheet ten pages long.

A lot of assault with a deadly weapon, a few breaking and entering, theft, along with several drug possession charges. Not a nice guy."

"But no murder charges," Jason pointed out. "I can't help but be grateful for that."

"True," the sheriff allowed. "Of course, that could also mean he just hasn't been caught yet."

He had a point.

"If you somehow manage to find out who hired him, let me know."

"Will do." They chatted for another couple of minutes about inconsequential things like the upcoming holidays and how the sheriff's department had finally gotten the decorations up on Main Street before the sheriff ended the call.

When Jason relayed this information to Abby, she shook her head. "I was hoping they'd find out who hired him."

"Not yet. Maybe they will," he replied, though he doubted it. "But for now, we need to be extra vigilant. His bosses might decide to send someone else."

Expression troubled, she nodded. "Do you think we ought to load up your Jeep and head somewhere else? I'm not feeling too safe here in the cabin."

She had a point. "Not yet," he said. "Right now, with the hit man in custody, they won't have time to get someone else out here right away. I hate to be forced out of my own home without a fight."

Despite his brave words to Abby, as the day went on, Jason couldn't shake the feeling that something else was about to happen. He'd long ago learned not to ignore these gut instincts so, as bedtime approached, he found himself restless and unwilling to allow himself to relax.

Rick called again finally. He sounded much more upbeat than he had the last time. "How's everything going?" he asked.

Jason told him about the hit man and everything else.

"Damn." Rick cursed. "Both of us would be dead if we'd hung around Kabul. Right now, I'm working on gathering up enough evidence to save my own ass," he joked. "When they realized finding me wasn't going to be as easy as they thought, they concocted a hellacious story about me and my motives. They're trying to make me out to be some kind of traitor to my own country."

"That's ridiculous. No one who knows you would believe that," Jason protested.

"I know. But that way, they're covering all the bases. If they locate me, they can shoot me dead on sight with no questions asked. Easy cleanup."

Suddenly, the unspoken truth hit Jason like a punch in the gut. "You saw too, didn't you? Abby wasn't the only one." He took a deep breath. "Rick, do you have video?" The urgency in his voice caught Abby's attention. Though she'd been puttering around in the kitchen, she immediately dropped whatever she'd been doing and joined him.

The silence on the other end of the line stretched out so long that Jason wondered if he'd lost the connection. "Rick?"

"Yeah. I'm still here. And you're correct. I didn't want to involve you, because the less you know, the better off you are, especially if you have to testify under oath." Rick's grim tone left no doubt he'd thought all this through.

"You have a point."

"Yeah. But I have a reason for my call. I'm putting together a press release, to be emailed simultaneously to various news outlets worldwide. I've got the text typed up, and the video."

"But why?" Jason asked. "That's what I don't understand."

"Russell Stovall is the vice president's son. Once word of this gets out, and everyone knows the VP tried to cover it up, any chance he might have had at winning the presidency is gone."

The magnitude of what his friend had just revealed stunned Jason. "That never occurred to me. But then, I tend to avoid politics."

"Yeah, good for you." Rick sounded stressed. "Anyway, I'm wondering if you could shoot me a few of the more graphic photos you must have."

Stunned, Jason gripped the phone. "That's just it, Rick. I have tons of shots I took during the bombing, even one of Abby being brought out on a stretcher. But I wasn't there when whatever went down with Russell Stovall. Abby was, and she didn't take any photos."

A thought occurred to him. "You've never explained how you were involved in this. You were supposed to meet up with me at the hotel, yet I never saw you. I figured once the bomb went off, you stayed away. But you didn't. You were there, weren't you?"

Silence again. When Rick next spoke, his voice had gone rough. "Yes, I was there. I was assigned as a bodyguard for the vice president. He asked me to watch his son. When he sneaked out, I followed him. I heard the first woman scream, so I rushed in. Abby came in after. The pimp, or whatever he was, pulled out his phone and recorded everything. I paid him $500 for that phone."

Rick took a deep breath. "It was pretty bad, bro. If Russell had been one of the soldiers or, hell, even a civilian, he would have been arrested. But since his father has both power and money…" His voice trailed off. "When I tried to jump him after he first punched Abby, two of his own men held me back. I fought like the devil, but Russell nearly killed her, Jason. I couldn't leave her there like that. I tried to get her taken to the emergency field triage that was set up after the bombing, but I knew Russell would come back and finish the job."

"So you arranged to get her to US soil. How? I know how much red tape is involved in something like that."

"I have my contacts," Rick replied. "You know how it is."

Jason had to admit that he did. When you'd been around as long as he and Rick had, there was always a back door somewhere.

"As for the rest," Rick continued, "ask Abby. It sounds like her memory has come back. Apparently, Russell Stovall believes she died there in Kabul. He has no idea she's still alive."

"Seriously?" Jason swore. "I hope he doesn't find out."

"Don't worry. By the time he does, I'll have started

the wheels in motion to take him down. Oh, speaking of which. If you have a shot of her after he beat the living hell out of her, email it to me." He rattled off an email address, one he'd clearly set up as an extra.

Jason jotted it down, promised to send what he had and Rick said he had to go. He said he'd be in touch, especially once his media bomb went public. Jason sure hoped the satellite was working that day. He could only imagine the media frenzy.

"That was Rick," he told Abby, placing the phone in the cradle. "He finally got around to telling me how he got involved with the whole Russell thing."

She nodded. "I think I remember. Wasn't he one of the guys assigned to Russell's security detail?"

"Bingo. What else do you remember about Rick?" Jason asked. "You're sort of right about his duty assignment. Though he said he was assigned as a bodyguard to the vice president, but ended up watching over Russell instead."

"That's right. Russell wasn't too happy about having people following him around. At the time, I couldn't understand why. We were all warned about the dangers. It wasn't like we could go wandering around on our own."

"Though Russell did," he pointed out. "And you followed him. Lucky for you, Rick was right behind him."

"True. But honestly, I don't remember anything that happened after Russell started beating me. Even thinking about it makes me feel sick to my stomach."

Though she made a face, probably to downplay her words, her unease showed in her jerky movements and the way she kept shifting her weight from one foot to the other.

What could he do but go to her and pull her into his arms? As he gathered her close, inhaling the light feminine scent of her, he thought Russell Stovall was damn lucky he wasn't anywhere near right now. The thought of what that excuse for a human being had done to Abby turned Jason's vision red with fury.

And the fact that Vice President Stovall wanted to cover it up made Jason even angrier. Like Rick, he knew he'd do whatever it took to bring the VP down.

They stood without moving, clinging to each other, lost in their own thoughts. Jason thought of all the injustice he'd seen in his time as a photojournalist, most of which he'd managed to photographically chronicle. While all of it had hit him hard, none of it had been as personal as this.

"Make love to me," she murmured, her mouth against his throat. "Please. I need to lose myself in your body."

Instantly aroused, he let her take the lead. She kissed him as if she wanted to eat him up, climbed up on his lap and shed her own clothes before practically ripping his off. Once they were both naked, she rode him hard and with a single-minded purpose. He tried to slow her down, to make it last longer, but she took him rapidly over the edge and joined him there.

Later, after cleaning each other up, they'd put their clothes back on and headed into the living room. He made a quick detour to his laptop and sent a quick email with the photo attached. Rick had given him. Instantly, he received a response thanking him. Rick also told him to watch the evening news and to expect a call from the FBI.

Anticipation high, Jason joined Abby on the couch and turned on the television. The evening news would be starting in just a few minutes. As Abby snuggled into his side, pulling a blanket over them for warmth, he filled her in on what Rick's email had said.

"Do you think he's already gone public with the info?" she asked, her voice breathless.

"It sure sounds like it."

"Talk about breaking news."

Sure enough, as soon as the music began to play announcing the news was about to start, a red and white banner appeared on the screen. *Breaking News*. The anchor, expression properly serious, began to talk. "A video has been released that appears to show the vice president's son abusing and torturing women. Warning, the video is extremely graphic and violent."

Abby gripped Jason's hand as it began to play. The women's faces had been blurred out, as had some of their naked body parts. Russell wielded a thick deadly-looking whip and used it with apparent delight on three women who were not only naked and kneeling, but possibly underage.

One of them screamed. There was a blur as a large man—Rick—rushed into the room. Then Abby, bewilderment turning to shock as she took in the scene before her. When Russell turned the whip on her, the video cut off.

"They didn't show all of it," Abby protested, her voice shaky. She had a death grip on his hand and he could feel her trembling. "I wanted to see what happened after he started punching me."

His gut twisted, though for her sake, he forced himself to appear calm. "I'm sure the FBI has seen the rest of it." He held close until her shaking slowed. "I'm sorry. I know this must be traumatic for you."

Attention once again riveted on the television, she didn't immediately respond.

The vice president appeared on camera. He denied everything, despite the fact that the video evidence clearly showed his son. "There must be some rational explanation," he declared.

"He's looking at the end of any hope he had for becoming president," Jason mused.

"I just want Russell to face charges," she said, her jaw set. "He can't be allowed to get away with what he'd done."

For the first time, Jason realized she might yet have to continue to be involved. "Are you willing to press charges?"

Her chin came up. "Yes. I am."

"Even if you have to go to court and be cross-examined by his attorneys, who will try to make you out to be a liar?"

Eyes flashing, she lifted her shirt. "I have scars to prove what happened. We have the video and your photos. I will do whatever it takes to make sure Russell Stovall pays."

Chapter 15

Now that she had herself back again, there were two things of which Abby Tomblin was certain. One, she'd do whatever it took to take Russell Stovall down, no matter how difficult. And two, she wanted to spend the rest of her life with Jason Sheffield. Hopefully, he felt the same way.

First things first. Clearly, now that the video had been leaked, Jason should be safe. As long as no one realized she hadn't actually died in Kabul. She'd been there, as had Rick Engles, and with both of their personal testimony there was no way Russell would get away with this. Since he'd demonstrated clear proclivities toward abusing and torturing women, she wondered if it would occur to the police to check a list of unsolved rapes in the DC area. If they didn't investigate, she planned to make sure they did.

One thing she'd learned working at the top luxury car dealership in the metro area was how to present herself to the public. She'd do well in court, and even on television if it came to that. Plus, she had truth on her side.

"I'm really in the mood to get outside now," Abby declared. "How about you?"

Jason looked up, his expression slightly distracted. He'd once again grabbed his laptop and appeared to be frantically going through files. "Maybe in a minute," he said.

"What are you doing?" Curious, she went closer.

"Looking to see if I can locate Rick in any of the photos I took. I mean, clearly he must have been wearing a disguise. But any physical proof of his presence can only help prove our case."

"That makes sense." Leaning over his shoulder, she watched as he perused photograph after photograph. "Did you double-check the one of me on the stretcher? I have a feeling he never left my side."

He nodded. "That's the first one I checked. There is one guy whose back is to the camera. That might have been him, but I can't prove it."

"Let me see."

Instantly, he located the file and clicked to open it. Once he had it up, he enlarged it until the image filled the computer screen. "Here you go."

Taking a moment, she studied the photo. The first time she'd seen it, she'd been in too much shock to really take it in. The woman on the stretcher—her—

looked awful. Huge purpling bruises on her grotesquely swollen face. And blood. So much blood. She could definitely understand why anyone viewing this would believe she'd been gravely injured in the explosion.

Instead, a man she'd once trusted had done this.

For the first time, she allowed anger to well up inside her. Anger? Hell, more like fury.

Something must have shown in her face. Jason leaned in and kissed her softly on the cheek. "He'll pay," he said.

"I know." She'd never been more certain of anything. "I plan to make sure of that."

The old-fashioned phone rang, startling her.

"I don't recognize this number," Jason said. With a grimace, he went ahead and answered. A moment later, he held the phone out to Abby. "It's for you."

Surprised and more than a little leery, she crossed the room and took it. "Hello?"

After verifying she was actually Abigail Tomblin, the caller identified himself as Derek Leahy with the Federal Bureau of Investigation. He launched right into the fact that the FBI had received evidence from Rick Engles and that they were in ongoing conversation with him. Rick had mentioned a woman witness by the name of Abigail Tomblin and indicated she wanted to press charges. When Derek asked if that information was correct, Abby didn't hesitate. "Yes," she answered. "I do wish to press charges."

"Where are you?" the FBI agent asked. "We'll need to send someone to take your statement."

"No." Again, Abby didn't have to think twice. "You

don't need to know that. Right now, forgive me if I don't trust anyone. Russell is the vice president's son."

"Understood," Agent Leahy replied. "Rick mentioned you'd been subpoenaed by NCIS. Is that correct?"

"I wasn't," she clarified. "Jason Sheffield was. How does this work? Are the FBI and NCIS working together? I thought they were looking for Rick, since they consider him AWOL."

Instead of answering, he asked another question. "I left word at NCIS for an agent named Paul Groesel. Tell your friend Jason to hold off from taking you to NCIS or anyone else until we get this all straightened out. Believe me when I say we take this very seriously."

"I'll try," she promised. "But again, right now I'm not inclined to trust anyone. Even though you have a lot of information, I have no way to verify whether or not you're working for the vice president and his people or whether you're a legitimate good guy."

Her words made him chuckle. "I like to think of myself as a good guy, but I completely understand. I'll be in touch again. Is this a good number, or do you have another I should use?"

"This one is fine," she replied, waiting until he'd ended the call before hanging up the phone. She relayed the entire conversation to Jason, curious to hear his take on things.

"He sounds legit," he mused. "But then again, when you're dealing with people at the vice president's level, you never know who could be in his pocket. Since this story is already out, he couldn't accomplish much by taking you out. I'd say his chances of a successful run at becoming president are over."

"If he had me killed, he'd silence a witness. I have to think he'd consider that."

"Maybe." Jason shrugged. "But he'd also have to get rid of Rick. He'd have to think of how that would look. Especially since Rick took care to provide lots of evidence. Your and Rick's testimony is really just icing on the cake."

Torn, she had to admit that what Jason said made sense. "I'd still feel better if you'd verify with Rick that this FBI agent is legit." She wrote down the name *Derek Leahy*. "For all we know, he could be another hit man like that Stephen Colter guy."

"Who is safely in police custody," Jason pointed out. "Of course, we don't know for how long."

Restless, she began to pace. "I feel like we should *do* something. Be proactive."

"I don't have a snowmobile," he said. "And since the roads aren't plowed, we have no way of going anywhere."

She stopped her pacing and gestured toward the skis. "Can't we ski into town? I mean, what is it? A couple of miles?"

"Five at least. Even if you were an experienced snow skier, it'd be risky. I'm going to have to say no."

His answer made sense, even though she didn't like it.

"Plus, even if we were able to make it into Cedar, what would we do there? Sure, we could stop at the sheriff's department. But then what?"

Again, another valid point. She made a face. "Logic

wins," she said. "Surely, there must be something we can do."

Jason shrugged. Before he could say anything, the phone rang again.

Eying the caller ID, Jason told her that this time it was the sheriff. He put it on speaker phone so she could hear.

"What's up?" Jason asked, locking eyes with Abby. Part of her suspected she already knew the reason for the call. Clearly, Jason had the same suspicions.

"I thought I'd better warn you," the sheriff said. "Stephen Colter is out."

"I was afraid of that." Jason cursed. "What the hell happened?"

"He got an attorney. He was charged, bail was set and he paid it so he could be released. You know as well as I do that we couldn't hold him indefinitely."

"I know." Jason dragged his hand through his hair. "I'm guessing he's going to come back and try to finish the job. I need to take Abby somewhere safe."

Abby stepped forward and spoke up. "With all the breaking news, do you think whoever hired him might have called the hit off?"

"If they could get ahold of him," the sheriff answered. "But for now, it probably wouldn't hurt for the two of you to take precautions. Jason, do you want me to send an armed officer up there to help?"

"Might not be a bad idea," Jason replied. Abby nodded her agreement.

"All right. Let me see who I can get. It'll be dark in a few hours, and I don't think anything's going to happen tonight. I'll send someone in the morning."

"Sounds good." Jason ended the call. "Looks like we're on our own for tonight."

She stared longingly out the window at the blinding white snow. "Do you think we could get outside for a little bit? Even a half hour would make me feel a little better."

"Sure." He glanced at his watch. "Let's snowshoe up the ridge. We should be able to get to the top and back in less than an hour."

Suiting up, she felt as if she vibrated with nervous energy. Maybe she should have initiated lovemaking instead. Hell, if this hike helped dispel her unsettled feelings, they could also indulge in some vigorous sex.

The thought immensely cheered her. Stepping outside, she squinted in the waning sunlight. Inhaling the chilly air into her lungs steadied her. She looked up to find Jason watching her.

"Are you ready?" he asked.

She caught herself grinning. "Yes. Let's do this."

The physical activity turned out to be exactly what she needed. By the time they made their way to the top, her legs ached and she found herself pleasantly out of breath.

Standing at the top, they gazed down at the cabin. The bright blue of the afternoon sky had begun to fade with the sun's slow descent into the west.

"It'll be dark soon," Jason said. "We'd better head back down."

"I know." She didn't move. "Give me just another minute or two. This feels so good."

He kissed her then, his lips as cold as hers, though

they both warmed up fast. Kissing him back, joy bubbled up inside her and she almost told him she loved him. But he pulled back and stepped away and the moment was lost.

"Let's go." This time he led the way, not even looking to see if she followed.

The sound of a snowmobile somewhere close had them both stopping in their tracks. They were out in the open, halfway between the group of trees and the cabin. They couldn't move fast, no matter what they did. The snowshoes wouldn't allow that and if they took them off and tried to go without, they'd founder in the deep snow.

"Come on," Jason urged. They continued slogging forward as the snowmobile noise grew louder and louder.

They were still fifty feet from the front porch when the machine came roaring up where the driveway would be. Heart pounding, Abby leaped forward in a last-ditch effort to reach the safety of the front porch. Instead, she landed face down in the snow.

Jason grabbed her arm and yanked her to her feet. "We're okay," he told her, helping her brush the snow from her face and jacket. "It's Sheriff Jeffords."

Turning, she watched as the snowmobile pulled up, coming to a halt sideways with an impressive plume of snow. "Maybe he's come to get us out of here," she said.

"Who knows? It must be urgent if he took the trouble to come all the way up here so close to twilight."

"There you are," the sheriff hailed them. "I tried

calling several times and got worried when you didn't answer."

"Worried?" Jason asked. "Because of Stephen Colter?"

Abby had started to shiver so she trudged past Jason toward the cabin. "Come on. Let's get inside, where it's warm. Then you can tell us what's going on."

The two men exchanged glances but followed her lead. On the front porch, everyone stamped as much of the snow off their boots as they could. Leaving the snowshoes there, they all filed into the warmth of the cabin.

"I can't stay long," Sheriff Jeffords began. "I don't want to get caught trying to make it back to town in the dark. I got a phone call from someone named Derek Leahy with the FBI. After I spoke to him, I double-checked on the internet and he's legit. He's probably been trying to reach you as well."

"What's going on?" Jason asked.

"Well, you know that Paul Groesel fellow you've been dealing with at NCIS? Agent Leahy spoke to them and they don't have an agent by that name."

Stunned, Abby and Jason exchanged incredulous looks. "Does that mean the subpoena isn't real?"

"It's possible," the sheriff replied, pulling out his phone and squinting at the photos. "Hard to tell from the snapshots I took. Actually, since I have no idea what an NCIS subpoena would look like, I'm not the best person to answer that. Call Leahy back. And watch your back."

Looking from one to the other, he shook his head. "How about I give you both a ride into town? You can stay at my place for a few days."

Abby looked at Jason, trying to read his expression. He appeared to be deep in thought.

Finally, he nodded. "Abby, go with him. It's better if you go somewhere safe."

"What about you?" she asked, struggling between disbelief and dismay.

"I'm staying right here," he declared. "If that hit man comes back for me, I want to settle things once and for all."

Jason waited for the sheriff to say something along the lines of not taking the law into his own hands, but he didn't. Instead, he turned to Abby and asked her how long it would take her to pack.

Instead of answering, her jaw tightened. Jason's heart sank. He recognized that look.

"I'm staying with Jason," she said, her set expression defying either of them to argue.

Brows raised, Sheriff Jeffords looked from her to Jason. Finally, he shrugged. "Suit yourself. But please, the two of you be careful."

"Are you sure you can't stay too?" Abby asked, inadvertently revealing the actual depth of her worry.

"I would if I could," the sheriff answered. "But I've got a sick wife and my town responsibilities. I've got a man coming up first thing in the morning. Are you both sure you don't want to spend the night in town?"

Jason nodded. "Go on home, Sheriff. I installed security cameras outside, so we'll know if anyone approaches. We'll be fine." He hoped he spoke the truth.

After the sheriff left, Jason powered up his laptop

to double-check the cameras and make sure they were operational.

"Will they even help show anything once it gets dark?" Abby asked.

"Only as far as my outdoor lights reveal," he answered. "In other words, someone would be right up on the cabin before we know he's there."

Someone. Oddly enough, he didn't want to utter the name. As if saying *Stephen Colter* might summon him or something.

"Are we going to take turns watching the feed?" she asked next. "How else will we know if someone approaches?"

She had a point. "You watch the feed," he directed. "I'm going to suit up and sit outside in the dark with my night-vision googles." As plans went, it wasn't the best. Maybe he should have taken up Jeffords on his offer and gone down into town. No. He wasn't going to second-guess himself. Hell, for all he knew, Colter might wait a day or two before making a second try at finishing the job.

Darkness had just settled over the mountains, going from dim to utter blackness as if someone had flipped a switch.

As a precaution, he went around the cabin turning off all the lights. When he'd finished, only the glow from the woodstove remained.

"Good thinking," she said, immediately understanding.

"Thanks. Still, stay away from windows just in case." He crouched down beside her. "Why didn't you go into town, where you'd be safe?"

Her lips parted as she met his gaze. "I'm not leaving you. All of this is happening because of me. No way would I bail to keep myself safe and leave you to deal with this alone."

What could he do but kiss her? But this time, he made it quick and hard, hoping he could convey a myriad of emotions in one kiss. They couldn't afford to be distracted.

"I wish this was over with," she said, speaking out loud exactly what he'd been thinking.

"Me too," he answered. "Me too."

Outside, the sharp crack of a gunshot echoed through the mountains. Jason cursed. "Go get in the closet. Stay low to the ground and don't come out until I tell you to."

Eyes wide, she shook her head. "No. Give me a gun. Give me the one I had before."

Halfway to the gun safe, Jason turned. "This isn't the time to argue," he said, punching in the code to unlock the door.

"And I'm not arguing." At his side, she reached into the safe and retrieved the pistol and some ammo. "We're a team, Jason. Start acting like you get that."

Her courage and determination made him grin. Taking his own gun, he kissed her again before locking down the safe. "Are you ready?"

She nodded. "Let's do this. What's the plan?"

"Get suited up. We're heading outside. If we stay in here, we're sitting ducks."

Immediately, she grabbed her parka. Luckily, they still had on most of the layers they'd donned earlier.

Thirty seconds later, they were out the door and quickly strapping on their snowshoes.

"Follow me," he said. "Stay close."

"We're not going back up the mountain?" she asked, keeping her voice low.

"Not this time. There's a small cave on a rise near the edge of my property." He didn't tell her the last time he'd checked it out, a couple of foxes had made it their residence. That time, he'd left them alone. If they were there now, he'd have to chase them out.

Another gunshot, much closer this time. Jason rechecked his pistol, making sure it was ready in case he had to use it. Out of the corner of his eye, he saw Abby doing the same.

"Come on," he said. They went around the opposite side of the house from their trail up the mountain, staying close to the evergreens that bordered the edge of the yard. Abby stayed next to his side as the darkness enfolded them. Away from the cabin's outdoor lights, it became much more difficult to see.

Luckily, they made it into the trees, heading away from the cabin. They wouldn't have nearly as good a view out here; in fact, they couldn't see the cabin at all. While that wasn't ideal, he knew their route would be safer. After all, a sniper's natural instinct would send him to higher ground. But first, Jason suspected the hit man would do something to smoke them out of the cabin so he could pick them off as they emerged.

At least that plan would fail.

At the last moment, he decided not to go to the cave. He whispered the change in plans to Abby. "I want to try and keep my house in my view."

She nodded. "I get that, but what are you going to do if he sets it on fire? Unless you have a clear shot, you'll be forced to stand back and watch it burn."

"Maybe so," he admitted. "But I'm hoping to catch Colter in between the cabin and me. The element of surprise is a hell of a big advantage."

And then what? The question went unspoken, though he knew they were both wondering. He couldn't shoot the other man in the back, no matter how evil and dangerous the hit man might be. The very best he could hope for was to get that one perfect shot.

A man emerged from the woods near the trail, barely discernible in the dark except for the fact that he appeared to be carrying some sort of small flashlight and using it to light his way. Amateur.

As he drew closer to the cabin, he stopped. Hunching over, he fiddled with something in his hand. A moment later, flame flared as he succeeded in lighting something. Jason squinted, trying to see. Best he could tell, Colter appeared to have some sort of homemade Molotov cocktail.

A second later, when Colter sent it crashing through the living room window, Jason's suspicion was confirmed.

Bracing himself, stomach churning, Jason continued to watch. He fought the primal urge to rush at Colton. Not just yet. The perfect moment came a minute later. It took the fire a moment to catch. But when it did, flames quickly engulfed the small wooden cabin.

Now. While Colter stared fixated on the front door, expecting them to come running out.

Motioning at Abby to stay put, Jason crept forward.

The other man remained intent on the house, enabling Jason to get right behind him, completely undetected.

"Freeze," Jason ordered. "Drop your weapon. Don't make me shoot you."

Colter froze. But he made no move to discard his gun.

"Drop it," Jason barked. "Last chance. Make a move and you're a dead man."

Instead, Colter dropped to the ground, twisting around at the same moment, and fired. Probably because of the uncoordinated movement, he missed.

Jason shot him. Colter crumpled in the snow, finally letting go of his gun. Jason went close, kicking the gun away before turning Colter over. He'd made a clean shot, straight through the heart. The hit man was dead.

And Jason's house continued to burn. The fire engulfed the entire structure, roaring hungrily through wood, sending huge smoke clouds up into an already-inky sky. There would be no saving it, not this time. Sorrow welled up in him but was tempered with the knowledge that he could—and would—rebuild.

"Don't move." Another voice, vaguely familiar, came from behind him. "Drop your weapon."

Groesel. He finally put a name to the voice. Paul Groesel, the NCIS agent.

Jason dropped his gun. Hands in the air, he slowly turned.

"Who was that guy?" Groesel asked, his tone conversational despite the pistol he had trained on Jason.

Jason raised a brow. "A hit man someone hired to take me out. I'm surprised he wasn't working with you." He kept his gaze trained on the other man so he wouldn't look beyond him to the woods. Right now, Abby was his last hope.

Groesel laughed. He appeared to be around five foot four, with dark hair and a slight stature. He looked nothing like the way Jason had pictured him after talking to him on the phone. In fact, he appeared so blandly innocuous that people probably didn't consider him a threat. Therein would be his hidden advantage.

"What do you want, Groesel?" Jason asked, careful to keep his hands up. "If that's even your real name. Who do you work for?"

Behind Groesel, Abby stepped carefully out from the cover of the trees.

"That's none of your concern," Groesel said, smirking. "But I'll tell you since in a minute you're about to be dead."

"It's the vice president, isn't it?" Jason asked, mainly to distract him.

"Hell no," Groesel boasted. "Though I'm sure he's aware. The president wants this little episode shut down. Orders came to me directly from his people."

Momentarily stunned, Jason gaped.

Groesel laughed, clearly enjoying Jason's reaction. A second later, Abby pressed the cold steel of her pistol into the back of the short man's head. "Drop your gun," she snarled. "Now."

Groesel complied immediately. Jason grabbed the other man's gun as well as his own. Shoving the spare pistol into his holster, he trained his own on Groesel.

"Now," Jason said. "Don't make the wrong move or you'll end up like him. Abby, take my cell phone out of my pocket, grab Colter's flashlight, and go up the ridge and call the sheriff. Tell him to get up here with some men right away. Even if it is dark. That snowmobile has lights. Tell Jeffords to use them."

Groesel laughed, the cold sound letting Jason know he wasn't worried. "Don't tell me you honestly think your small-town sheriff is going to arrest me."

"I do and he will."

"Just wait until I make my one phone call."

Jason shrugged. "I guess I don't have a choice." If Abby wasn't able to get enough cell reception to make the call, he wasn't sure what they'd do. Sure, he could tie Groesel up, but they'd all get hypothermia if they spent the night outside in the cold. He had his Jeep, but they couldn't get anywhere. Of course, if they stayed as close as possible to the fire burning his house down, the blaze should provide enough warmth to enable them to survive.

After what seemed like forever, Abby returned. "I got through," she said. "The sheriff and some of his men are on their way."

"Good."

Groesel only smiled smugly and gazed at the fire.

Later, what appeared to be not only most of the sheriff's department but the entire Cedar Volunteer Fire Department roared up on snowmobiles. They weren't able to bring a water truck due to the road conditions.

They took charge of the prisoner, reading him his rights and handcuffing him, before loading him up in the snowmobile cart and taking off. Since there wasn't anything the fire department guys could do, they all stood and watched while years of Jacob's family history burned to the ground. Several of them said they planned to stay and make sure nothing else caught on fire. They got started digging a trench between the house and the woods. With all the snow and the lack of trees close to the cabin, that scenario seemed unlikely, though he couldn't blame them from wanting to make sure.

"Let me give you a ride into town," the sheriff said. "A couple of my men will bring Colter's body down to the morgue. I'll call and have the coroner come up tomorrow. I'll need to take statements from both of you. After we're done, you're welcome to stay at my place until you figure something out."

With one last look at his still-burning cabin, Jason agreed. Though the sense of loss crushed him, he also planned to make a new beginning, hopefully with Abby. He could rebuild on the land, put in a house that would be their home. If she was willing, that is.

"After we give our statements, I'd like to speak to the reporters," Abby told him, still holding his hand. "Will you stay with me while I do?"

"Of course." He smiled reassuringly at her. Inside, he couldn't help but wonder if this would be the prelude to her saying goodbye and going off to build her own life. Moving on. Without a doubt, he knew she would if he didn't tell her how he felt.

Go big or go home. This had always been his motto and one of the things that got him the good shots and made him an excellent war photojournalist. With that in mind, he planned to go all the way. He wanted to purchase a ring and propose. Since Cedar didn't have a jewelry store, he'd need to get to a large town like Colorado Springs.

How and when were the problems. He couldn't leave Abby alone but he somehow wanted to surprise her. And it appeared time was running out.

Back in town, the sheriff took Abby back first, promising to make this as brief as possible. Jason nodded, pushing back waves of exhaustion.

Absently leafing through a magazine on Sheriff Jefford's coffee table, Jason saw an ad for a jewelry chain. The photo featured a stunning emerald cut diamond in a simple setting. Exactly the type of ring he could picture Abby wearing.

Without even stopping to think, he quickly tore out the page, folded it neatly and stuck it in his pocket.

"Hey there," Abby said, smiling as she walked into the room. As usual, the sight of her had his heart somersaulting in his chest. "What are you doing?"

Feeling slightly self-conscious, he dropped the magazine back onto the coffee table. "I just left a message for the insurance company. I'll have to file a claim on the cabin."

"True." She perched on the arm of the couch near him. "I suppose I need to make some phone calls to co-workers back in DC." Tucking a strand of hair behind her ear, she grimaced. "I confess, I've been putting it off. The explanation is rather lengthy. And they'll see it on the news anyway."

She had a point. "What about friends and family?" he asked.

"My parents died twelve years ago. As for friends…" Her voice trailed off. "Russell kind of managed to drive a huge wedge between us. There's no one I really want to call."

"Then don't." He patted the space next to him, relieved that she didn't sound too dejected. "It actually doesn't sound like there's much tying you to DC."

"There's not. And I wouldn't feel safe there. Not until Russell is actually doing time for his crimes. He has too many powerful connections." Her gaze searched his. "What about you? Are you planning to go back to work in the war zones now that you no longer have your cabin?"

Though she tried to sound casual, he could sense how important that question was. They were still feeling each other out, trying to gauge how important each was to the other.

"I'm going to rebuild," he said quietly. Then, deciding he wanted to put an end to the uncertainty, he reached into his pocket and pulled out the magazine ad. Though he really would have preferred to have the real thing, his entire existence up until this point had been about photographs. He honestly felt Abby would understand. Plus, if she said yes, then they could choose the ring together.

If she said yes. He didn't want to think about what his life would become if she turned him down.

Dropping to one knee in front of her, he unfolded the paper, unsurprised to see that his hands were shaking. "Abby, I'd like to rebuild the cabin with you. Redesign it and expand it, making it into more of a home for the two of us to share." He took a deep breath, swallowing before he continued. "I don't have a ring, but maybe this will do until we can go together and choose one." Feeling slightly foolish—and a hell of a lot more vulnerable than he'd expected—he handed her the magazine page.

"Abby, I love you. I want to spend the rest of my life proving to you how much. Would you do me the honor of becoming my wife?"

Eyes wide, she accepted the paper, laughing out loud as she realized he'd handed her a photograph of an engagement ring. Eyes suspiciously bright, she studied it intently before raising her gaze to meet his.

"Cedar doesn't have a jewelry store, and since we couldn't exactly drive out of the valley, I couldn't get a ring," he said, realizing he might be babbling. "Since photographs are such a big part of my life, I figured this would work until we could shop together."

Still, she didn't speak. Finally, she placed the paper on the coffee table and knelt down in front of him, knee to knee.

"Yes." Her simple answer electrified him. "I've never been more certain of anything in my life." And then she tackled him, laughing and crying all at the same time. When she kissed him, he tasted the salty sweetness of her tears.

"Don't cry," he begged. "Please don't cry. I love you."

"Tears of joy," she murmured, her mouth once again claiming his. "Tears of joy."

* * * * *

#2087 COLTON'S UNDERCOVER REUNION

The Coltons of Mustang Valley • by Lara Lacombe

Ainsley Colton hasn't seen Santiago Morales since he broke her heart years ago, but he's the best defense attorney she knows. To get him to agree to defend her twin brother, though, she has to pretend to be Santiago's wife while he goes undercover to save his sister—and they reignite their passion in the process!

#2088 DEADLY COLTON SEARCH

The Coltons of Mustang Valley • by Addison Fox

Young and pregnant, Nova Ellis hires PI Nikolas Slater to find her missing father, who could make her a Colton. They work together, uncovering danger and mutual attraction—and a threat that's after them both.

#2089 OPERATION SECOND CHANCE

Cutter's Code • by Justine Davis

The only one who blames Adam Kirk more than Amanda Bonner for her father's death is Adam himself. And yet the tragedy brings them together to uncover one last secret. Can the truth of what happened that night bring forgiveness to them both?

#2090 INFILTRATION RESCUE

by Susan Cliff

FBI agent Nick Diaz enlists Avery Samuels, a former cult member turned psychologist, to help him take down the cult—undercover. She's just trying to save her sister, but the unexpected attraction to Nick is proving to be more than a mere distraction!

She ended up on his lap. And the first thing he saw when he caught his breath was Cutter, standing right there and looking immensely pleased with himself.

"He bumped me," Amanda said, a little breathlessly. "I didn't mean to...fall on you, but he came up right behind me and—"

"Pushed?" Adam suggested.

She looked at him quizzically. "Yes. How—"

"I've been told he...herds people where he wants them to go."

She laughed. He was afraid to say any more, to explain any further, because he thought she would get up. And he didn't want her to. Holding her like this, on his lap, felt better than anything had in...at least five years.

"I'd buy that," she said, as if she didn't even realize where she was sitting. Or on what, he added silently as he finally had to admit to his body's fierce and instant response to her position. "I've seen him do it. But why…"

Her voice died away, and he had the feeling that only when she had wondered why Cutter would want her on his lap did she realize that's where she was.

"I…" she began, but it trailed off as she stared down at him.

He could feel himself breathing hard, felt his lips dry as his breath rushed over them. But he couldn't stop staring back at her. And because of that he saw the moment when something changed, shifted, when her eyes widened as if in surprise, then, impossibly, warmed.

She kissed him.

In all his imaginings, and he couldn't deny he'd had them, he'd never imagined this. Oh, not her kissing him, because sometimes on sleepless nights long ago he'd imagined exactly that. He'd just never known how it would feel.

Because he'd never in his life felt anything like it.

Don't miss
Operation Second Chance *by Justine Davis,*
available May 2020 wherever
Harlequin Romantic Suspense
books and ebooks are sold.

Harlequin.com